T0208599

Kissed by an Angel

Kissed by an Angel

a novel

Robert M. Workman

iUniverse, Inc.
New York   Bloomington

Copyright © 2009 by Robert M. Workman

All rights reserved. No part of this book may be used or reproduced by
any means, graphic, electronic, or mechanical, including photocopying,
recording, taping or by any information storage retrieval system
without the written permission of the publisher except in the case
of brief quotations embodied in critical articles and reviews.

This is a work of fiction. All of the characters, names, incidents,
organizations, and dialogue in this novel are either the products
of the author's imagination or are used fictitiously.

iUniverse books may be ordered through booksellers or by contacting:

iUniverse
1663 Liberty Drive
Bloomington, IN 47403
www.iuniverse.com
1-800-Authors (1-800-288-4677)

Because of the dynamic nature of the Internet, any Web addresses or links
contained in this book may have changed since publication and may no longer be
valid. The views expressed in this work are solely those of the author and do not
necessarily reflect the views of the publisher, and the publisher hereby disclaims
any responsibility for them.
ISBN: 978-1-4401-4660-2 (sc)
ISBN: 978-1-4401-4658-9 (dj)
ISBN: 978-1-4401-4659-6 (ebook)

Printed in the United States of America

iUniverse rev. date: 06/01/2009

Acknowledgements:

When one accomplishes the completion of a Novel there is a long list of those who should be thanked. Professor James McKweon worked unselfishly with his Creative Writing Class, calling for excellence. Bob and Cookie Vigue, who for twenty-four years reminded me of the importance of completing this project. Lisa King and Christi Raley who read bits and pieces until it was completed. And my beloved wife who not only read and reread the manuscript but also worked overtime so I could take creative writing classes. And finally my editor Judy Schuler.

Thank you

I would like to dedicate this book to the most loving, understanding, visionary I have ever known. My beloved wife, Kimara Jo Ten Eyck Workman

"Elisabeth, do you remember when times were simpler? When there was a sense of order to life here in Heaven?" Gabriel looked out over the streets paved with gold, at the Pearly Gates. At the same time he expanded his enormous wings to their fullest and filled his chest with air. It was obvious that he was enjoying his position as 'Head Archangel.'

"You know, it seems just like yesterday angels would greet me with Sir or Archangel Gabriel. Now, since the Master said there will no longer be any male or female genders here, I can't say Miss or Mrs. Or even that new one, what is it, oh, Ms. Something or other. Yet the other day walking down Emerald Avenue, I heard, 'Hi, Gab, how they hanging?' I mean, who cares how my wings are hanging?"

Elisabeth, Gabriel's Office Administrator, sat quietly at her desk, knowing that it would make little difference to voice her opinion. Gabriel was on his soapbox and no one but the Master was going to get him off, or so she thought.

Out of the corner of his eye Gabriel saw the solid-gold door of the office open slowly. A little head appeared. Just as quickly, it disappeared. "Who's there?" Gabriel shouted.

1

"It's Ken, sir. Remember Ken …the one who is trying to get his permanent wings? He has passed his studies and wants to speak with you." Elisabeth answered.

"Tell him I'm too busy. Come back later." Gabriel folded his wings back into place.

"Sir, I don't mean to be disrespectful, but that's what you said a month ago, then two weeks ago. Can't you take a little time, Sir? He's so small. All he wants to do is get his permanent wings so he can help people." Elisabeth pleaded.

"Help people! *Help People!* Like he tried to help Lot's wife! He whispered in her ear, she turned and what happened? She became a pillar of salt. What about the time Joseph had those dreams and Ken explained it to him? What happened? He told his family that he was going to be over them, so his brothers decided to kill him. He helped all right; his brothers sold Joseph into slavery before I could intervene. Oh, then there was Balaam, remember that, Elisabeth? Balak, the king of the Moabites hired a diviner called Balaam to curse the nation of Israel. Ken whispers in Balaam's ear telling him to just go and pretend to curse Israel. He gets on his ass to ride out to curse Israel and I had to talk through that ass to stop him. Oh, you don't know what I have gone through with this one." Gabriel paused, and then started to chuckle, "Remember the time the Master sent me to the classroom. There was Raphael standing on his desk his robe pulled up past his knees, screaming. Ken changed himself into a snake and didn't know how to change back. Whoever heard of an Archangel scared of a little grass snake? Oh, bring him in. Let's get this over with."

Before Elisabeth could get up from her desk, Ken was in the room, smiling from ear to ear. "Archangel Gabriel, Sir, I finished my studies. I was first in my class. All I have to do is get an assignment from you, do it, and I'll be able to get my permanent wings. Do you have anything for me to do, Sir? Please, please, Archangel Gabriel?" Ken's crystal blue eyes started to fill with tears.

"Congratulations, Ken, job well done." Gabriel smiled. "Listen, right now I have a lot to do. However, I will meet with your teachers and discuss what your best fields of study were. Then I'll find something for you to do so you can pass the final test. I remember when I was your size. I know how eager one is to get their permanent wings, but this will be your third try. If you don't get them this time, you won't be coming back. You do know the rule don't you, Ken? Another thing Ken, it is 1935 down on earth it is not the same as when you went with me to bring the animals in the Ark. Elizabeth, did I tell you what happened? Ken couldn't tell the difference between the genders of the fly or mosquito or fly so he just put a bunch of them in a container. Since then all the Master has heard from the human race is 'why we have so many mosquitoes and flies?'"

Ken dropped his head sadly. He knew the many times he had tried to do right, never making it, wondering if he would ever get it right, so he could get those precious wings. "Yes, sir," he mumbled.

Ken was about to leave when Elisabeth said, "Gabriel, I just received a message from the Master. He wants to see you and Ken immediately."

With that they found themselves in the Great White Throne Room instantaneously. The brilliant white light was blinding to Ken. The cherubim and seraphim flying around; calling out "Holy, Holy, Holy" confused him so he couldn't remember how to approach the Master. Was he to bow or prostrate himself before Him? The great angels and the saints of old all standing in His presence, His son sitting beside Him, poor Ken just couldn't remember. Before Ken could get his thoughts together, the Master's voice rang out, "Ken, I am sending you and Gabriel on a mission. You must leave tonight and you can't take more than one hour and twenty minutes of our time to fulfill it."

"My Lord," Gabriel bowed so low that his face almost touched the golden floor. "You know how far behind I am. Can't you ask someone else to go with Ken, someone like Raphael?"

"Gabriel, you know the rules," the Master said. "Once you have an apprentice, they stay with you until they earn their permanent wings. It doesn't hinge on you being busy or how long it takes. You have him until he receives his wings. The rule hasn't changed, nor will it ever change. Maybe if you didn't stop at the ice-cream stand or stand around expanding your wings, you would have your work done."

"Now Ken, I want you to know what is at stake here. You have failed twice before. If you fail this time, you will remain on the earth plane until you find a family you can attach to, live a life as a human and then die. Don't take this assignment lightly, Ken. You are kind, but sometimes you let it control you. You do that and you will fail." Once again Ken hung his head in shame for past failures.

"Now let us get to the assignment. There is a child of mine whose name is Sarah." The Master pointed to the overhead screen showing a young woman with all the relevant information: height, weight, date of birth, the lineage. He continued, "She is nineteen, full of dreams and promises. Like you Ken, she sees only the good in everyone. *Ken noticed that Sarah had dark red hair, deep brown eyes, a slight frame; one could say she had a body that King Solomon wrote about in the Sacred Text.* The same man raped her two sisters. Her father said that they must have asked for it. This has caused Sarah sleepless nights. Her boss, Frankie will proposition her, then he will threaten her life. All you have to do, Ken, is to assure her that I know her every need, I have heard her prayers for help, and everything will be fine.

"Don't try to save her. Don't try to change history or have something happen to him. They both have lessons to learn. You do this and, when you come back, I will have your wings ready for you. Once again, if you fail, you won't come back."

With that, they both found themselves on the streets of the west side of New York City. Ken couldn't help but comment on how big and expensive the buildings looked compared to the poverty of the people. It had just rained and there should have been a fresh clean smell in the air, instead it smelled of death and poor hygiene. Dead rodents and rotten food lay in the gutter; drunks were sleeping against the buildings. Ken quickly moved from person to person touching them with healing, hope and assurance of a new tomorrow.

"That isn't your concern, Ken," Gabriel said. "Remember, you are here on an assignment. Now this is Saint Anthony's Church. Sarah comes here every morning at 10 a.m. for Confession and prayer. You know what she looks like. Listen to the conversation between the priest and Sarah so you can be sure it's her. You can give her the message through the voice of her priest, an idea or a dream. Nevertheless, don't try to intervene."

"I must leave now. Do you have any questions? If not, I will meet you here on the steps of Saint Anthony's if you pass the test. If you don't, I won't be seeing you again." With that, Gabriel was gone.

Ken spent the night looking around the neighborhood. Touching the lives of the hopeless and healing the sick, ministering in every possible way that would glorify his Master. In the morning as the sun was rising he went to Saint Anthony's to wait for Sarah. He sat through the service listening to the priest, wondering, *what hope was there in this form of religion.* The priest was an old gentleman, small boned, but spoke with a definite conviction, genuine concern for his flock. The old priest went on and on about how hopeless they were in their sinfulness, that only if they lived with a repentant heart could they find happiness.

Ken lost interest and started looking at the images of the saints that were standing in the sanctuary. He'd met every one of them, St. James, St. Jude, St. Anthony, and of course St. Joseph with the Blessed Mother. Finally, the sermon was over. A transformation occurred with offering the Sacrament. Hope radiated throughout each person as they went up to receive the Host.

The sanctuary emptied and only a few remained. Ken

spotted her as she sat in the shadows of the back of the sanctuary with her head bowed. Her red hair had a glint of gold from the stained glass windows. Her eyes looked sad, much sadder than any nineteen-year-old should have. Her shoulders bent as if she had the troubles of the world on them. Her clothes, though well-worn, were clean and pressed.

Ken sat next to Sarah through the confessional and her prayers. He tried to explain that everything was going to work out, but she wasn't listening. There was something different about this young woman. On one hand, she was a child wanting to grow up, and on the other, bound to a life of disappointment and hard work. Her sins were what Ken thought of as just a child's desires. But she was sincere and this impressed him. Her prayers weren't for herself but for her family and friends. They were much more mature than he had expected from someone so young. It was no wonder the Master called her "My Child".

Sarah left the church, walking slowly to the café. Looking in the windows of the stores, she dreamed of a time when she could spend her own money. Wondering how long she would have to work to help support the family. Why couldn't her father get a job, was there something physically wrong with him? Suddenly she stopped in front of a pawnshop. In the window was a display of stilettos. "I wonder," she said aloud, with a mischievous smile, then went on to work.

The café was in the usual pre-luncheon void. It was nothing more than a large room with pillars decorated in the bright colors of the Italian flag. The tables each had a checked vinyl tablecloth and a wine bottle with a candle stuck in it for what Frankie called "romance". The curtains, once white cotton now yellow from cigar and cigarette smoke. Frankie, her boss, was putting the final touches on the special for the day. She hated this part of the day. To sign in she had to squeeze between Frankie and the counter. He was a big man. Besides being six feet in height, he weighed nearly three hundred pounds.

She found it repulsive, with his constant belching, the smell of old grease that reeked from his skin and clothes as she passed him. His hair was always oily, he hardly ever shaved and every time she passed him he would reach out and pinched her bottom. As usual, she blushed and he laughed his vulgar laugh.

Business was always good at the lunch and dinner hours. The smoke-filled café always had laughter and a sense of joy in it. Yes, the men were smelly and crude, but the tips were good. When someone went too far, someone else would step in to defend her. She felt like a princess with a group of protective knights waiting to save her.

Ken noticed how she listened to the customers and related to them. She moved easily from topic to topic, touching each life, encouraging those who needed encouragement, comforting those who were in sorrow. *This is an exceptional woman. How can I save her from this trial?* Ken thought. Suddenly he heard the Master's voice in the back of his mind say: *"If you fail…"* A chill went down his back, as he thought of the outcome of not just doing as directed.

As the dinner crowd thinned, Frankie ran his hand over the side of her breast as she squeezed by him. Without thinking, she turned and slapped his face.

He smiled and said, "So, you liked it? How about coming over tonight? I'll make you feel like a real woman."

"You could never make me feel like a real woman, Frankie. You may be my boss, but you will never, never be my lover," Sarah snapped.

"That's what you sisters thought," Frankie held up a stiletto, "but my friend here convinced them differently."

"You, *You!*" Sarah shouted. "You RAPED my sisters." The stored-up hatred suddenly gripped her. The instinct to kill came on her in waves as she looked for a knife or something to attack this monster that stood in front of her grinning. The café suddenly became quiet as they listened to Sarah and Frankie.

"Yep and they enjoyed it, no matter what they said. You will too. I just hope I don't have to use my friend on that beautiful face." He once again waved his stiletto in front of her face. "It would be a shame to spoil that beauty. By the way don't go to the police or your father, I have them both covered." Frankie smiled, almost drooling with desire. Suddenly he realized the few customers in the café understood what he had said. Turning to them, he waved his stiletto and called out, "That goes for you too."

Sarah cried all the way home that night. She was thankful for the darkness as she walked so no one would see her tear-stained face. As she went into the apartment, the family was sitting down for dinner. She asked if she could talk with her father alone. She wanted to hear him say that he didn't know who raped Joyce and Alice. She wanted him to get angry at someone besides her mother, sisters or herself. She wanted him to be the head of the house, the protector that she had always dreamt him to be. He got up from the table. He was an overweight, bald man who didn't take care of his appearance. They walked into the living room and he sat in his worn-out chair. For the first time Sarah realized the room symbolized her life, dull and abused.

"Father, I know you said you didn't want us to talk about what happened to Joyce and Alice in this house, ever again. I know that you are the head of the house; I am to honor you for that and obey you. But today I found out who raped Joyce and Alice. It was my boss Frankie, and I think you should know it." Sarah was crying uncontrollably by now. To her, rape is the greatest humiliation a woman could bare.

"Sarah, Sarah, don't you think I don't know who did it? I knew it was going to happen three days before it did. There was nothing I could do. Frankie owns this apartment building; he has the police in the palm of his hand. I feel bad for Joyce and Alice, but there was nothing I could do to save them. If he comes at you, all I can say is what I said to them, don't fight it. He will cut you with his stiletto. Sarah, please promise that you won't fight with him."

Sarah ran out of the room crying.

"What's wrong with Sarah?" Her mother stood in the doorway like a ghost with clothes hanging on it.

"Oh you know how emotional she gets. It must be that time of the month," replied her father.

Sarah cried herself to sleep, hating a father that could be so cold and indifferent about his daughters.

Ken came to her in a dream that night, but somehow it turned into a nightmare. She dreamed of her sisters screaming for help and her father just standing there laughing. He tried talking to her, assuring her that everything was going to work out. He knew that she wasn't listening.

He brought in the bright light of the Master, but she just curled up with her knees to her chest and cried in her sleep.

The next morning she got up and fixed breakfast as if nothing had happened. Her mother rushed out to work, while her father sat back and had another cup of coffee. As she was finishing, he said, "Listen Sarah, life is rough. You have to learn to roll with the punches. If your sisters weren't behaving so provocatively nothing would have happened. So far you've behaved yourself. Keep acting like a lady and he'll leave you alone."

Sarah didn't say a word. She just got herself ready for church and left. For the first time in her life, she didn't say good-bye and kiss him. Somehow she just lost all feelings for him and couldn't pretend that she loved him. As she walked to church, she thought of her father. What made him so callused? Why didn't he work? What was it that Frankie had over him? She just couldn't figure him out. Mother always said to her, "Marry a strong man, a man who will protect you and provide for you, a man who will let you lean on his shoulder." Was he that much of a weakling? She suddenly realized that she would never see her father as her daddy again. She took a deep breath and walked into church.

She sat in the confessional thinking. Was it her actions that brought this on, or was it just society taking what wasn't theirs to take? How could a person protect herself, from animals, like Frankie? Or was it God punishing her for not forgiving this fiend who molested her sisters. Would she ever be able to give herself to the one she loved?

Suddenly she heard the priest say, "Yes my child."

"Forgive me Father for I have sinned. No wait, I haven't sinned. It wasn't me. I mean I have sinned, but Father I want to talk about something else. I mean, I know you are busy. I should be confessing my sins and I have to get to work, but what am I supposed to do?" With that, the story flowed from her lips and the tears began to fall.

Her Father Confessor sat quietly for a moment. Then with a gentle voice said, "Pray, my child, the Blessed Mother will give you strength in the time of need. She will not fail you."

She went to the altar and prayed for help.

The next few days all Frankie did was look at her as if he was undressing her. She disliked it, but didn't say a word. However, on Tuesday before Holy Week, he said to her, "I'm going to have you," and showed her his stiletto.

A cold chill went through her. She had to think fast or she would become his victim like her sisters. "Listen Frankie, you are a man. There isn't much I can do to stop you. You also need me here to work. You will close the cafe Friday because it is a Holy Day so why not wait until Thursday night?" *What am I saying*, she thought, *am I crazy?* "But I will not go to your house nor do it in the alley like my sisters."

"Just don't try to get out of it." Frankie drawled.

After church, the next morning Sarah stopped once again at the pawnshop and looked at the stilettos. She went in and asked to see one.

"What do you need one of these for?" The clerk asked. As

he led her to the stiletto showcase, she grew accustom to the darkness. The items on display looked like the history of someone's life, some items shiny and inviting, as if cared for, others broken and foreboding, as if no one cared at all. The man waddled more than walked; his pants hung so low she could see that vulgar crack that men seem so proud of. He smelled like old beer and the cigar hanging from his mouth smelled as if he had relit it a dozen times. Suddenly, she realized the only way out was blocked by the clerk.

"I walk home in the dark and I think I might feel safer with something to protect myself." Sarah felt the hairs on her neck rising and cold chills ran through her body.

"Well, this will work. It's four inches long. You push this button and the blade comes out, like this." He pushed the button.

Sarah jumped back as the blade snapped out. "But I don't always have my purse. Do I have to walk around with it in my hand?"

"No, you can get this sheath that you can attach to your wrist."

The clerk was starting to look at her like Frankie did. It made her nervous. "How sharp is it?" She asked.

"Honey with one flick of the wrist you can change a man from a bass to a soprano." The clerk laughed.

She bought it and headed to work. She was late and knew Frankie would be upset. As she entered, Frankie yelled, shaking the mixing spoon at her, "You are late. I'm gonna dock you."

"I know Frankie, but I was buying something for tomorrow night. I want it to be a night that you will always remember." She turned her head to avoid misleading him with a tentative smile. *Believe me, what I have in mind for you, you will never forget,* she thought. She squeezed behind him, hiding the sneer on her face.

"Well if that's the case I'll let it go this time. Hurry up now we are gonna to be busy today." There was a sudden softness in Frankie's voice, a softness that she hadn't noticed before.

Time flew by as she rushed from table to table. The customers were in a festive mood and the tips were good.

As the day ended Frankie offered to take her home, but she made an excuse.

"Get here as soon as you can in the morning, Sarah. It's going to be busy tomorrow. They'll want you here to wait on'em, so get a good night's sleep." Frankie smiled.

Once again, Sarah thought she heard softness in his voice. The next morning Sarah woke up early. Fear had her tossing and turning all-night. *What if he overpowered her? What if she couldn't protect herself? What if…* The thoughts went on and on. *Oh, how do I stop this mind of mine from running?*

In the morning she slipped into Frankie's favorite green dress and put on some perfume, then went down the hall to serve breakfast, ignoring her sisters and mother.

Sarah skipped going to church that morning. What she planned on doing wasn't something to bring into God's house. Frankie was in a good mood when she came into the café. He was wearing a clean shirt, had shaved and even washed his hair. As she squeezed past him she smelled aftershave. He leaned back, forcing Sarah to rub her body against his, *Forgive me God, but I hate this man,* she thought, as he tried to pinch her.

Once again, it was a busy day. Time flew by, but Sarah made several mistakes. At one point Frankie asked if she was there or maybe she left her brain at home. She kept rehearsing what the evening would bring, how it would unfold. Her mother once told her that once a man gets in the 'mood' the woman is in control. "God didn't give him enough blood to think with both heads at one time," she would say.

The last customer left, and Frankie locked the door. "Let's sit down a minute and catch our breath." There was a definite softness and need in his voice.

"Let me have a cup of coffee first. I am tired." Sarah hoped that Frankie would call it off. "You don't have to go through with this, Frankie," she said. "I don't understand what pleasure you can get from cutting up women, then forcing yourself on them."

Frankie looked down at the floor for a moment. Then with an evil look he grabbed her arm and asked, "Trying to back out, bitch? I had your sisters and I'll have you." Once again, he pulled out his stiletto, only this time he opened it.

Suddenly a peace came over Sarah that gave her strength to face this monster. "Frankie, I'm not afraid of you. No, I'm not backing out, but you look tired, I thought you might want to rest for a little while." *What is wrong with me?* Sarah thought, as she looked him in the eyes.

Frankie started to walk away as if to get the coffee then suddenly whirled around and grabbed Sarah. "You thought you could out-smart me did you?" With a grip that bruised her arm, he pulled her roughly to him and began kissing her. As his kisses became more intensive, he let go of her arm and reached for her breast with one hand and her buttocks with the other.

To Sarah it seemed as if his hands were everywhere at once. All she could do was try to fight him off as he tore open her dress. Fighting the bile rising in her throat, she suddenly remembered the stiletto and prayed that his wandering hands would not find it. It took all of her strength to keep from screaming at him. Feeling the rising bulge of his manhood, she knew she would have to do something soon or it would be too late.

Using well practiced moves, Frankie had managed to undo his pants while holding onto Sarah. Unexpectedly, he grabbed her hand and wrapped it around his penis. "This is what a man uses to teach his woman a lesson. You are now going to learn what a woman is for. I'll make sure you'll learn your lesson well!"

As if in a dream, one minute Sarah was standing there in fright, the next in revulsion. Somehow she had managed to pull out her stiletto, in anger and fear she lashed out at Frankie, cutting off his penis then watching him fall to the floor.

Looking at Frankie as he fell holding his groin, she said coldly, "I guess you won't be using that anymore," throwing his penis into his lap. "Oh, by the way Frankie, blow the candle out when you leave."

She walked over to the cash register, took out her pay and walked out, leaving Frankie bleeding on the floor.

2

As she opened the door of the café, the cold wet wind of early spring slapped her in the face, bringing her back to reality. She had just brutally cut a man. Pulling her coat close to her body, for protection, she started home wondering, *"What have I done, what have I done?"* Suddenly she turned around.

"Why not see Father Tom." Whispered Kenneth in her ear, "He'll tell you what to do."

As she passed the café's open door, she could hear Frankie talking to someone. Fear swept over her like a wave as she realized she might get caught. Frankie could be telling the police that she had done this to him. In the distance she heard the wail of the sirens and another wave of fear swept over her. *I have to get out of here.*

She ran in fear, then slowed to a walk so no one would think she was guilty of something. The walk to Saint Anthony's was into the wind. With the mixture of rain and tears falling down her face, she rehearsed her speech to Father Tom. Every person she passed slowed down as if they knew what she'd done. The holiday traffic looked like every other car was a police car. The police officer, who tipped his hat and asked her where she was going in such miserable weather, had his hand on his weapon as if he already knew.

Finally, she arrived at Saint Anthony's only to find the huge doors to the Basilica locked. Sitting on a step, Sarah put her head in her hands, crying hysterically.

A priest she had never seen before sat down beside her. "Can I help you my child?" He handed her a handkerchief. "I'm Father Ken." He was taller than the other priest and had a quietness about him. His hair was dark red, his eyes crystal blue, and they had a glow of reassurance and concern.

Sarah jumped away in fear, hearing the stranger's voice. But the kindness in his eyes, the softness in his voice called her back. She sat back down and broke again into sobs. The priest put his hand on her arm to reassure her, "I won't hurt you my child."

Between sobs, Sarah tried to tell him what had happened.

Finally, Father Ken said, "Why don't we go inside, before you become chilled, then you will be no-good for anything."

"The church is locked, Father," said Sarah.

"I know the Man with the key, my child." Father Ken smiled.

Suddenly she felt at peace as she got up to walk the stairs once again.

Ken wondered *what do I to this child of the Master. Was she in this predicament because of me? How could I have done it any differently? Who would protect her now that she was on the run?*

Father Ken ushered Sarah to one of the inner offices and closed the door. It never occurred to Sarah that he didn't use keys or the room was all ready fully lit. On one wall were hundreds of books; the other wall had pictures and certificates hanging. The desk sat a little to one side of the room, allowing chairs to face it. Sarah knew that she was safe, safer than she had felt for years.

Father Ken said, "Sarah, tell me once again what happened. I'll take notes so we can figure out our next move to keep you safe."

Once again, Sarah started to tell the story, but this time she could do it with fewer tears.

When she finished, Father Ken pushed his chair back, reached into his pocket and took out his thinking stone. As he rubbed the cool, smooth stone, he collected his thougts, deciding what needed to be done next. "Did you know who you were working for? Frankie is the head of a group of evil people. They steal, kill, rape at will. They own the police. Your father has a reason to fear them. He should have told you. I'm sure Frankie will live, so stop worrying about being a murderer. After all, you did stop him from ever raping again." Father Ken rose chuckling from his chair and walked around the desk.

"Now we have to figure out what we're going to do with you. Frankie's family and friends are going to be looking for the person who did this to him... I doubt that Frankie will mention your name because of his pride. No man wants to admit that a woman cut him the way you did."

" Why don't you go, light a candle before the altar and pray to the Blessed Mother while I do some research, maybe find an answer."

Sarah got up and went to pray.

Sometime later Father Ken came into the sanctuary with two light blue envelopes and some money. "Here are two envelopes, one addressed to you and the other to someone you haven't met yet. He will help you. I should tell you to go to the police, but not in this case. Take this money, get out of town. When you're out of town, open your envelope and follow the instructions. Go with God's peace, my child. My prayers will be with you. Remember you are never alone." He took her arm and walked her out the door of the church.

She turned to thank him, but he had already left. She tried the door, it was locked.

Sarah hurried home, knowing that her family would be worrying about her safety.

Her mother greeted her at the door with the fear of the

unknown in her eyes. Her small tired body hung on her skeleton frame. "What happened to you, why are you so late? I walked down to the café to see what had happened. The place was swarming with police. I asked one of them what happened, and he said that some man broke in, took all of Frankie's money, then cut him. He said Frankie would recover, then he could tell them more. Darling, I was so worried about you. I thought maybe they took you or maybe even killed you." She was getting hysterical.

Sarah knew she had to calm her down. "Get everyone together, mother. I have to talk to all of you and I don't think I can say it twice. Oh, mother, thank you for caring. When I left home this morning, I didn't think anyone did," Sarah whispered as she gave her mother a reassuring hug.

Sarah began telling her story to the family—it was easier this time. She told of Frankie's proposition, his boasting of hurting her sisters. Joyce's hand went to the stub of the ear that Frankie had left and Alice's hand went to the scar that ran from her right ear to the base of her nose. When she told her father's response, she expected him to react, but he just sat there staring as if she were lying. She told of stopping at the pawnshop, buying the stiletto. When she came to the part about cutting Frankie, her father flew out of his chair, hitting her as hard as he could. She fell to the floor unconscious.

When she came to, she could hear her father shouting. "That slut has no idea what she's done to this family. We're as good as dead, just because she didn't want to lose her virginity."

Her mother was kneeling beside her, wiping the blood off her face. She helped her get up and walked her to her bedroom. Her nose and mouth were still bleeding, her head hurting. "He doesn't understand Sarah. He never will. Don't be hard on him," her mother whispered.

Her mother pulled out a suitcase and opened Sarah's bureau. Quickly she started to pack. She began to speak quietly as if she didn't want anyone to hear, "I think you should go to see my mother in Columbus, Ohio. I wouldn't tell father, he would tell Frankie's friends. You need to get out of town as quickly as possible. You won't be able to write us, but remember we do love you. Your sisters and I are proud of you. I have a little money saved up if you need it."

"I have money, mother. I was paid tonight, so don't worry about money. I told Father Ken at Saint Anthony's about what I had done. He gave me an envelope and told me not to open it until I was out of New York," she added.

Her mother stopped and stared at her. "Father Ken…at… Saint Anthony's? We don't have a Father Ken at Saint Anthony's. I know every priest that comes and goes out of our church and there is no Father Ken. Are you sure that you spoke to a Father Ken?"

"He said that was his name—tall, about three inches taller than me. Hair about my color but a little gray in the temples. His eyes were crystal blue that flashed with light when he became upset." Sarah said.

"Honey, there isn't a priest there who fits that description. You had a visitation. Saints be praised, everything is going to be okay. Just do what he told you to do." Her mother seemed much less worried.

Sarah finished packing, and then said good-bye to Joyce and Alice. She went to her father to say good-bye, but he stormed out of the house. "I'll tell him you love him, Sarah," said her mother. "We called a taxi. It's waiting."

She got into the taxi with her suitcase and headed to the Grand Central Terminal. Suddenly she felt alone and scared. The people in the cars looked as if they wanted to stop and drag her from the taxi, accusing her of her crime. As she slouched down to hide, she heard a voice from the front seat.

"Sarah, are you okay?" It was the cabby. "I've been talking up a storm and there hasn't been any answer." He was looking through the rearview mirror at her, smiling from ear to ear.

I've seen those eyes, heard that voice before, she thought. "Yes I'm okay," Sarah mumbled. "How did you know my name?"

"I-I heard your mother," Ken stammered. "So are you off to see the world, or are you just going to visit family? I hear Paris is lovely this time of year," he went on with a laugh.

Sarah wasn't amused. *Who is this guy?* She wondered. "I'm just taking a trip out of town." She hoped that would end the conversation.

"Well, I guess you have your reasons, but you have to do what's good for you, Sarah."

"Right now, your family is healthy and can fill the gap of your absence. No one is after you, so you don't have to fear the unknown." Ken went on, trying to get Sarah to relax and talk, but it was no use.

Sarah was caught up in her own little world. Wondering what to do if Grandma wouldn't take her in. "I know she's unpredictable, but she's all we have right now," her mother had said.

They arrived at the train terminal; Sarah got out and paid the cabby. Pausing, she looked at him as if she knew him, then turned and went her way. The voice, the eyes, even the smile reminded her of someone, but whom? As she turned and looked at the huge limestone building with its pillars, she felt a chill pass over her. The chill seemed as cold as the building looked in the darkness of the night.

As she walked toward the terminal entrance, a police officer with broad shoulders, his voice full of authority stopped her, "Where are you going, Missy?"

She looked at him and fear swept over her. At first she tried to answer but nothing came out of her mouth. Her feet felt like they'd been glued to the concrete. Her heart pounded so loudly she was sure the officer could hear it.

"I asked you a question, Missy." The officer's hand was on his revolver as if he knew how guilty she was.

"Why Officer, I'm going to see my grandma," Sarah

mumbled, thankful that it was dark and he couldn't see how guilty she looked.

"Don't get smart with me, young lady," he snapped. "We're looking for a man who's dressed like a woman. About your height, he tried to kill a café owner tonight."

"I'm sorry officer. I thought you were trying to be fresh. As you can see I'm not a man. I'm going to see my grandmother." *Good, Frankie hasn't told them the truth yet,* she thought.

"Go on in, but don't be surprised that you are being watched," said the officer as he turned to approach the next person.

Grand Central Terminal seemed as dark and lonely inside as it looked cold outside. As she walked the corridors looking for the ticket agent, even the echoing of her footsteps drove fear farther into her heart. The high walls of yellow limestone and the domed plastered ceiling caught every sound and magnified it. From the laughter of a sailor with his girlfriend to the cry of a baby, the sounds closed in on her. As she looked into the windows of the shops that were closed she thought she saw the image of Frankie laying on the floor pointing his finger at her. People seemed once again to be looking at her with an accusing eye. Finally, she saw the sign, *TICKET AGENT*.

Walking up to the window, she said, without even thinking "One-way to Columbus, Ohio."

The agent smiled. "Is that were you're from?"

"No, I'm from New York City. I'm going to see my grandmother…I don't know when I'll return," she replied, wondering why he asked where she was from.

"Ah, a biscuit in the basket," the agent laughed. "Well that happens when you're not careful, forty-three dollars please."

She paid him; he stamped the ticket, gave it to her, and she moved on.

Twice, sailors tried to hold a conversation with her, but she just got up and walked away. Another police officer stopped to talk to her, listening to her voice, checking to see if she was a woman. After what seemed forever, she finally heard the announcer say, "Train leaving for Columbus, Ohio now boarding on track four."

She quickly got up, picked up her suitcase, and boarded the train. Looking around, and trembling in fear, she saw a young couple sitting together and two businessmen. Relief came over her; she was finally on the train, it was nearly empty, no one had stopped her. *It won't be long and I'll be safe,* she thought.

"You will never be safe honey," said a voice from behind her.

Sarah looked back in fear. An old woman came toward her with a shopping bag. She had such a bad limp that she could hardly walk the aisle. Her hair was snow-white; her glasses hung barely on her nose and her eyes where a crystal blue.

"You'll never be safe traveling alone, honey. You need a traveling companion. You never know what lurks within the shadows of the night. I'm going to Columbus. Why don't I just sit with you, that way we both will be safe." The woman dropped her bag on the empty seat across from Sarah.

Sarah sat looking out the window, watching the lights of houses go by. The old woman opened a book and began to read. The sound of the wheels formed a rhythm in Sarah's mind. *I am free, I am free, I am free. But am I?* She wondered. Would Frankie live? If so, would he come looking for her? Would she ever have the luxury of just relaxing without the constant memory of this night?

She finally fell asleep. Somewhere in the night, she became the woman that took nothing from anyone. She woke up with a shawl laid neatly over her; the old woman had a ragged coat draped over her. *She looks so peaceful,* thought Sarah. *I wonder if she knows what I'm doing here. Could I talk to this stranger or is she a spy sent by Frankie?* Her mind was beginning to pick up steam; she had better slow it down. She thought of the priest who said he was Father Ken, then the cabby who knew her name. She was sure no one used her name when she got into the cab, now this old woman, who gave up her shawl so she could keep warm. *Who are these people, why are they here?*

The conductor came by and Sarah asked, "How long before the train gets to Columbus?"

He had a warm smile, almost seemed like the grandfather figure that she would pretend she had when she was little. "Not for another fourteen hours, sweetie." The conductor said as he tipped his hat.

Sarah laughed aloud. The conductor stopped and asked, "What's so funny?"

"Oh, nothing, it's just that I was stopped at the Grand Central Terminal and was accused of being a man in disguise. The ticket agent thought I was pregnant. Now you call me sweetie as if I were a child." Sarah laughed.

The conductor grinned and moved on.

The old woman woke up and stretched. "Well I see you woke up. Did you have a good rest?" She said with a smile.

"Yes," answered Sarah. "Thank you for your shawl." She handed it back to her folded. "I hear the dining car is four cars up, would you like to join me? I'll help you get there."

"Only if you tell me your name, I don't like to eat with strangers. My name is Jon," said the old woman.

"John?" Sarah asked.

"No, Jon, spelled J O N, my parents wanted a boy, but I came along. So they called me Jon without the h. It was my mother and father's sense of humor."

A chill ran down Sarah's back. *That laugh where did I hear it before?*

"I'm Sarah McGee. I grew up in New York City on the Westside; this is my first trip away from home alone. I'm glad you came."

They slowly moved through the different cars, bouncing around, sometimes on each other, sometimes grabbing a seat just before falling. Finally, they came to the dining car and ordered breakfast. They talked for hours about everything except what Sarah was doing there; she was able to dodge that question.

They went back to their seats and sat, quietly watching the

scenery pass by. They had left the big cities, now there were fields and hills; once in awhile Sarah saw a stream or waterfall. She noticed that Jon had fallen asleep again. She got up, took out the shawl and covered her, smiling at the old woman, wondering why she was there.

Suddenly she remembered the envelopes from Father Ken. She opened her purse took out the envelope addressed to her, and opened it. The stationery matched the envelope but it had a small angel in the lower right corner. The handwriting was bold and clear as if the writer was convinced that he was doing right. She began to read:

Dear Sarah,

By now, you are on your way to Columbus. Don't ask me how I know, I just do. When you get into the Columbus Station, you need to make a decision to play it safe, stay with Grandma or go on. Remember, what looks safe, isn't always safe. I would warn you that Frankie's organization has a long reach into our society. Therefore, please consider my proposal.

By now your father has found out where you are headed. Trying to save his neck, he will go to Frankie and tell him where you are. Frankie will come looking for you. It won't be safe for you or your grandmother.

Change trains in Columbus and go to Crestline, Ohio. I have a friend there who will give you a job. Give him the envelope with Mr. William Strowe on it. He will give you a new name and a new place of former address.

Do what he says and you will be safe. Remember, you are loved by many. And someone will always be there for you.

Father Ken

Sarah sat back and closed her eyes. How did she get into this mess? Maybe to avenge her sisters' virtue wasn't worth all this pain and confusion. Maybe she should have just let him have her. Her family would be safe; her father wouldn't have to betray her mother.

She folded the envelope up and put it into her purse. She took out the magazine that she had bought and began reading. The world seemed quiet except for the clanking of the train wheels. She got up to go to the powder room and when she came back, the old woman was gone.

When the conductor came by, Sarah asked, "What happened to the old woman that was sitting here with me?"

The conductor gave her a strange look. "Lady no one has been sitting with you since you got on this train." He walked away.

A chill came over Sarah as she thought, *first the priest, then the cabby, and now the old woman. What's going on am I cracking up?*

Suddenly the conductor called out, "Columbus, end of the line. Everyone out."

As Sarah started to pick up her belongings, she saw the shawl with a scrap of paper pinned to it.

"Keep this shawl; it will remind you that you can make it and that you are loved. Remember you are never alone."

Love, Jon

She put on her coat, picked up the suitcase, shawl and purse, and left the train. To her surprise the air smelled fresher, the sky was clearer than she remembered of New York City. Yet in the back of her mind she still knew she was fleeing for her life.

Quickly Sarah went to the ticket window and asked if there was a train going to Crestline, Ohio.

"Yes Miss, in twenty minutes, would you like a round-trip ticket?" The ticket agent replied.

He reminded her of the rats that ran the streets of the city at night, with his pointed nose, ears that stuck out and hungry eyes that darted back and forth in a searching way. It gave her the impression that he could see clearly beneath the clothes she wore.

"No, one-way, how much is it?" Sarah silently prayed, *Hurry up before I change my mind.*

"One-way? Why would you want to go to Crestline one-way? That's just a little one-horse town with no work, no housing, just farmland and unemployed people. Two dollars please." The agent laughed.

Sarah quickly paid for the ticket and headed for the departure area. *Am I doing right?* She wondered. *What if Father Ken isn't the person he pretends to be?*

What if this is a trap? He's right, if Father tells Frankie of Grandmother, Frankie will come or send someone to her house and then Grandmother will be in danger. But the ticket agent said Crestline had nothing to offer. Maybe Father Ken doesn't know of the economic condition of Crestline.

Sarah jumped as the train whistle sounded while it came into the station. As she picked up her suitcase, she glanced into the crowd and there stood a man. He just stood there looking at her, dirty shirt, greasy hair and a scrubby face. *Could it be?* She tried to glance back toward him to see if it was Frankie. But when she did, the man wasn't there. Fear gripped her as she boarded the train.

The ride to Crestline was only an hour and a half long. As she looked out over the farmland, she felt once again the peace that she had felt before. The farmland had already experienced the spring thaw and some green was appearing. *It won't be long before the tulips and daffodils are blooming, a new season of growth and a new start for me. This is good.*

Checking her purse to make sure the envelope for Mr. Strowe was still there, she saw an edge of cloth. As she pulled it out of the purse, there came memories of her high school days with it. It was a partially finished handkerchief. As her finger ran over the tatted lace, her mind went back to the many dreams of what her knight in shining armor would be like. A man who had saved himself for her, who would be faithful and always there when she needed him. She could still hear Miss Ghast when she explained, why she couldn't finish it. It only had her first initial, and she would finish it when she found such a man.

"That only happens in the movies, Sarah," replied Mrs. Ghast.

"Crestline, Crestline all-out for Crestline," called the conductor.

Sarah got up and went to the door waiting for the train to stop. Suddenly she felt alone and scared. 'What ifs' were once again running rampant. She stepped off the train and put her suitcase down. In front of her was a large Catholic Church, which on one hand gave her a sense of security and on the other reminded her of why she was there. Crocuses were blooming in the little flower bed between the station and the loading area.

She looked up at the sky and prayed silently, "Help, I don't know where this person is or how to get a hold of him."

"Did you call?" Asked a voice from behind her. It was a police officer. He was short, a little overweight, but with a jolly face. He didn't have a gun on his side, but he did have a nightstick. Another chill went down Sarah's spine and the hair on the back of her neck stood on end.

"You got me officer," Sarah held her hands up, thinking, *it's over. I'm caught.*

"Got you?" The officer laughed. "Mr. Strowe stopped by the police station and asked for me to pick up a Naomi from Lookout Ridge. The description fits you. Come on, I'll take you to the estate. By the way, I'm Jerry. We're casual here. Everyone goes by his or her first name except Mr. Strowe. I don't think more than five people know his first name."

"How did he know I was coming?" Sarah asked. "I didn't even know myself until two hours ago."

"Oh what he knows would amaze you. Why just the other day he came by and suggested that we put an extra guard on at the bank. He felt that someone was going to try to rob it. Guess what, someone did try to but we caught him. Yep, we don't question Mr. Strowe's word and you shouldn't either," Jerry went on as if it were a one-sided conversation. "If he's on your side, you'll be safe from any shadow you might have left behind in Lookout Ridge.

She got into the squad car with a sense of fear that she might end in jail. They went about three miles west out of Crestline on Highway 30 and turned right. They traveled about another mile and turned right again. All the way Jerry held a one-sided conversation; Sarah was too scared to talk. He turned right one more time on a crest of a hill. There, before Sarah, was a gorgeous landscaped field filled with cattle grazing. Jerry turned onto the lane, Sarah couldn't help but notice that every tree was pruned the same height, about six feet from the ground. The white fence, the trees and the buildings behind them blended into a perfect picture. They went another quarter of a mile and suddenly in a hollow stood what looked like a white stone castle. Sarah never saw a house so big and beautiful. The gardener, in old patched-up clothes, was working on some bushes in front of the house. Sarah got out of the squad car, thanked Jerry and walked up to him.

"Excuse me sir," said Sarah trembling, "I'm looking for the servant's entrance."

"There isn't one," he replied. "We're equal here. If you want to talk to someone, you go through that door and tell them whom you want to speak with. You must be Naomi. We've been waiting for you." He got up, took off his gloves, and offered her his hand. "I'm Mr. Strowe. You have an envelope for me?"

Sarah put down her suitcase, opened her purse and handed him the envelope. "I'm sorry, but I am Sarah McGee, from New York City," she corrected him, as she once again picked up her suitcase.

"Not only are you Naomi, but from now on you will be Naomi from Lookout Ridge. It's for your safety. Father Ken told me of you. I have a job for you if you want it. If you don't like it, you can quit, but then you will have to leave my protection and never come back. The pay will be your room and board plus a wage. If that is acceptable I will take you to your room," replied Mr. Strowe. Acting as if it was already a done deal he continued. "You can leave your suitcase. We don't talk about our past troubles here. Everyone has their own shadows to hide from, and they don't need to hide from yours. Besides, if they know too much they can say something by accident to those outside the estate. And you wouldn't want that would you?"

Mr. Strowe was a large-boned man, taller then she and stocky built. His hair was thick and black except for his temples which were pure white. He walked in the cadence of a military officer and yet his large soft brown eyes gave Sarah the feeling that he would take care of everything. With every gesture, or move, there was a sense of command about him, except for his clothes that said. *I wish I could be a commoner like you.*

"By the way you are not being held captive here. There's a town just west of us called Bucyrus and a city a little farther east of us called Mansfield. If you need to go shopping or just get away, I'll see to it that you have transport to and from. We have cars to go to town, but horses and buggies for Willow Creek Estate. Also, if you feel that you need to talk to someone about your past, talk to me. Remember if no one knows of your past, no one can find you. Don't trust the police, the priest, or even my wife—they might talk. I have put my life in your hands by having you here, so be careful."

The house was as beautiful inside as it was outside. From foyer to kitchen, everything was spotlessly clean and brightly painted. The rooms went on endlessly as he moved from room to room. There was a large library where she was given permission to take out books to read in her spare time. A ballroom with pillars and gorgeous chandlers hanging from the ceiling, everything looked like it just came out of a book.

Naomi stood in the middle of the ballroom and just stared at the surroundings.

"What's wrong Naomi?" Mr. Strowe asked.

"Oh, I just can't believe there are rooms like this. I dreamed of them, this is beautiful.

"Yes, and when we have parties for the staff, you will be dancing in your own dreams." As Mr. Strowe laughed, it seemed as if the building shook.

He took her to her room on the third floor. The room was large, the walls off-white, the ceiling a bright white, and the curtains Irish green. It looked as big as the apartment back home. She almost said so and then thought better. After all, she wasn't to speak of her past.

Mr. Strowe smiled. "Its okay, Naomi. You'll get used to it. I'll have one of the boys bring your suitcase up."

Naomi looked at him for a moment wondering if he was psychic; he knew what she was thinking.

As they went back down the stairs, Mr. Strowe explained the rules and her job description. The rules were simple: no speaking of one's past, no real name, do your job as needed. She was going to be one of the laundry women; there were two others working with her. Once a month, sometimes more, she would have the responsibility of getting ready for, and then cleaning up after, the parties.

"We work together here when we have a party;" Mr. Strowe said, "so don't get overwhelmed. Oh, I'd like to introduce you to my wife. She should be here somewhere."

They walked into a large room filled with plants, formal furniture and many flowers. A woman was sitting all dressed in black, and writing what looked like a letter. "I'd like you to meet Mrs. Strowe. Sweetheart, this is Naomi, a new employee."

Naomi smiled and said, "Hello," and offered Mrs. Strowe her hand. Mrs. Strowe simply nodded, gave her a cold look and went back to writing. *Strange woman,* thought Naomi, *no smile, no light in her eyes, almost as if she isn't here, even though her body is.*

"We lost our only child a few years ago," said Mr. Strowe. "She is still grieving our loss."

The dinner bell rang and the two of them went into the dining room. It was a servant's eating area. The curtains were white cotton and the walls had a fresh painted look to them. A long table was set for about twenty people. "We eat together, except the married employees. I'll introduce you, but don't try to remember their names, you'll learn them later," suggested Mr. Strowe as he looked over those seated at the table.

The names went into one ear and out the other as Mr. Strowe went down the table. One name did stand out, however, Garrett Adams, a tall man, with flaming red hair and warm smile, although he tried to hide it as fast as he showed it. He wore a dark blue work shirt that was stained with perspiration and blue jeans that were tight in all the right places. Mr. Strowe introduced him as the Head of Buildings and Grounds. For some reason she made a note of that. *Cute,* she thought, as she sat across from him. When all the people were introduced, they said grace and began eating.

"Do they feed you like this all the time, Garrett?" Naomi blushed as if she was a little girl again.

"Nope, this is the light meal. The big meal comes at noon. Now that's when we have a feast," Garrett said, without even looking at her.

His food is more important to him than I am, Naomi guessed, as she ate her soup and sandwiches, with banana pudding as dessert.

It took Naomi about a week to learn her responsibilities, washing the clothes, hanging them out to dry, starching and ironing and putting them away. Five-thirty a.m. was wake up time, breakfast at 6:30 a.m. Naomi tried talking to Garrett during the meals and when he brought his dirty clothes, but he just didn't seem interested. She asked if he had someone that he was seeing.

"Only the barmaids at the local pub," was the only answer she got.

Four months later a staff party was announced. Everyone was asking one another whom he or she was going with. Naomi knew whom she wanted to go with, but would he ask her? She asked her new friend, Jenny, a large boned, opinionated woman, what she should do.

"That's a strange one, Naomi. He comes and goes like an easterly."

By now, Naomi knew what the term easterly meant; no-good weather comes from the east.

"Well I'm going to ask him," Naomi said.

"You can do it, but you'll only get hurt," replied Jenny.

Naomi was washing clothes when Garrett brought in his weekly laundry. They had some small talk and then Naomi took a deep breath and said, "Garrett, I'm planning to go to the party and I want you to take me!"

Garrett stood there with the dumbest look on his face. Naomi almost broke out laughing.

"W-Why?" He stuttered. "I mean you can go with any man here. I heard them ask you. Why me?"

"I have been asked, but it's you I want to go with." Once again she blushed. "So are we going or not, Garrett?" Naomi asked, scared to death the answer would be no.

"I don't go to those." Garrett's face turned bright red.

"I know you go and see the barmaids at the local pub. But this time you're going with me," Naomi was determined to get a yes.

"I don't have to get all dressed up, do I?" Garrett was squirming now; Naomi could see that he was hoping to get out of there before she asked for anything else.

"No, you don't even have to pick-me-up. I'll just meet you there."

"So you got Garrett to go out with you." Mr. Strowe came around the corner. "Just be patient with him. He's a good catch, he has been deeply hurt, so be patient with him." With that, he was gone.

The party was in full swing and Garrett hadn't shown up. A live band played on the balcony of the ballroom, which was decorated with special flowers and streamers. *Maybe he isn't coming,* she thought as she once again turned down a request to dance. She stood off to the side of the room, wearing a gown of forest green chiffon, suited to accent her peaches-and-cream complexion. The scalloped edge of the neckline encircled her shoulders and swooped enticingly low over her breast. She wore her dark red hair swept up to frame her face, with a few stray tendrils cascading down her back. Suddenly there was a trembling hand on her shoulder and she heard his voice.

"Can I have this dance?" He asked.

Naomi turned and found herself in the arms of the man she wanted to spend the rest of her life with. He wore a navy blue blazer with brass buttons, a white shirt open at the neck and gray dress slacks. His clothes looked a little large in the waist and short in the legs, as if he had borrowed them from Mr. Strowe. Naomi didn't say a word. They danced until the last dance was over. They went walking in the moonlight, talking about everything and nothing. Finally, she suggested that they should get back; hoping he would suggest a kiss, but none came.

They saw each other more and more over the next six months. One day Mr. Strowe said that he needed to speak to Naomi alone. There was a sense of urgency in his voice and she wondered what had happened. Did someone find out she was there? Did he find out what she had done and want her out of there? *"God I love this place, don't let them throw me out, please Lord,"* she prayed as she went into his office. Garrett was sitting there, looking scared and out of place.

"What's wrong Garrett?" Were the first words out of Naomi's mouth as she knelt beside him.

"I guess you're right, Garrett, she is twitter pated," Mr. Strowe said. "Garrett here has come to me with a problem; he feels that he has fallen in love with you. You have just proven your feelings for him, by asking about him even before you knew what we're here to talk about. Now this is the problem: you know the rule of not telling anyone about your past. But should a husband and wife keep secrets from each other? Garrett thinks not, how do you feel about it Naomi?"

"S-Shouldn't he ask me to marry him first?" Naomi stammered.

"Normally, yes, but Garrett feels that he doesn't deserve you. He didn't know what to do, so he came to me. Remember when you first came here, I told you if you needed to talk with anyone,

I was here to listen? Well he needed someone to talk to, and I listened. So what do you think should there or shouldn't there be secrets, Naomi?"

"No…I don't know…am I good enough for him?" With the blood rushing to her face, Naomi felt like she was about to explode.

"Well, I guess we'll have to find out. I don't play God, so what I'll do is let you have my office to talk alone. Take your time. You can talk about anything except giving your real name, place of birth and former address," Mr. Strowe got up and left the room.

Suddenly the room became quiet; Sarah sat next to Garrett, waiting. Looking around she noticed the beautiful walnut desk and the hand-upholstered chairs. Finally she decided that if they were going to talk she would have to start the conversation.

"Garrett," Sarah placed her hand in his, "usually now days when a girl gets engaged the man says something like, 'I love you.' Now I know that for some men that is hard to say. I don't ever remember my father saying that to my mother, but I do know that she wanted to hear it. Because I do love you, Garrett Adams, I will tell you about my life."

They talked into the night about their pasts. At one point Garrett suggested that they turn on the light. Sarah countered with suggesting that he light the fireplace. When Naomi spoke of Frankie, she noticed Garrett's reactions. He got mad when she spoke of the raping of her sisters and the threat she got from Frankie. When she spoke cutting off Frankie's manhood, Garrett pulled his legs together tightly and laughed nervously.

Garrett explained that he had gotten into a fight in a pub and was accused of killing the son of someone important. The law was after him, even though it was self-defense. His witnesses said that a shot rang out after Garrett was knocked unconscious, but his witnesses suddenly disappeared. So he fled, leaving behind a pregnant wife. He had heard that when they couldn't find him, they killed his wife and unborn child, but he couldn't prove it.

He spoke of his many barmaids. He gave his virginity to a barmaid before he was married; since then, he enjoyed making love to them because there were no strings attached. You just do it, get your physical release, pay them and then move on. And when memories came to haunt him, they made them go away. Naomi felt cheated hearing this part of his life. *Would he stay faithful to her? What would happen if she couldn't satisfy him?*

Finally, they kissed and Naomi knew everything was going to be okay. She would make him faithful no matter what it cost. She loved him. And for the first time someone loved her. As they kissed, she wanted him more than anything in the world. He held her tightly in his arms and she knew that if he asked to make love to her, she would say yes.

"You haven't eaten, my love," she said to Garrett, but he ignored her.

"I guess we better go and tell Mr. Strowe," said Garrett as he took her hand.

The next six months flew by with the work that had to be done and the planning for the wedding. Mr. Strowe arranged for the wedding to be at the Catholic Church and then the reception at the estate. Jenny was going to be the maid of honor, Mr. Strowe the best man.

One day Garrett arranged for Naomi and him to have a day off. He told her to be ready at 1:30 p.m. because he was going to take her to his favorite spot. He had a picnic dinner made up and he came to the door with Mr. Strowe's best horses and carriage. A shiny black surrey pulled by Satin and Silk, World Champion Hackneys. They rode down the back driveway, past the barns, across the road and into the woods. Naomi sat as close as she could to the love of her life feeling that her heart was going to burst.

Suddenly they came to a sharp turn. There before her was a new house being built. It was a white bungalow with a porch wrapped around it. "It's going to be done in a week," said Garrett. "It's Mr. Strowe's gift to us as long as we work for him."

"It's lovely, Garrett, can we go in and see it?"

"Sure, everything is done but the hardware on kitchen cabinets and the trim in the living room. It has three bedrooms, a living room, bath, kitchen, and laundry room so you don't have to go up to the house all the time for your laundry work. The laundry room has a stove so you can boil the sheets without going into the kitchen. Oh, he's going to have me build a shop in the back, so we can spend more time together. He said that he wants to hear the sound of a baby crying by next year."

Shyly, Garrett took her through the house. Explaining each room as they went through, "and I thought this room would be our 'playroom', it overlooks the lake and when the moon is full, it will shine through our window. Mr. Strowe thought maybe we should have a fireplace in the bedroom, but I said no. We'll keep each other warm." Garrett laughed nervously.

Naomi blushed, but kept quiet; it was obvious that Garrett didn't understand the many uses of a fireplace.

Garrett was bubbling over with joy and pride. "Mr. Strowe has some furniture we can use until we can buy some of our own."

"That will work just fine, Garrett." Naomi reached up and kissed him.

They got back into the carriage and followed the road around the lake. There in a clearing was the most beautiful sight Naomi had ever seen. Waterfalls, swans swimming, the trees were the perfect combination of hardwood and pine. Across the lake she thought she saw a deer drinking with a fawn standing next to her, the brilliant color of the changing leaves behind them.

The air smelled so pure and clean, birds were singing and only the sound of small animals running through the fallen leaves broke the silence.

Garrett placed a blanket on the ground and took out the picnic dinner. "Mr. Strowe gave me this wine; he said it would go well with the meal. He also said that if anything happened, we were to break the glasses against a tree for good luck."

Garrett was nervous, Naomi could tell, because he was talking a mile a minute. What happened to the man who would never say more than five words to anyone? She sat down on the blanket and reached up to Garrett and whispered in his ear, "Then let's make something happen."

They kissed passionately and let their hands explore each other's bodies. He slowly undressed her, amazed at the beauty of her body, her firm breasts, inviting him to kiss them. As his lips touched them, Naomi flinched for a moment and then yielded to his touch.

As their passion mounted she rolled over on her back and welcomed him. First a twinge of pain, then complete ecstasy. With each thrust she wanted more and more. When she finally came with a "yes" her body relaxed.

They ate the picnic dinner and then made love again. Once again, she felt him fill her with his passion. All she cared about was that she gave herself for the first time to her man; no one else would have that privilege.

As the moon rose, Garrett filled the last of the wine in their glasses and toasted to their life together. Throwing their glasses against the tree, they shattered their past into a million pieces.

They were married a week later. Naomi wore a plan white dress, holding red roses and a tatted lace handkerchief with S.A. on it. Garrett wore his borrowed blazer, but this time he had a gray tie. The priest, Father Van Horn, a tall thin Dutchman who took his duties seriously, told them that they needed to get their hearts right with the Almighty. For when a man finds a wife, he is blessed by God Himself. And to put one's wife and his physical pleasures before God's service would be to live outside God's love. To live outside of His love is sin and damnation to the soul.

The party was the usual Strowe's party, a live band, much food and liquor. Everyone was there, mayors, committeepersons, important people mixing with the disadvantaged, laughing, drinking, eating and dancing. The cake was a four-tiered lemon cake with cream filling, a real masterpiece. The bride and the groom danced with everyone at least once; finally they had to sit down exhausted.

Mrs. Strowe dressed in a black floor-length evening gown, came to give the happy couple her blessings, and then left for a walk. Naomi noticed that Father Van Horn left a few minutes after she did in the same direction. But the day was hers and she was having fun, she would worry about Mrs. Strowe tomorrow.

They moved into their new house that night and after an easy pregnancy, nine months later Henry was born. Mr. Strowe brought in a midwife to help Naomi. Henry gave both of them a sense of security in their marriage. Now they had something that was the fruit of their love. Time moved on, parties, repairs of the building and laundry. One day passed on to the other, like a never-ending wheel.

Ken had a habit of sitting on a fence rail by the house in the evening, thinking of heaven. How he wished he was there, but he felt compelled to stay near. Did he make the right choice? Had Gabriel waited at the church steps for him? Suddenly a breeze blew, he looked up and there was Gabriel.

"Well you didn't come looking for me, so I decided to come looking for you, what happened?" Gabriel asked.

"You know, Sir, I just couldn't leave her alone. I did what I was told to do, nothing more, and nothing less, just what I was told to do. What does she do, but takes on this man, cuts him and then flees. I had to help. No one cared. I couldn't leave her alone," Ken replied.

"So my little angel has finally learned what it means to be an angel," said Gabriel as he gave Ken a big hug. "You did well, but we do have a problem. Because of this decision, you will have to become a human again either within this family or another one.

But you have to do this, or else you will just float around as a spirit for all eternity."

"How do I do that?" Ken asked.

"That's not for you to know, just that you are willing. The Master will do the rest," Gabriel answered.

"I would like to be in this family," said Ken.

"You haven't changed have you Ken." Gabriel smiled at Kenneth's reaction, "You are always ready to jump into something you know nothing about. To become a human means that you will have only a haunting memory of your former life. You will have to learn all over that which you now know. The one thing you will keep is your desire to help people."

"But if I don't become a human, you said I couldn't get my wings," Ken stated with a confused look on his face.

"You're right," Gabriel started to leave. "Oh, by the way, the Master is proud of you. And wants you to know that you will never be alone, call and He will answer you."

The moon was rising over the lake as the music from the house came gently through the trees. Garrett and Naomi slowly swayed in each other's arms in rhythm with the music, dreaming of the day they could have a house just as beautiful as the one that supplied their music. Instead of champagne, they had to be content with the left-over wine from the boss's previous meal. Nevertheless, life was good. Garrett kept the buildings in good working order, and Naomi kept the linen and clothes clean. When the sun set, the parties would begin, Garrett and Naomi would step out of reality, into their own little world of make believe. It was a time to dream.

"Is Henry sleeping, Mother?" Garrett asked with a sheepish smile.

"Yes, dear," whispered Naomi. They danced their way to the bedroom, tenderly undressing each other. The love that flowed between them lasted throughout the night. By early morning, Naomi had conceived Kenneth in a love that should not be broken.

Kenneth wasn't easy on Naomi as she carried him. It seemed like every little thing that bothered her bothered him. The time

Garrett slipped off the balcony and strained his shoulder, she felt the pain; in so doing, Kenneth suffered too. Henry, who was two, came down with the chicken pox. The doctor told Naomi to stay away from him or the child she was caring could catch the disease and be born blind. Kenneth wondered if she knew how much fear he experienced because of the hidden fear she carried. However, for each cause of concern and fear that Naomi experienced, Kenneth retaliated. Morning sickness lasted all-day for the full nine months; it became so bad that Mrs. Strowe asked Naomi, "not to come to the house." She looked like a walking skeleton. Garrett had to pick up the laundry and bring it down to the house so she could continue to work.

What amazed Kenneth was that as the unborn child, he had more peace than his mother. There was some pain when the sperm penetrated the egg when he was conceived. Yet that was the pain of creation. The security felt by the unborn child is second only to the peace and quietness that comes as death calls one home. There was never any hunger or loneliness for the mother was always present. Still, the motherly instinct that existed within her draws fears. Fear of the unknown, of the past haunting her. Could it be that God was already preparing Kenneth to linger within His presence? Whenever Naomi started to live in the past fears, she would see that little piece of paper: "Remember you are loved by many. You are never alone." Not only giving her the confidence to go on, but to minister to her unborn child the peace that all was well.

Days turned into weeks and weeks into months. Kenneth could tell it was getting colder because Naomi's blood was getting thicker. The joy that Naomi was experiencing was causing happiness to vibrate throughout his body. As sick as she was, Naomi enjoyed her pregnancy.

She slipped on some ice and that upset Kenneth's security. In a few hours, he was back to normal, listening to the laughter that existed around him. The smell of the pine needles didn't agree with him, neither did the wine Naomi drank when Garrett wasn't around. Kenneth knew why she was drinking. Her mother always said, "The redness of the wine is good for the blood." But it was the loneliness she experienced when Garrett was gone. She knew that he was with Missy the barmaid. Naomi never realized that that same blood was feeding her unborn child. Thank goodness, she wasn't a smoker like Garrett.

By now, Kenneth had become a little person. His brain was almost fully developed; his organs were all in place. The room that Naomi had for him had become a little crowded. Maybe if he turned a little this way—not that damn cord again—that way maybe…still no good. He knew there was a better way; God wouldn't want him to be this uncomfortable. Better be a little more careful; Naomi was beginning to worry. Well, it's time to sleep…try again tomorrow. During the night peacefulness fell on him. A light surrounded him. Gently someone moved him into a new position…ah much better.

March winds, April showers, all bring May flowers. Kenneth didn't know about the latter part of the poem, but March was turbulent. He could hear Naomi and Garrett arguing more and more those days. Garrett said the doctor told him the baby was overdue. Naomi claimed that everything was normal; the doctor didn't know what was going on. *That is funny, Garrett got her pregnant and she carries the child for nine months. Then Garrett lets a stranger tell him that she doesn't know what is going on. Don't they remember how comfortable and safe it is in the mother's womb?* Kenneth wasn't sure he wanted to be born. Besides, his lungs weren't developed to their fullest potential, and everyone knows how important it is to have a good pair of lungs once you get into the world. However, something was wrong out there. Naomi was talking about being miles from the nearest doctor. There are no-good midwives in the area, as there was when Henry was born. Still, Naomi wasn't in the best of health. Kenneth noticed the quality of food from her blood wasn't as good as before. Maybe he was being too hard on her, but he did have to eat.

Garrett was gone for the day. He said it was on business, but mother said it was to see that woman at the bar. A strange easterly wind was in the trees; Naomi said it meant a big storm was coming up. Kenneth hoped that someone knew it was time for him to be born. He tried to send his mother a message, *Mother, now is the time you should be worrying. I do hope you have someone to help you. How do you do this now, headfirst or feetfirst? God, where is the doctor? Mother I need help and I need it NOW! So you decided we could do this alone. There is that light again coming toward me.* He felt its peace. It helped. Naomi wasn't breathing in rhythm to the messages that Kenneth was sending her. *There's that stupid cord trying to go around my neck, and I know that isn't right. The light is trying to say, relax, everything is going to be all right. Headfirst, down the tunnel, easy now. Don't panic. Everything is okay. A little farther…that's it. Ah, it's over. So this is what birth is all about?*

Naomi spanked him on the bottom to get him breathing. Kenneth started to cry. "I haven't done anything wrong, mother. Mother is that you? Yes, yes I hear the beat of your heart." Kenneth could recognize that sound anywhere; he heard the soft cry of Naomi's voice. *Don't cry Mother!*

Strange sounds were still all-around him. The wind was blowing the newly fallen snow. Naomi said Garrett wouldn't come home tonight. There was disappointment in her voice as she looked out the window and whispered, "What is wrong with that man? Every time there's something important, he's out." Tears fell again as she laid Kenneth in the top-drawer of the dresser and called, "Henry! Henry, come in here and watch Kenny while I go out and get wood for the stove."

Henry toddled to the dresser and stood up to peek in. "So you're Henry. Ouch stop poking me! I thought that maybe we could be friends. Mother, he's hurting me. Mother! Mother! I want my mother!"

"Henry, what's wrong," called Naomi as she ran into the room. "Go into the living room, Henry." Naomi picked Henry up, turned him around, patted his seat, and then picked Kenneth up.

Naomi wasn't the same. She cried a lot. It sounded like a cry of relief though. Kenneth knew that she missed his father.

Kenneth's favorite time was eating. He got to be alone with his mother and enjoy the warmth and tenderness of her touch. He thought that he could handle Henry as long as he had her love. Kenneth wondered if he was going to have this problem with Henry all his life. It was funny; Henry and he were already competing for their mother's attention.

There was a knock at the door and Naomi put Kenneth down. "Garrett!"

It must be Father.

"Where have you been? I've been worried sick. What took you so long? God I missed you. You're frozen clear through. Come, sit down by the fire and I'll get something to warm you up."

Ah, it is father; mother doesn't have that fear in her voice any longer. Here come the tears again.

"Say, Mother, you've lost weight. What happened, you put yourself on a diet?"

It is Father, you can tell by the strong laughter in his voice.

"Oh, I forgot all about our son. Come on in the bedroom and meet your son dear," said Naomi.

So this is my father. You don't look like what I thought you would. All the hair on your face, I don't think I'm going to like it much, but the red hair and blue eyes, and that laugh—oh the laugh won my heart.

"Well, well, let me see this good-looking young man." Garrett laughed and held Kenneth. "We did proud, dear. What did you name him? I hope it isn't Garrett."

"I didn't name him, Garrett, I named him Kenny Edward Adams," said Naomi with some hesitancy. She knew how important it was to Garrett that his children had good solid names. As Garrett held Kenny in silence Naomi came over, trying to read the look on his face. "If you don't like it, we can change it. I just thought that—"

"Know what, Mother," Garrett interrupted, "you did a good job naming my son. Only one minor change, no son of mine is going to be called Kenny. He will be called Kenneth Edward Adams." He handed Kenneth back to Naomi with a smile. "You did it again to me, didn't you woman? You knew I should have something to say about naming him. What did you do but set me up so I can feel a part of naming our son. Did I ever tell you I love you?"

Naomi and Garrett were sitting at the dinner table one evening discussing different things. Suddenly, Garrett said, "I was talking to Mr. Strowe this morning. He feels that we should move to a larger house. He said we could design it." Garrett was talking to himself more than to Naomi. "But why would I want to move? We're making it in this three-bedroom house. What's wrong with this house? What do I want with a house with no view, no privacy and no real feelings?"

"Memories, dear, memories, not feelings," corrected Naomi. Tears of fear were filling her eyes.

"Now Mother, no crying," Garrett said. "I'll just tell old man Strowe, that he can stick his 'larger' house where the sun doesn't shine. If he thinks he can push Garrett Edward Adams around, he is sadly mistaken. After all I was looking for a job when I found this one."

"Garrett, we have hardly any money. How can we JUST . . . just . . . just leave?" Naomi was getting a hold of herself, but fear was running rampant through her body. She knew that she had to do something, or Garrett would have them on the street.

"Tell Mr. Strowe that he is so kind for thinking of us. And since he is the boss, if he wants us to move to a larger house, we will be more than happy to do so. But he would have to remove the trees so we can see the lake," replied Naomi.

"Do you think Mr. Strowe is going to touch his precious trees?" Asked Garrett, surprised by Naomi's reaction to moving. "I mean those trees are almost like God to him. He planted them with his own two hands when he first moved on the land. His wife was in labor, and had to sit and wait while he fought the brushfire so the trees wouldn't get burned. And in the meantime, she lost their child. No, no he wouldn't hear of it."

"I know," whispered Naomi with a mischievous smile. "But this way we can give him a chance to change his order. You see, I don't plan to move from our house, unless it's into our own home.

"By the way, I asked Father Van Horn to baptize Kenneth. He said there's more to Christian baptism than getting a kid wet. I told him that no matter what, we want Kenneth baptized." What she meant was that SHE wanted Kenneth baptized. "He said that he would be over tomorrow for dinner to talk about it with us. But we shouldn't count on him baptizing Kenneth." There was worry in Naomi's voice. She heard that Father Van Horn was strict about baptisms, plus if you didn't agree with him, he would embarrass you in public.

"Let him come," Garrett said, "I'll talk with him, but he better remember that we are members of the church."

"He said that can be changed. After all, we haven't been in church for almost three years. You don't think," she went on, "that he can have our names removed from the membership roll just because we haven't been in church do you? I couldn't show my face in town if our friends found out that we were thrown out of the church. Please don't say anything that would upset him, dear. I know you don't like him but our son's soul is in his complete control," Naomi pleaded.

"Sweetheart, don't worry. We'll have Kenneth baptized in the church." Garrett leaned over the table, kissed her forehead, and took her hands.

The touch of his lips and hands sent peacefulness throughout her body. Somehow, Naomi knew it was going to be all right.

"Oh, by the way, I love you." Garrett smiled and walked out of the house.

The next evening Father Van Horn drove up in his fancy car just before dinner. He was heavier than Garrett and about six inches taller. Naomi had been sure to remove all the wine from the house so Father Van Horn wouldn't think they were drunkards. She gave Garrett and Henry a last-minute lecture on manners. Dinner was served on the best china; the fireplace was burning brightly, and everything seemed to be going well. Both Henry and Garrett were behaving, nothing but small talk, weather and the crops.

Suddenly, Father Van Horn turned to Garrett. "So you expect the church to drop what it stands for just so you can have your son baptized." There was disgust in his voice and hatred in his glare.

You could hear a pin drop as Garrett looked him in the eyes. His jaw tightened; his face turned red, and the muscles on his neck stood out. With a voice that could hardly be heard and yet cut to the marrow of the bone, Garrett replied. "Father Van Horn, I believe in Jesus Christ. I believe that each day is a gift from God, a chance to live, to follow Christ. Part of following Christ is to practice His teachings. Now, Kenneth is a gift from God. He will be baptized in the church."

Naomi's heart had just stopped beating. Garrett never spoke in this manner unless he was mad.

"What he means, Father Van Horn, is that no matter what we have done, this child is a gift from God. We would like to recognize that and in a sense give Kenneth back to Him."

She was trying to break the tension. It feels like she's ready to cry.

"A gift from God," Father Van Horn laughed. "You must be kidding. This child isn't a gift from God. He's a product of sexual lust, like between a sow and a boar. In other words, this child is a product of sin. You cannot give a product of sin to a Holy God and expect everything to be okay. And I won't be the one to give a stamp of approval to the sin of sexual lust."

Naomi's temperature suddenly rose. She felt as if she were about to explode. Kenneth felt tears coming, but he didn't see any. How could she keep control of the emotions that Kenneth felt vibrating through her body as he lay in her arms? Kenneth sensed the strength of a woman who loved her family.

Garrett too was on edge; he rose from his chair and walked over to the fireplace. As he looked into the fire, he took a deep breath. No longer was it an issue of baptism. The line had been drawn; Father Van Horn had gone too far. To call his wife a sow in his presence was reason enough to beat this man to death. Garrett didn't like it when Naomi cried or was upset. He didn't like it when someone compared his wife to a pig.

With a voice that could cut cold steel, Garrett turned to Father Van Horn. "Let me tell you a story. Last summer I was walking with a friend, a deacon of my church, through the orchard when we heard sounds. It was the sound of someone gasping for breath and yet yelling in ecstasy." He paused as if he was about to say something and then changed his mind. "We followed the sound until we came on this couple passionately embraced. We saw the woman's face clearly. The man's face we couldn't see, but there was a large mole on his right shoulder. There was also a large birthmark on his right buttock, which we both can describe. Now I never condemn what one does with his or her life that is between them and their God. What I saw is what I saw and that cannot be denied. Now, I will have my son baptized in 'my' church."

"If you're trying to say something, say it," mumbled Father Van Horn. "If not, let's not stray from the subject. I must say I'm appalled that you would slander such a fine Christian woman as Mrs. Strowe. Let me say that no man should talk in such an obscene manner before his wife and children. If you had any respect at all for womanhood or for me as your priest, you would be more careful with your language." After a long pause, Father Van Horn continued. "Well it's getting late and I have people waiting for me. What your story had to do with your son's baptism is beyond me. Let me think it over, but remember God has called me to protect His laws." He got up to leave.

"By the way Father, I never said it was Mrs. Strowe, so how did you know?" Garrett asked quietly as he opened the door for him.

"Yes you did Garrett, you're not going to trick me," snarled Father Van Horn as he hurried out to his car.

Garrett stood there smiling, as if he had just won the war.

Naomi and Garrett talked long into the night about the meeting. Naomi was furious with Garrett for telling a story that would put their jobs and Kenneth's baptism in jeopardy. No way would a woman of Mrs. Strowe's stature be involved with another man. Garrett didn't say much that night. He would only smile and repeatedly say, "Don't worry, mother, our jobs are not in jeopardy and our son will be baptized in our church."

On July 3rd Kenneth was in the church waiting to be baptized. The church was about half-full, mostly with friends of his parents and the Strowe's. The sermon title was "Be Not Deceived." Kenneth sat on his father's lap as Father Van Horn preached. The sermon content was about a child who was conceived in the sin of sexual lust and should not be recognized by the church as a child of God. Therefore, the Church of God shouldn't compromise her purity by rubber-stamping children through baptism. Garrett was about to burst into laughter. What was so funny was beyond Kenneth, but his blood was bubbling merrily along. It was as if he had won and no matter what was being said, he knew he was the victor.

Naomi on the other hand didn't see anything funny and took the sermon personally.

With the service over, Father Van Horn went into the Rite of Baptism. The Strowe's were named godparents. As Kenneth was placed into Father Van Horn's arms, he had an accident.

The whole congregation burst into laughter. Father Van Horn just stood there with Kenneth's breakfast all over his white robe mumbling, "Damn child of the devil." Then with a clear voice, he called out, "By what name will this child be called?"

"Kenneth Edward Adams," replied Garrett, trying to hold a straight face.

"Kenneth Edward Adams, I baptize you in the name of the Father, and of the Son, and of the Holy Ghost. Let us pray, O God, we offer to you now, your son, Kenneth Edward Adams. We realize that he came into this world from you; we now give him back to you to protect, guide and bless. We ask that you might bless him in his coming in and going out, his work and his play, in his rising up and lying down now and forever more. Amen."

Turning to Naomi and Garrett, he once again warned them of their sinful ways. "For if you don't change and come to church, as your priest, I must warn you, God will bring judgment on you and your household."

With that they went home and the party started. The Strowe's had it in the main house on top of the hill. Once again the live band played, people danced. This time, however, there were only about thirty families present. Naomi said she wanted it small.

Father Van Horn came over to share in the joy. Garrett was talking with him while holding Kenneth. "Have you forgotten something, Garrett?" Father Van Horn asked.

"What do you mean, Father?"

"The fee for baptizing your son, normally the parents of the child give a generous gift of twenty dollars to the Church," replied Father Van Horn. "But if you don't have the money, I understand. Of course, I could speak to Mrs. Adams; she is more concerned with Kenneth's soul than you are. You know his name hasn't been listed on the church records yet for Christian Baptism."

"Twenty dollars…that's-that's two days wages," Garrett

stuttered as he turned to go to the house. Finding Naomi, he placed Kenneth in her arms. "I'll be right back."

Garrett went home and took the money out of the jar that was for emergencies. When he came back, he found Father Van Horn. As he handed him the money, he said, "Here is your money Father. I hope it blesses you as much as you have blessed others."

Kenneth remembered the music and the laughter. All was well as sleep came on him.

Sometime later Kenneth was waking up, when Mr. Strowe asked, "Garrett, my wife is gone, and I can't find her. Have you seen her?"

"Yes, sir, half an hour ago she was talking to Reverend Van Horn. Then she went up the north path by herself. I guess she wanted to be alone. If you go that way you probably will meet her coming back, or by the waterfall."

"That's her favorite place. What that woman does there is beyond me. Thanks, I'll go find her." Mr. Strowe turned to go.

"Garrett, Father Van Horn followed her there not five minutes later. You don't think—no. Forgive me Lord for even thinking it," said Naomi.

"Honey, it takes more than one to tango. I don't think Mrs. Strowe or Father Van Horn is as innocent as you may want them to be," said Garrett.

Mr. and Mrs. Strowe came back shortly after that. What happened to Father Van Horn, no one ever heard. The party broke up shortly afterward, something about Mrs. Strowe becoming ill. During the next Mass, Father Van Horn announced his resignation effective immediately.

Mr. Strowe asked Naomi and Garrett to the main house about a week later. It was a long meeting; Mrs. Strowe stayed with the children while they talked. It was decided that because of Mrs. Strowe's illness, it would be better that they go abroad. Garrett was asked to move into the main house so he and Naomi could keep an eye on it and the employees.

5

As winter broke and the birds began to return, sickness came to the Adams family. Henry had a temperature and a sore throat. No matter what Naomi tried, it just became worse. He couldn't swallow any food or liquid. All-night Naomi and Garrett took turns sitting with him, humming a tune. Henry could only lie there looking up at the ceiling.

The doctor was finally called and after sometime of poking and checking, he called Naomi and Garrett together: "Henry is in the latter stage of scarlet fever."

Kenneth remembered that moment because Naomi was holding him. The fear just swept through her like a hot knife through butter. Her body trembled as she got up to look out of the window. Garrett just buried his head in his hands and sighed. They both knew what the verdict would be, yet not grasping the meaning of the doctor's statement.

"What are the chances, doctor?" Naomi asked.

He just shook his head and got up to leave.

"You know you must quarantine the house. Everything he has touched must be burnt. As far as the chances of him recovering, they are maybe one out of five hundred at best. I'm sorry, but you called me too late." The door closed behind him. All was quiet.

Lying Kenneth down, Naomi picked Henry up and held her firstborn in her arms. Tears flowed on the fevered body. Garrett kicked the fire in the fireplace, sending sparks flying. "I'll be back," he said. Taking his coat, he walked out of the house. Naomi knew where he was going.

Days seemed like weeks as Henry lie on the threshold of death. Nothing Naomi did, helped. Then one night he was gone. Kenneth heard the scream; he felt the pain—Henry was gone.

Naomi and Kenneth were alone in the house, the single staff had moved into other quarters. Garrett hadn't come back from his "walk".

The next morning, as the sun was rising, Naomi knew what had to be done. Taking Kenneth and a shovel, she headed out to the hillside overlooking the lake. Going back to the house, she carried Kenneth in one arm and Henry in the other. Setting Kenneth beside a tree, she laid her firstborn in the grave that she had dug with her own hands.

Picking Kenneth up and holding him so tightly he could hardly breathe, she quoted the 23rd Psalm, the Rosary and the Lord's Prayer. Setting Kenneth down once again under the tree, Naomi covered her firstborn with dirt. The sun was setting before they headed back to the house. After that day nothing was the same, no matter what the occasion, Naomi was empty.

About a week later Garrett came home from his "walk". They moved themselves back home, boarding up the main house and rearranging permanent living quarters for the single staff.

Garrett kept saying, "Don't worry everything will be all right." But he knew better. Once again, he had failed Naomi. Once again, she needed him standing beside her, to comfort and encourage her, but he was gone doing things that shamed him.

This time the news he had to tell her, he knew would break her heart.

Missy from the bar just had his child, a baby girl, named Sara Lynn. Missy was going to have trouble raising her. What he wanted was to be able to help her financially. But Naomi would have nothing to do with it, "Let that whore take responsibility for her actions," was her final statement on the matter.

Mr. Strowe came home without his wife that summer. With him came a clergyman, a teacher, and a supervisor for the farm. The priest was a gentle man. He spent hours with Naomi and Garrett talking about Henry and the hope of seeing him again. The issue with Garrett was God's judgment for the sins in one's life, especially what went on while he went on his "walks".

Father Hubner would just quote Scripture of God's love. Slowly Garrett began to listen. But Naomi became a stranger to both Garrett and Kenneth. The laughter in her voice was gone; there was no longer any singing in the house. Naomi would go to the hillside that held her son. For hours she would just sit and cry.

Just before Christmas, Garrett left again for a short time. Naomi said, she didn't care what he did and slammed the door. Two days later, he came back with a baby girl in his arms. "Her name is Sara Lynn," he said as he handed her to Naomi, "Woman, this is my child, take care of her."

Naomi stood there for a minute, holding the bundle that he had given her, with a strange look on her face. Then her face became red and for the first time Kenneth heard her swear. Laying Sara Lynn down, she began calling Garrett every name she could think of, throwing any object she could find and threatening his life. She made it clear that she wasn't about to have a bastard child in her house.

That night Garrett slept in the spare bedroom. With him was Sara Lynn, who, like Naomi, cried throughout the night.

Garrett tried to get out of the bedroom, but Naomi had secured the door by tying a towel around the knob and then to a chair.

The next morning Naomi calmed down enough to talk with Garrett about the night before and to feed the baby. Somehow she got him to admit the baby belonged to the barmaid; she couldn't take care of her because she possibly was carrying his second child. Naomi just smiled and assured him that she would take care of everything.

That evening Naomi asked Mr. Strowe if she could be taken to Crestline. On arriving at the bar, Naomi asked Eugene, the driver, to wait for her while she went into the 'I'm Not Here Bar'. She sat in the car sat in the car for a few minutes, holding the baby and trembling uncontrollably. Naomi always dreamed of having a baby girl that she could call Sarah; now she was holding one that wasn't hers. *How could he do this to me?* She thought. *I never thought he could be so cruel, so insensitive. How could I have fallen in love with such a bum?* The trembling changed from the fear of facing the woman who ruined her life to anger toward the one who cheated her out of so much. Was Father Van Horn right about loving someone so much, that it was sin?

"Well, Naomi, what will it be?" Eugene asked.

"Eugene, how could he do this to me?" She asked, not caring if he answered.

"Well Naomi, the last time I checked it takes two to make one of those you're holding. And sometimes it takes three to cause two to get together to make it. So maybe instead of asking how this could happen to you, you should be asking why this has happened to you. Or better yet, what will happen to this child I'm now holding? Remember the moment we are in now is the future of our lives. You don't know, but maybe the good Lord has given you an unexpected gift. So what are you going to do with it? You know in the end, we all choose what lives inside us."

"Now that's a man; put the blame on the woman. Make me responsible for the wrongs of my husband. What about Missy?

She's the one who's determined to break up my happy home. Why not blame her?" Naomi shouted.

"No, I'm saying, stop casting stones and look into the face of that child. And ask, why am I holding her right now, and what future does she have here at the 'I'm Not Here Bar'? Look up there on the second floor. See that window? On the other side of it, that child was conceived and born. There's no electricity or running water up there. The heat in the winter is provided by the downstairs heaters. The mother of that child has to give a portion of her earnings to her boss to live up there in those conditions. She eats leftovers from the food bar; if she wants to bathe, she has to wait until everyone is gone and then use the bathroom downstairs. Need I go on?" Eugene asked.

"No, I am going to get rid of this bastard child and nothing you can say will stop me. Please just stay in the car and wait for me." She got out of the car, walked to the door and opened it.

She stood in the doorway for a moment; the smoke and stench of liquor nearly knocked her over. A woman, who looked pregnant, walked up to her. She had hair the color of the sandy beaches, a pale complexion and an exhausted look about her. As she walked, the men would pinch or pat her bottom. She didn't even flinch at their vulgar touches. "Can I help you?" She asked. "You know babies are not allowed in here."

"I'm looking for Missy," said Naomi.

"That would be me. I'm called 'Missy' here. What do you want?" She asked coldly.

"How can you stand this dirt and smell?" Naomi asked without thinking. "And it looks like you're in the family way, what about the baby?"

"That's the life that was given me to live. I don't judge you in your highfaluting life style, why judge me? I have tables to wait on, so what do you want?"

Naomi looked Missy in the eye and said, "I just wanted to thank you for trusting me to bring up your child. Her name will be changed; but she will be brought up to know love." With that she turned around and walked back to the car.

"Let's go home, Eugene." She got into the car with the baby.

When she arrived back at the house, she woke Garrett up and with her stiletto in her hand said, "If I even hear of you cheating on me again, I'm going to castrate you." After that Garrett didn't go on his walks as often, and if he did, he was home before dinner.

6

Mr. Strowe started to expand his estate. New barns were built for the horses, dairy and beef cattle. Fence lines were changed from split rail to barbwire. There was a sense of excitement each night when Garrett sat down at the table to eat. Even Naomi, as she took care of the baby whom she called Mercy, was changing from the dark shadow of a shell to once again a vocal, loving individual.

On Kenneth's ninth birthday Garrett announced, that it was time for him to earn his keep. Mr. Strowe had offered to give him an apprenticeship. With the training, Kenneth would continue to receive private tutoring from Dr. Schade, the new schoolteacher, he brought from Germany.

The days that followed were happy ones for him. He was taught to train horses for show and racing. Mr. Schmidt was an expert equestrian and loved his work. Daily he went over the tack with Kenneth, explaining how to judge what was good for the horse. Learning how to feel the energy fields on the animal's body, detecting trouble before it occurred, the art of judging livestock for quality and breeding purposes. And of course Kenneth spent hours listening to the stories of the European Equestrian Circuit.

The evenings and Saturdays were spent with Doctor Schade, doing his spelling, grammar, math, writing, reading, how to use his special gifts and much storytelling. Oh, those were the glorious days. Both men had a common saying: "Let there be no waste." Kenneth was always being challenged to find new ways of using leftovers. So when there was no longer any use for something, it returned as energy into the ground.

One summer they had a bad draught and there was no bedding for the animals. Kenneth suggested that they go to Mr. Strowe's sawmill and use the shavings. This not only saved Mr. Strowe money for straw that he couldn't find, but also gave a use for all the shavings that lay rotting on the ground outside his mill.

On Kenneth's twelfth birthday, he asked Mr. Strowe if it was time to get paid for the work he was doing. Garrett was furious. Kenneth didn't know that Mr. Strowe was giving his father three dollars a day for his work. When Mr. Strowe came to the house that night to discuss the request, a new war was declared between Naomi and Garrett.

Mr. Strowe stood before the fireplace, his pipe in his hand. "Garrett and Naomi, we have gone through many difficult times together. When Kenneth was born, didn't I allow you to lighten your responsibilities to be home with Naomi? I'm not sure you're aware that when Kenneth was baptized, I gave the priest fifty dollars for doing the service. When Mrs. Strowe was ill, you stood by me and oversaw the complete estate while I was in Europe. I brought back the best teacher money could buy so your son could receive a solid education, but you decided that he needed an apprenticeship. I rearranged my staff's schedule so Mr. Schmidt could teach him. For the past three years, you have asked for three dollars a day for his labor. I gave it. Yet he eats at my table more than he does at home. Not that it matters—he has become a son to me. This morning he came to me with the idea that he should be paid for the work he does around the estate. Until now, there was nothing I wouldn't do for him. But I won't be fleeced by him."

Garrett's face turned red; veins stood out on his neck. Kenneth knew that he was in trouble. He only remembered one whipping up to that point, but his father wasn't half as mad as he was now.

"Mr. Strowe," Garrett said, "I wasn't aware that Kenneth had intended to speak to you about money. If I had, he would have been stopped. We haven't brought him up that way. He knows that one receives pay for his labor, yes, but his training and education are enough. He will apologize now for this disrespect and greed shown toward you. Kenneth, apologize to Mr. Strowe, *NOW!*"

"I'm sorry, Mr. Strowe; I didn't know Dad was getting the money," Kenneth sobbed.

A short time later Mr. Strowe left the house, Garrett said he was going to teach Kenneth a lesson he would never forget.

"Haven't you done that already, Garrett?" Naomi asked coldly. "Haven't you taught him how to connive and cheat? How dare you judge our son, when you have lied and cheated all your life?" Naomi was only getting started. "Oh, yes you've cheated him all right, and you've cheated me. Now I know where you got your money to stay out all-night with that whore at the tavern, the one who is carrying your child. Don't deny it; I've seen you with my own two eyes. Don't think I'm going to raise that child, because I'm not. There's talk that you promised her that you would leave me to marry her. It will be a cold day in hell before you leave me, Garrett. You don't know it, but I'm carrying a child in my belly and it isn't yours. Therefore, you touch my son, and I will see you in hell."

There was a pause and Naomi continued in a much gentler tone, "I love you Garrett, and I did a foolish thing, but I won't have you hurt my boy. What he asked for was done with my blessing. You didn't tell me you were being paid for his labor.

From now on you will give me the money, or I will have Mr. Strowe give it directly to Kenneth. The choice is yours."

With that Naomi went into the bedroom and slammed the door. All was quiet that night. When Kenneth got up to start the fire in the morning, Garrett was asleep in his favorite chair. He woke up as Kenneth tried to put wood into the fireplace without disturbing him. "Kenneth, you and I will have to go to Mr. Strowe's house today and talk with him," he said quietly.

As Garrett and Kenneth walked up the hill, they didn't say a word, and yet somehow they were communicating with every step they took. Kenneth didn't know what was going to happen. He had the fear of losing his job working with Mr. Schmidt, or even worse his education with Dr. Schade. And yet the lesson that Kenneth learned that day was one of the keys to his success.

As they reached the top of the hill Garrett stopped. "Son, I want you to listen carefully to what I have to say. No one knows what's going to happen in that house. You'll hear some things that you won't understand; you can ask me about them later. What is spoken in this meeting is between you, Mr. Strowe, and me. You mustn't speak of them ever again. Do you understand, Kenneth? Never are you to speak of them again. They will hurt your mother, me, Mr. Strowe, and even yourself."

Fear swept through Kenneth. His father was dead serious; his face looked ghostly, as if he had seen death.

"Remember our exercise? Before we go in, take a deep breath and let it out slowly. As you do, ask yourself what's going on, on the other side of the door."

Kenneth took the deep breath and, as he let it out, he felt that everything was secretive. Something was going on that Mr. Strowe didn't want anyone to know about.

He tried to explain it to his father, but Garrett smiled and said, "Yes, son, everyone has secrets -- hidden shadows that follow us. Remember, unless you're God, you don't have the right to judge. The reason we get along here at Willow Creek is because we let each person deal with his or her own shadows."

They rang the door pull and were welcomed in by Sarat, the housekeeper. She had a warm smile as she welcomed them. "Come in Garrett and Kenneth."

"Never mind the welcome, Sarat," Garrett said sternly, "We came to speak to Mr. Strowe. Is he up yet?"

"Oh, yes Mr. Adams, he is having breakfast. Have you eaten this morning? Maybe I can fix something for the boy." Sarat suddenly seemed nervous. She never was nervous around them before. *What's going on?* Kenneth wondered.

Garrett walked past Sarat and into the dining room unannounced. Mr. Strowe was reading the paper while drinking his coffee. He looked up and laughed. "Garrett, Kenneth come on in. Boy did I open a can of worms last night. Come on in. Sarat fix something for our guests."

"We are not your guests this morning, Mr. Strowe," said Garrett. "We have come to talk about our future here and what has happened in the past. I've brought Kenneth because it not only concerns me, but him as well. I also feel he is of age to enter manhood and should be a part of this discussion. Naomi doesn't know we're here and Kenneth has been told not to discuss anything that is said here this morning with anyone, including his mother."

"Oh Garrett let bygones be bygones. Life is too short to worry about the past. And the future, well who knows what it holds? I wonder if God even knows. Anyway why worry about it?" Mr. Strowe laughed, but the laughter was nervous, not his usual laugh that was always strong and reassuring. Kenneth guessed that he knew his father came there to clear more than just the air over last night.

Garrett was about to speak when Father Hubner came into the room still putting his shirt into his trousers. A look of surprise and fear swept over his and Mr. Strowe's faces. "Garrett…Garrett…This isn't what it seems. Let me explain," Mr. Strowe stammered.

"Maybe I should just move on," said Father Hubner. "I thank

you for your Christian hospitality. You see, I was caught out late last night and Mr. Strowe, the fine Christian man that he is, took me in. Thank you for the act of kindness."

"Sit down!" Garrett demanded. "I know what's going on here and you might as well know that I'm tired of being played the fool."

"What about the lad? Surely you don't want to make a scene in front of him, do you?" Mr. Strowe begged.

"Oh, what my son hears today won't damage his life. There's no doubt in my mind about that, but I would rather have him be here listening than hearing it out there.

So listen real well, because if you don't, I know others who will," Garrett growled. Once again, those veins were sticking out and his face was bright red.

"Fourteen years ago I was sitting at a bar, broke, discouraged, without a job, wanted for murder, with a bride who was expecting, not knowing what had happened to her. Who should come into the bar, but generous Mr. Strowe. I didn't know it then, but I found out later, that you knew I had been fired. You promised you'd get my wife for me, but she got killed before you even tried to find her.

"Remember that night, Mr. Strowe? Well, I do. I do. You sat beside me and asked if you could help me. I pulled away from you, but you knew I was vulnerable. And you played it to the hilt, didn't you. You said that you had a job for me for as long as I wanted one. All I had to do was keep my mouth shut about your sexual preference. Which is still no problem with me, it's your choice. Later you came to me and said you couldn't have any children so for twenty dollars, I was to get your wife pregnant. She told me that you never even tried to get her pregnant. She told me that you preferred men. But who am I to talk, I prefer women. I never have been, and probably never will be, faithful to my wife. When I confronted you, you said, 'What's one man's meat is another man's poison.' Then twelve years ago, you caught your wife having sex with Father Van Horn. You sent her away and brought back a lover. Oh don't worry I won't blow the whistle. But don't touch my boy."

"Garrett, Garrett, you're making a mountain out of a molehill. First I have no intention to approach your son with my sexual preference. I never have done that to a child and never will. Secondly, do you think I, your benefactor, would harm your son? I love him like my own. I don't deny what you say, but why are you making such a fuss in front of the lad?"

What Mr. Strowe was getting at, Kenneth didn't know, but his father didn't like it.

"Stop where you are, Mr. Strowe. I'll tell you what I want, and you, Father will be our witness. I want Kenneth to continue his apprenticeship and education. In addition, I want you to teach him to be a businessperson and then set him up in a business. If you can't do this, I will have to tell what I know." By now Garrett was standing between Mr. Strowe and Kenneth. "And if you think that you can get rid of me, I have an insurance policy written up that will hang you."

"Well, I had every intention to help Kenneth get started. I have no children to leave my inheritance to. You know that I'm a generous man, so why not? What about Kenneth, can he keep quiet? What assurance do I have that he won't break the agreement?" Mr. Strowe had gone back to his chair.

Kenneth was getting sick to my stomach. "I got to go to the bathroom," he said, as he tried to pass his father.

But his father grabbed his arm and stopped him. "There will be time for that later, Kenneth. First Mr. Strowe wants to have your word that you won't speak a word of this meeting to anyone. If you can, then give it. If not, then the deal is off."

"I won't say a word to anyone, Mr. Strowe, I promise." With that, he ran out of the room.

For months, Naomi fumed around the house, talking to herself and crying. She knew her marriage was frayed. But she hadn't realized that it had gotten so bad.

On top of the frayed marriage and her pregnancy Kenneth's hormones were running rampant. Kenneth would do things that were uncharacteristic of his mild nature. He would disappear for hours on end, talking to the animals but refusing to talk to his parents, talking back to Mr. Strowe and Dr. Schade. He would take his slingshot and hit the bull's testicles to make him mad and break out of its pen to chase him. Catching frogs and putting them in a can of water. Then putting the can over an open fire to see how long the frog would live.

Although the pregnancy was easy on Naomi, it played havoc on her emotional state. One minute she would be laughing and suddenly tears would flow. She was like the weather, if you didn't like one mood wait five minutes, it will change.

Each day as Naomi washed the clothes, she would wonder who was talking about her and Garrett. Did they know who the father of her baby was? Would Mr. Strowe fire them? What would happen if they were thrown out in the streets in the middle of nowhere? Would Garrett be man enough to stay with her? Or would she be out in the cold with two children, plus one on the way, with no father to provide for them? She had some money saved, that Garrett didn't know about, but she knew it wouldn't last long.

First, she decided to talk to Mr. Strowe. He always had good advice, plus he was the one who would decide on her and the children's future. So getting up early one morning Naomi declared to Garrett and Kenneth that she was going up to the main house so they needed to hitch up the buggy. Garrett just grunted. They went out and hooked up the horse to the buggy. Garrett made an excuse for having to work around the main house and Kenneth had a lesson with Dr. Schade.

The ride to the house was quiet; Naomi and Garrett didn't say a word. Kenneth was engulfed with his history lesson on Alexander the Great. As they got out of the buggy, Naomi said to whoever would listen, "I'm talking to Mr. Strowe about our marriage."

Garrett still didn't say a word he just picked up his tools and went to work. Kenneth watched him walk away noticing a darkness around his father. When he mentioned it to his mother she told him to go find Dr. Schade, start his lesson, and then went into the house. Leaving Mercy with one of the ladies, Naomi went looking for Mr. Strowe.

Mr. Strowe was sitting at his big black walnut desk reading his ticker tape as Naomi walked into his office. He offered her a chair as he finished his work and then turned to her. "Naomi, what can I do for you?" He asked with no emotion in his voice. He looked tired and upset.

"I can come at another time, Mr. Strowe," said Naomi nervously.

"No, no that's okay. It's the market. Lately it's been one step forward, three steps back, believe me it's not you, or the Estate" replied Mr. Strowe with concern written all over his face.

"I came to talk to you about the ramifications of Garrett and me separating. We are not getting along, he cheats on me and now I have cheated on him. We can't go on like this, either we make up or we part. I think Kenneth is reacting to our frayed relationship with his disrespect, cruelty and anger. So I am trying to look at all the possibilities before it comes to that," said Naomi.

"I don't think it's that bad Naomi. I know that you might be caring Hershel's baby, I think everyone does except Garrett. That is because of his shear love for you that he refuses to accept the fact. Or he has heard it and is waiting for you to tell him. And frankly I'm surprised he hasn't gotten into it with Hershel. He has shown a great deal of restraint. Kenneth, well he is growing up, if it wasn't this problem he would find another. Don't worry, he will outgrow it. But then that isn't why you came is it? What would happen if you two separate? First, I would be put into a bad position because I have given my word to hide both of you from your enemies. And believe me, they are still looking for you. I have also given my word to make Kenneth my heir. To do that, I need him here to be trained. I am looking into a Business School in Mansfield for this fall." Mr. Strowe stretched his large frame as he spoke, looking out the window into the horizon. "So what would happen is this, you and Garrett would have to leave the house you are in. Both of you will be given an apartment by yourself. You would keep your jobs as long as you live peacefully on the grounds of Willow Creek. But my suggestion to you, Mrs. Adams, is that you make peace with your husband as soon as you can. Life is too short to hold grudges. I don't approve of Garrett's actions, but you will not find a better man than Garrett. And he would be hard-pressed to find a woman that can hold a candle to you. I haven't had a chance to say it, but I am proud of you for accepting Mercy. God will bless you for this act of kindness."

"Now about your work," he went on, "as you probably have heard, Sandra is leaving us in about two weeks. The man she is marrying doesn't want to live under our rules and frankly I don't want him here. This means you will have to pick up her workload as laundress. You will get her pay plus I will have her washing machine brought to your house for you. Both you and Garrett have been a blessing to me and to this organization from day one. So please work this out. If I have to be the intermediary I will do what I can." With that he got up and opened the door for Naomi to leave.

Naomi walked out of the house, seeing Garrett out of the corner of her eye turned the other way. She quietly went around the building, sneaking up behind him and planted a big kiss on his cheek. He jumped with a startled look on his face. Before he could say anything she said, "Garrett, we will work this out," and hurried away.

That night Garrett came home early for dinner. Somehow Naomi knew he would and had dinner ready. The talk was light at the dinner table. When Kenneth would try to bring up a subject they just ignored him. When dinner was done Naomi said: "Kenneth do your chores and then go to your room. I'm going to put Mercy to bed early so please be quiet. When you come back don't go through the living room, use the back entrance." Which meant either he had messed up or Naomi and Garrett planned on a long night alone? Or in this case Naomi planned that they were going to be alone. Garrett was not willing to stay in the room.

"I have to brush the horses," Garrett got up to go; "dinner was good tonight."

"Garrett, sit down, Kenneth can do that," Naomi said with authority. Kenneth quickly left the room to do as he was told.

It is hard to say what happened next, Kenneth was out in the barn, all he could hear was shouting, name-calling and things breaking. He went down to the lake to feed the swans because of the turmoil within the house, Kenneth was torn. Trying to figure out what was going on, what if they did separate, who would he and Mercy end up with. Unable to stand it any longer Kenneth just walked into the living room. He shouted, "What is wrong with you two, don't you love each other?" And then ran to his room crying and locked the door.

There was quietness for a longtime. Neither Naomi nor Garrett spoke, lying in his bed, Kenneth was beginning to wonder if they were even alive. Then he heard his mother say, "Kenneth is right we are adults, I love you, and we should be able to act like adults. Now can you tell me what attracts you to other women? Is it that I'm not enough of a woman for you? I mean no matter what I do, I feel that it isn't enough. I feel like I'm in competition with women I don't know nor do I care to know."

"No, no it isn't that, I love you too, and when you are in my arms I curse the nights that I have cheated on you. Yet in the back of my mind I hear my father telling me that women are here for one purpose. Men aren't like women, we don't brag about our new dress or stove or whatever you talk about, we talk about the women that we have made love with. It is nothing personal it is just raw animal instinct," explained Garrett.

"It isn't personal? Raw instinct! What are we a piece of meat? Oh, she was just like a tough piece of rawhide, she was like a prime steak, have you tried her she's a sausage? It's not that I don't believe you Garrett, my mother told me about men. I didn't believe her; I thought you were above all this male instinct stuff. When you get to the bar, do you compare notes and the best story gets a free beer? I just don't get it," she cried.

"Why did you cheat on me?" Garrett asked trying to redirect the blame.

"Oh my God, you where pushing all the right buttons, I mean if I had a gun I would have shot you. I looked for two days for my stiletto, so I could castrate you. I never was so mad at anyone in my life. You not only flaunted your affair with Missy, in everyone's face, you brought the baby home with the name I had planned for our daughter. And then someone came to me and said you told them that you promised Missy to leave me and marry her. How I prayed that you would show up in our bedroom and see us together. Why did I do it? Because I was too proud to ask you why I wasn't enough of a woman for you, and then I prayed that I wouldn't get pregnant, but I guess one cannot sow wild oats and then pray for crop failure," Naomi cried.

"Listen, I don't understand why you have to have all these women. When a woman marries she has this idea that he is the man for the rest of her life. That's the way we think, or at least the way I thought. I knew you had affairs before we got married. And if that is what you need then I will have to bear that, but please try not to rub it in my face. I forgive you for the past hurts and disappointments. I am asking you to forgive me for all that I have said and done," she said as she kissed him, "and please come back to our bed."

"So who is the father?" Garrett asked coldly, "I won't forgive you until you tell me who the father is."

"I don't know," said mother, "I just don't know."

That night Naomi woke Garrett up a little after midnight. It's time, Garrett you will have to wake Kenneth and have him help you."

"Help me with what?" Garrett asked half asleep.

"Delivering the baby, my water broke and the pains are about five minutes apart. Now get Kenneth up and have him put water on the stove. Tell him it's his job to keep the water hot until the baby is born. Then come back with towels. Oh, oh, that's a bad one," cried Naomi holding her back.

Garrett got Kenneth up and they put the water on and the towels stacked up. Naomi kept them moving with orders and cries of pain. Finally, there was silence, then a cry of a baby. Kenneth heard Garrett say, "It's a girl."

"What should we call her, mother?"

"Sarah, that name is dear to me," said Naomi.

That evening Naomi and Garrett were talking about Sarah and the rest of the family when Naomi said, "Garrett, sit down here beside me. I want to ask you something and I want you to be honest with me. You wanted me to tell you whose child Sarah is, and I said I don't know. If she was three weeks later she would be Hershel's, but she was born on time so she is yours. But either way I would like to have your name on the birth certificate. The world doesn't need to know that we had problems, Garrett. Heaven knows I don't want Hershel's name on our daughter's birth certificate."

Garrett leaned over and kissed Naomi and said, "Put my name on it mother, I have to pass out cigars for my baby. I think the first one will go to Hershel."

"Don't start a fight Garrett," Naomi said.

"Don't worry mother, the Adams babies are always on time," Garrett laughed.

8

As promised, in the fall Kenneth started 'The Mansfield Academy for Business.' Mr. Strowe gave Kenneth his Model T Ford for transportation and rented him an apartment in town for the times that he wanted to be alone to 'study' other things. Kenneth attacked his courses with great vigor. When he reached his seventeenth birthday he was told that he needed to move on to maybe a University, he had finished all the courses the school had to offer him. The closest University was OSU – Ohio State University – in Columbus and the trip took an hour and fifteen minutes. *Surely, Mr. Strowe would need me around Willow Creek,* Kenneth thought *he would want to get some of his investment back.*

Kenneth closed up his apartment and said good-bye to his friends. He said good-bye to Rachel, it took all-night, but he got it done. The next morning Rachel begged him to take her with him, but he drove off not even looking in his review mirror. He drove home to face the challenges ahead for him at the Estate. He didn't know what to expect, up to this point he just came home to get clean clothes, visit with his parents and Dr. Schade.

About two o'clock that afternoon Mr. Strowe asked for him

to come up to the main house. As he walked into the office he saw Mr. Jenkins, his mentor at the business school, Dr. Schade, a stranger and Mr. Strowe. They all had a glass of something, laughing, having a good time. Kenneth stopped at the door and knocked lightly. "Come in, come in, Heir Scholar," laughed Mr. Strowe. "We are celebrating your success; Jenkins here said you finished first in your class and in record time. The good Doctor and I are proud of you Kenneth. Dr. Kenton here is from OSU, he was a fellow student and then my mentor over the years.

"Kenneth, good meet you, Jenkins, Schade and Strowe has been bragging about you for two years now," said Dr. Kenton as he held out his hand to Kenneth.

"We would love to have you come to the Ohio State University. With the transfer of credits you will finish quickly."

"To do what?" Kenneth asked.

"Whatever you want to do, the world will be yours to conquer." Laughed Mr. Jenkins. "We spoke of many opportunities that would be offered to you. Now don't just think that because you are done at Mansfield you have to make a decision. Dr. Kenton here is offering another door for you to enter."

"Believe me I have thought about it gentlemen. I don't know what I want to do. I would love more education, and OSU is an opportunity of a lifetime. I also know this, I owe everything to Mr. Strowe and it is time for me to start paying him back." Kenneth explained.

"If I know Strowe here, he will get every penny out of you that he has spent and then some. He hasn't become the tycoon that he is by being kind. He will siphon the last drop of blood from your dying body to make a buck." Dr. Kenton laughed as he refilled his glass.

"If that is the case gentlemen then you do not know the same Mr. Strowe that I know, he has been more then generous to me and my family. If it hadn't been …"

"Kenneth, Kenneth, its okay, they don't need to know about

those things. After all I worked hard for this bad reputation, so don't ruin it." Laughed Mr. Strowe.

A few days later, Naomi was sitting down at the kitchen table counting money. Garrett left early for work. Mercy and Sarah were asleep in their beds. Slowly at first she counted the pennies and nickels, but as she moved to the dollars she got more excited. Each denomination of coins was stacked neatly in five dollar groups, so it could be rechecked. The tens and twenties were in hundred dollar increments.

"Kenneth can you help me?" Naomi asked. "What I need you to do is to count the number of piles of each denomination, total it and then on this piece of paper figure out the total."

There were fifteen large coffee cans full of money. Some of the cans had already been divided into pennies, nickels, dimes and quarters. One can had nothing but ten dollar bills, another twenty dollar bills. As the money filled the table Naomi and Kenneth started to talk about what seemed so far away.

"If you could buy anything you wanted mother what would you buy?" Kenneth asked.

"Oh, that's easy; I would buy some land so we could have our own home." She said.

"But this is our home, isn't it? Kenneth asked.

"Well technically no, it isn't. Mr. Strowe had given it to us as a wedding gift. But if we leave the Willow Creek we lose the house," explained Naomi. "We understood this when your father and I got married. I would like to just have my own home and have enough land for your father to be self-sufficient."

"By the way your father isn't to know about this money. I want to surprise him. So you have to keep this a secret," she added.

"We better hurry before dad comes home," he said.

"He won't be back until tonight for dinner, but yes we need

to keep moving. What would you do if you could buy whatever you wanted?" Naomi asked.

"Oh, I don't know, I guess I would open a savings account at the bank, save for my college education and my future." Kenneth answered.

"You're lucky; being a male you can do that. I can't because I am married so I have to have your father's name on the account. But he can have an account without my name on it. Someday you will see women having equal rights in all areas of life. It won't happen in my lifetime, but it will in yours. I just hope you will be part of helping all people to be equal and free to live their life to the fullest." Naomi's tone and facial expression made it clear that it was important it her.

They counted until mid afternoon, finally the job was done. Kenneth was exhausted and Naomi looked tired as well, but she had a look of excitement on her face. The total was $23,972.14 enough to buy a piece of land and start a home. She was going to have her home after nearly nineteen years of struggling, scrimping and saving.

Garrett came home just before dinner as Naomi said, he was tired but in a good mood. Naomi had dinner ready as always but this time she had Garrett's favorite dessert, strawberry pie with whipped cream. As they ate the pie Naomi reached over and put her hand on Garrett's arm. "Sweetheart, what would you buy if you could buy whatever you wanted, no concern about money?" She asked.

"I guess I would buy electric tools so I wouldn't have to do everything by hand," smiled Garrett as he looked at his sore hands.

"Oh," said Naomi with the look of disappointment on her face.

"I know you wanted me to say, buy some land and build a house, but that isn't practical. That would take 15 to 20,000 dollars and unless the good Lord drops that into our lap we will never have that much money. So let us face reality." Said Garrett with discouragement written all over his face.

Naomi turned to Kenneth and said "Kenneth go get the cans from heaven."

He brought them out one at a time because of their weight. With each can his father's mouth opened a little more. When the final can was placed before him Naomi announced the total amount of $23,972.14. Garrett just sat there speechless. Finally he got up and gave Naomi a big hug, with tears in his eyes he whispered, "What did I do to get a woman like you, I love you Naomi."

"Thank Kenneth as well, all the money he has given to me has gone into the cans," said Naomi. "You see Kenneth in a sense you have been saving for your future." She smiled. Little did she know the truth of her statement.

Every day for the next few months Naomi and Garrett spent hours going over ads, reading newspapers and talking about what they wanted in their new home. Naomi wanted was a fireplace in the bedroom and a private bathroom, with a big tub. Garrett wanted a wood shop big enough to build cabinets. Kenneth prepared to go to OSU. Mr. Strowe offered him a partnership on the condition that he would graduate from the University. There was a sense of excitement and unity in the home. Finally they decided on a piece of land about five miles away. It was wilderness now but it had a waterfall and a stream. There was enough flat land to farm and the house could be built on top of a hill overlooking the countryside. They went and walked the land many times. Twice Kenneth was able to go with them, listening to them talk about the future, 'Adams Farm.' Watching the leaves change and listening to the Canadian Geese as they flew south, telling them the cold weather was on its way. Their dreams kept them warm, even during the carriage ride home.

Then came the day, Friday before Thanksgiving, Garrett and Naomi wanted to take one more look before they bought the land, they rose early. Garrett harnessed the horse as Naomi made a picnic lunch. It was cloudy with a slight wind coming from the east. Garrett made a remark of a Chinook front coming in, but they laughed and continued to prepare for the trip. They took the girls to the main house for the day. Kenneth spent the day talking with Dr. Schade about what to expect at the University.

Kenneth waved goodbye, watching them, as they sat close together, heading out into their unknown future. At first neither noticed the wind picking up, the temperature dropping and clouds rolling in.

"Maybe we should think about going back," Naomi said, as she pulled out her favorite shawl, the one Jon gave her on the train. "Let's put this around us, so we don't get sick"

"The wind has increased but we are only few minutes from the gate, besides the wind won't be so bad in the woods." Garrett wanted to be alone one more time with Naomi.

You know since we have talked out our problems I keep falling in love with you. What did I do to have a woman like you love me is beyond my imagination, the angels must like me," laughed Garrett. He gently reached over and pulled Norma a little closer and kissed her on the cheek.

"Either that or the devil is getting even with me for something I have done in my past," Naomi started thinking of Frankie, "Let's talk about happy things. Mr. Strowe said he would help us develop a herd if you want to go into dairy or beef. And that old Mogul tractor is ours if we want it, with all the attachments."

"Yep, he made that offer to me too, I said beef, it's slower but I would rather do other things instead of milking twice a day. He also said Kenneth could continue working for him while he went to the University and I could work hourly on the Estate. That would supplement our finances until we can get on our feet." By now it was sleeting and Garrett knew that something was in the wind. "Sweetheart, the wind is in the trees, we are in for a real storm. Here is the gate do we go in or turn around and get back to the house while we still can?"

"Since we are here can we at least look out over the countryside one more time from the spot where the house will be, besides it's changing to snow so it won't be that bad." Naomi said.

"I have seen these storms and we should get back on the road as soon as possible," Garrett looked worried. "Now that we have once again become a family I don't want anything to happen to my love," Garrett tried to smile reassuringly.

They went about a half of a mile when a shot rang out, Garrett slumped over, and then fell out of the carriage. The horse bolted and Naomi had trouble getting it under control to stop the carriage. Getting out of the carriage she hurried back to where Garrett laid bleeding from the neck. Snow had started to fall and she couldn't see twenty feet before her, all she could do was call out. "Help, help, is there anyone there, I need help. My husband is shot, help me please, Please Help Me!" But all she could hear was the silence of the woods and see falling snow. Death seemed all around her as she felt panic coming over her. *I cannot lose control,* she thought, *I have to keep my senses.*

Suddenly a boy came out of the brush with a rifle in his hand. "I didn't mean it; I thought he was a deer." Stammered the young boy about sixteen, "They're goin' to put me in jail, I just know it. I am sorry lady but I don't want to go to jail." And with that he was gone, just as fast as he came, Naomi was once again alone. She went back to get the horse, but had to go farther into the woods to find a place to turn around. By time she got back Garrett was barely conscious.

Trying to get him into the carriage was impossible; with his weight, the slippery footing, she just couldn't do it. Finally finding a rope, she tied it around his chest put it around a tree and tied it to the carriage. Slowly she pulled him till he was against the tree. Untying the rope she moved him to be out of the wind, covering him with her shawl, she kissed him and promised to be back.

"I love you, Naomi," Garrett whispered, "and I love the children."

"We love you too sweetheart; just hold on, we will be back

together before you know it. I am so sorry for not listening to you. I do love you darling."

With that she went back to the horse, threw the rope into the carriage and started to lead the horse out. She couldn't see in front of her face at times, so she made a few bad turns, she finally found the gate. Turning onto the road she got into the carriage and whipped the horse into motion. The drifts had already started to cover the road and the carriage couldn't break through them.

The horse stumbled in the snowdrifts and Naomi had to get off and break the path when the drifts were too much for the horse. By now the wind was gusting and snow was so deep that she had all but given up hope. She had to let the horse loose because of the snow; the feeling of death had started to grip her soul. No longer was it *'I have to get help for Garrett, but I have to save myself.'* Finally after what seemed a lifetime Naomi saw a light in the distance. Every part of her body felt like it was frozen as she staggered to the door of the milk house. Just before reaching the door she fell and lost consciousness.

Hershel came out of the milking parlor and stumbled over her. Brushing the snow off her face, he realized who she was, quickly got a blanket and wrapped her up. Taking her to the main house, Mr. Strowe called the doctor on the phone and started to give her warm fluids. She went in and out of consciousness for four days, finally, she could talk.

She described the area where she left Garrett, how many steps from the tree to the gate. But when they went to look for him they couldn't find him. That spring they found him wrapped in the shawl that Jon had given Naomi on the train.

More than Garrett died that year, each day Naomi died a little more. With his father gone and his mother declining daily, Kenneth rose to the occasion. Realizing that if Naomi died he would be left with two little girls to bring up, Mr. Strowe had no agreement to take care of the girls. The promise that was made to his father was done under the threat of blackmail and Kenneth knew not to push that issue.

Hearing that Hershel had given his notice so he could buy his own farm, Kenneth went to Mr. Strowe with the proposal to become the Farm Manager. He felt with his management training and his friends at OSU he could turn the farm into a profitable business. Mr. Strowe wasn't so confident, he said, "You know there's a big difference in managing a business on paper and managing a herd of cattle." But he gave Kenneth a chance with the agreement that he would report weekly to him about any changes.

In the years that followed Kenneth made the farm into a money making machine. Putting in a milk parlor with automatic milkers, changing from grass hay to alfalfa, giving supplement feed according to weight of production. Plus milking three times a day caused milk production to jump from 1,500 pounds to 4,250 a day. At the same time he culled the herd and brought in new heifers from high producing dams. Next he got rid of the bull and went to artificial breeding. All in all by the end of the fourth year the profits went from 12% to 74.6% profit, with plans to triple that profit in five years by doubling the herd.

Mr. Strowe had gone on a trip out east for six months when Kenneth's world began to fall apart. People where showing up from the different OSU graduate programs to examine the farm, asking questions that Kenneth felt was personal information, thus stepping on toes, and sometimes making enemies. Joe Murphy, an Irishman, who handled the beef enterprise would step in and make peace. Joe was a small man, with a big heart. He walked around with a hand carved cane his father had given him when he left Ireland and a pipe in his mouth. His clothes were always the same, plaid slacks and a green shirt. Sometimes if he felt like dressing up he would have a bonnet on his head. He didn't have the academic skills that Kenneth had but he could handle people. Thus they became a team, working wonders at the Willow Creek Estate.

They would rise before the sun broke the horizon and sit on the highest point of the Estate talking about the challenges before them. They had a gift that bound them, the gift of knowledge. They would sit on the hill and exercise the gift without fear of being judged, while looking for opportunities to help. Then one day Joe pointed to a break in the mist that covered Naomi's house. Both men knew that it meant death was standing at the threshold of the house.

Two days later, on Kenneth's twenty-first birthday, Naomi went to be with his dad for evermore, leaving him with two girls to bring up. On her deathbed she told Kenneth about the families past, their real names and why they had to give them up. She also gave him the handkerchief and the stiletto. For the next four months Kenneth just moped around the grounds of Willow Creek. He would start something but never finish it. The girls were turned over to Rose, one of the widows that lived on the Estate. Then one day Mr. Strowe decided to take things into his own hands.

9

"Kenneth, I have five companies averaging a seven-percent profit margin. I want you to use your skills to double the profit." Mr. Strowe said.

"Aren't you taking a risk sending me? I have no experience in the field nor do I have the people skills. Besides what happens if employees have to be dismissed because of work distribution? What happens if the factory is just out-of-date or the product line cannot support the profit margin that you are asking for? How much are you willing to invest in time and money in this venture?" Kenneth asked.

Mr. Strowe could see that Kenneth was getting excited about the challenge. "I will give you full authority to make any changes that seem necessary. I do have a few guidelines however; anyone over forty is offered severance pay if you cannot find a place for them in the plant. Anyone under forty must be willing to be trained for any new position or they will be released. Anyone who is forced to leave our employment will get severance and one year of health insurance. I expect you to be sensitive to those with children. Lastly, any expense over $300,000 must be approved by me. The companies are in Chicago, Cleveland, two in New York City and another one in Hoboken, New Jersey. Do you want the challenge?"

"How much time do I have?" Kenneth asked.

"Why don't you go out and look them over, then come back to me and we will negotiate the time frame," smiled Mr. Strowe. "Oh, by the way from now on when we are one-on-one you will call me Bill."

Kenneth sighed, "Give me a letter showing my authority, a list of companies with their exact address and annual reports. I will go over them and be on my way in ten days. Thank you for trusting me. Now can I ask you for a favor? I never did like the name Kenneth, can you call me Ken?"

A week later Bill told Ken that he had the papers, the tickets and hotel reservations ready for his departure. But before that happened he needed to talk to him. He had some concerns he said, something that maybe Ken was not ready to see.

Ken went up to the main house for a late dinner and spent most of the night talking about what was expected of him. And what would happen to Mercy and Sarah while he was gone.

"Ken, you have grown in the last six years," Said Bill as he handed him a glass of Port. "You have graduated with honors from the schools that you entered and have turned this Willow Creek around financially. No longer do I have to worry about my investments supporting it. The farm is doing more than its share.

"That's Joe's doings, sir, I had the ideas, but he carried them out." Ken said.

"I know the value of Joe, but believe me, you are the brains behind it." Bill said. "One of the issues that you are going to face in the big city is the problem of egos. You cannot let the opponent think they are better then you, Ken. You have to take the credit and then challenge them if they try to take it away. You now will be among the wolves. I want you to come across as the one who is in charge, because one of these days it will be yours to run. Always remember those who were looking for your parents – they are now looking for you – so be careful."

Ken let the latter statements slide, he remembered the conversation with Mr. Strowe and his father on the day that he learned to visualize. "What about Mercy and Sarah? I have money that I have invested so they will have something to live on, but are they going to stay here or do I have to make other plans for them?" Ken asked.

"Wait, wait, what investment, what money do you have? I always thought of you as the one being next to destitute? What do you know about the investment world?" Bill asked excited about Ken knowing something about investing.

"One thing at a time Bill," laughed Ken, "first the money that mother and father had for their farm was invested. I know everyone thought that they had paid for the land and Mr. Nimrod took the money and ran. But when mother died I went to him and asked about the money, he gave it back with interest. He made me promise not to say anything to anyone about it."

"When I was at OSU doing my Masters I developed a friendship with Abram Goldstein. He went into his father's business on Wall Street; he is now running their Chicago Office. While together at Columbus we developed a formula that would tell if a stock or commodity was over or under priced. By trading with this formula I went from $20,000 to $575,000, he went from $25,000 to 5 million. He buys and sells on margin, I don't. He limits his losses to $10,000; I limit mine to either 10% or $250 whichever is smaller. When he hits $100,000,000 he is going to retire, I don't plan to retire until I am seventy-five. So you see we have the same goals just different time frames."

"My God, here I am trading in the same market as you, worried from day-to-day if I can keep this place going, you come along and turn it into a business. I worry about my investments because my broker is the only one who is getting rich, and you are sitting here making a fortune without saying a word." Bill was sitting on the edge of his chair with the look of excitement all over his face. He got up and refilled the glasses with Port for Ken and himself. "Can you teach me the formula, Ken?"

"When I come back, Bill, I promise. What about Mercy and Sarah, what will happen to them while I am gone? Am I to look for a place to keep them or can they stay with Rose and be educated by Dr. Schade?" Ken asked.

"They stay here of course. They are part of your family which means that they are part of my family. I would suggest that they stay with Molly and Joe. I think they are getting on Rose's nerves."

"Ken, when I agreed to treat you as a son, I meant it. Oh, I know your father was trying to blackmail me. You kept your word and that is one thing I have found hard to find in this world. Now can you give me a little hint about this formula? I would like to know about it." Bill asked once again hoping for a glimpse of the formula.

"Thank you Bill, I knew what father was up to, so I hadn't expected much from that promise." Said Ken with a sigh of relief. "You have proved yourself as a man of your word as well, for that I am thankful. And no I won't give you any more information. What you need to do is start moving your funds from stocks to Treasury Bills. This will give you a strong base to work from and it will tell your broker that you are not happy without saying a word. Have the Treasury Bills sent here for you to hold. While I am gone start looking for the lower priced and higher priced stocks in the Journal that interest you. Pick out ten of them. So when I comeback I can sit down with you and begin turning your investments around. I promise you that when you control your assets you control your destiny. It's already 4:00 in the morning I need at least an hour of rest before I meet with Joe."

"Why do you meet him all the time on the hill?" Bill asked.

Ken just smiled and said, "Come out there and find out, it's a whole different world."

"No, I need my sleep, besides I don't like to mix with commoners and there is no one commoner then you and Joe," Laughed Bill as he let Ken out of the front door.

The morning light found Joe and Kenneth sitting on the hill looking out over the eight hundred acres. Joe was trying to relax by deep breathing and Kenneth by working his thinking stone. "Joe, what do you think of Mr. Strowe, not as the head of Willow Creek but as a person?" Kenneth asked.

"I don't think you can separate the two Kenneth. You take a look at this masterpiece and you see his handy work everywhere. And yet you look closer and you see that corners are being cut; buildings are in disrepair, the bloodlines of the cattle are slowly changing but not as fast as they could be. Because of that I look at Mr. Strowe and I see a proud man, hanging onto a dream that is falling apart. He doesn't have to lose his dream or even cut it back. I don't know his business I just know that when I came here your father had the buildings in top shape. The herds were questionable but had potential. Now when I suggest something he acts like I am trying to break him. While you were in school he changed a lot, he stopped coming down for meals, only spoke to us if we did something wrong, there hasn't been a staff party here since your father's death. No I think he is losing it and doesn't want anyone to know it." Replied Joe as he puffed on his empty pipe.

They sat in silence for awhile and then Kenneth spoke, "I was asked what we did up here by Strowe, I told him to come and see, he said he doesn't like to mix with commoners."

"So we are commoners now, well I take that as a real compliment. But I will have you know laddie, we get more work done here in five minutes then he does all-day behind that fat desk of his." Joe laughed then looking at Kenneth he added, "Ah, I am going to miss you laddie. Things will not be the same without you. You know one of these days I'm going to take up smoking," shaking the moisture out of the stem of his pipe.

"Well when he does come up here, and he will, be kind to

him Joe, You are right he is a scared old man, not knowing where he is going. Now his empire is crumbling and his 'friends' are starting to abandon him. He will need us 'commoners' around to pick up the pieces. Before I leave we need to talk about the girls, I guess they are getting on Rose's nerves. Plus they are not learning the common household duties that come with growing up. Can you and Molly work something out for me? They might want to live at home but they do need some guidance." Kenneth stated.

"Ah, laddie, as if you have to ask. Of course we will, we don't need to talk about it, consider it done." Replied Joe.

"Thanks, Joe, now I want to go and say good-bye to my parents, but promise me that you will keep an eye on him, Joe." Kenneth asked as he looked at the main house.

"Ah, laddie, I will be like a son to him, just you take good care of yourself and comeback soon." With that the two men hugged each other. "If old man Strowe saw this he would think we were one of his kind," Laughed Joe.

Kenneth spent a couple of hours at the graveside of his parents; finally Mercy came by to speak to him.

"Kenneth, why do you spend so much time here? You know they are in heaven don't you?" Mercy said as she sat down next to him.

"Yes, I know, but you were too young to remember the good times we had as a family. Like the time when the calves were making a racket. We had separated them from their mothers; you should have heard the noise. I opened the gates so they could get together. It took us two days to separate them. Father was furious, but mother got him to see the funny side of it. Father could get mother going and what a battle would erupt. Suddenly they would look at each other and laugh until tears would flow. I know they had their disagreements, but Mercy they loved each other and they loved us. And isn't that what's it all about?" Kenneth asked as he put his arm around Mercy.

"Did she love me Kenneth; I know she wasn't my mother?"

Mercy whispered as she played in the dirt with the toe of her shoe. "I often lie awake at night wondering who my real mother is and what it would be like living with her."

"Sit down Mercy; you are old enough to have some of those questions answered." Smile Kenneth. "Our father had a weakness for barmaids, or should I say for anything with a skirt. And out of one of those affairs you were conceived." And so for over an hour Kenneth told Mercy of her real mother and the mother who would give her life to save her. "When I come back I will do my best to have you meet your natural mother if that's what you want Mercy." They walked back to the house hardly saying a word. Mercy was deep in thought and Kenneth was wondering if he was as gentle and kind as he could have been.

When they reached the door Mercy reached up and hugged him, kissing him she said, "I know it wasn't easy for you to say what you did, but thank you for being honest. I love you Kenneth." And then she went inside.

Kenneth taking a deep breath followed Mercy into the house. Asking the two girls to sit down, he laid out his traveling schedule. Then he said, "Mother asked that if something would happen to me I would leave a Will for you. I have given my lawyer the Will, here is his number, and everything is to be divided according to mother's wishes. Mercy because you are four months older then Sarah you will get fifty-two percent, Sarah you will get forty-eight percent. This was mother's wish so it is what will happen, if either one of you protest the Will the other will get it all. Do you understand?" asked Kenneth.

Yes, sir," Answered the girls.

"Now tomorrow is the opening of the State Fair, I am taking both of you. Get a good night sleep; we leave at 7:00 A.M. sharp." Kissing 'his' girls on the forehead he pushed them off to their bedrooms.

That night he went over to talk to Eugene, Mr. Strowe's retired Chauffer; about that night when his mother brought Mercy to the bar. Eugene suggested that they go to the 'I'm

Not Here Bar' for a refreshment and do some questioning. All he could remember was the girl's name was 'Missy' and to his knowledge there was no follow-up contact made.

Kenneth thought it was an exercise of redundancy but tagged along, "after all any excuse for a drink." As they pulled up Kenneth suggested that they use the exercise his father taught him. Taking a deep breath and letting it out slowly he saw an old woman, with white hair and a mean look, waiting on tables. There was only two at the bar and one table with a younger couple. "Well let's go get drunk," laughed Kenneth and got out of the car and walked in. It was exactly as he saw it, except the old woman was not old, maybe 40, but looked like she had lived a rough life.

"Well, looky here, we have some new blood." Smiled the woman showing that she had teeth missing, "What will it be boys a beer, something stronger, or maybe something upstairs nothing too good for 'Missy's customers." She put her arm around Kenneth and rubbed her flabby breast against him. She smelled like a hog in rut and suddenly looked like one.

I would like some Bourbon," said Kenneth, "maybe 'Wild Turkey' 101 proof." He turned to Eugene and asked with a laugh, "What would you like? Nothing is too good for Missy's customers."

"Give me a scotch and water," said Eugene. "You're not the 'Missy' that was here fourteen or fifteen years ago are you?"

"That's me," laughed Missy.

When she came back with the drinks she said, "I washed the glasses out good, you two being gentlemen and all. By the way how did you know about me? I don't remember you." She said to Eugene.

"Oh, I just came here once with a friend, you won't remember a one-drink order." Laughed Eugene.

"No, but I do remember those days. We worked on our feet down here and on our backs up there. I got pregnant six times, once gave birth and the other five – aborted the bastards. The men would line up to be with me for fifteen minutes in bed." There was a pause she looked into the distance. "And then there was Garrett," she said with a smile. "Some bitch got my baby girl, changed her name. Then had the nerve to come here and flaunt her high faulting ways in my face. I should have punched her out."

"That woman was my mother, and I don't appreciate it that you call her a bitch. She brought your daughter up to be a lady, educated and useful to society, and I don't mean on her back," Said Kenneth. His face was turning red; he suddenly thought of his father and calmed down.

Missy didn't flinch, "Well where is the brat? I would like to tell her what happened."

"She wants to meet you too, Missy. I promised her that when I came back from my business trip I would find you. Now I wonder if I did the right thing. Let's go Eugene." Kenneth said as he paid the bill and walked out.

The next day Kenneth asked Joe to join them at the fair. He told Mr. Strowe it was a good place to pick up ideas for improvement of the Estate. The girls went on all the rides and Joe and Kenneth looked over prize winning cattle, picking up names of bloodlines and breeders.

On the way home the girls fell asleep and Kenneth told Joe of the meeting with 'Missy'.

"Ah, laddie, you are opening a can of worms," was Joe's reply.

10

"Good morning brother." Kenneth opened one eye and saw Sarah looking down at him smiling. "We made breakfast for you, so you'll remember to come back home." Kenneth sat up in his bed trying to wake up gracefully. Mother always said that women didn't like a grouchy male in the morning.

"What do I smell burning in the kitchen, water?" Kenneth grinned.

Mercy laughed. "No, we don't burn water anymore, do we, Sarah?"

"Well at least I don't," said Sarah. "We made your favorite breakfast, four pancakes, then a slice of ham off the bone browned, and three eggs over-easy."

"Don't forget the homemade maple syrup," Mercy called as she went to get the coffee.

Kenneth looked for the juice glass. "Where's the orange juice?"

"Sorry we're all out of vodka." Mercy placed the coffee on the tray.

"Do you really have to go, Kenneth?" asked Sarah.

"Yes, Mr. Strowe has some companies in trouble and I have

to see if they can be saved. He has always been there for us, now we have a chance to be there for him. I will miss you. I'm looking forward to the day I come home and see your faces again. Maybe I can make breakfast for you."

"Oh my God, please help us. We're going to die of poisoning," Sarah said. The girls grabbed at their throats and fell on his bed laughing.

The pancakes were runny in the middle and the eggs were overdone and the ham was dry. But the most important part of breakfast was excellent—the coffee.

"Great job girls," said Kenneth with a laugh. "Now, let me get dressed or I will make you eat my cooking."

They went up to the house where Mr. Strowe was waiting for them. He handed Ken a briefcase. "You'll find the introductory letter, letters of credit and authority to make changes all in place. Go with God's peace, my son." He reached out and gave Ken a hug, and whispered in his ear, "Our future is in your hands. Your Mother's enemies are aware of your coming so please be careful."

"Mercy, do you want to drive your brother to the train?" Mr. Strowe asked.

"What about me?" asked Sarah

"One can drive to and the other from, you decide." Mr. Strowe laughed.

Ken turned and looked at Mr. Strowe; his laugh had returned. That laugh was from the heart.

"What's wrong, Ken?" asked Mr. Strowe."

"Oh, nothing, I just heard something I haven't heard for years," Ken said.

They got into the car and started out for Crestline. They went over the travel schedule, the list of things that the girls wanted from each city. The twenty minute ride to the station seemed like a second, it went so fast.

When they got to the station Ken asked that he be left alone with Mr. Strowe for a minute. "Bill, remember not to mention the formula to anyone, especially your broker. I gave my word that I wouldn't share it with anyone but family, those girls are as much family as you are. You're as dear to me as my father was when he was alive. I won't fail you, I promise. Will I turn every plant around, I don't know, but you will stay above water. Now keep that belly laugh going, it's good to hear it again." He hugged Mr. Strowe and then called the girls over. "Let's get our hugs and kisses in before the train comes. You know I don't like wet good-byes."

They came up like two mature young women, smiling but no tears, and offered Kenneth their hands for a handshake. "What's going on? No kisses, no tears, am I a stranger?" Kenneth asked.

"You want us to act mature so we are," said Mercy. "If you want us to be ourselves, then brace yourself." With that, both girls attacked him with hugs and kisses.

Father was right, Ken thought, *there is nothing as good as family.* The train to Columbus was an express, so it hardly took any time. But there was a two hour delay for the Toledo-bound train. Kenneth used the time to get newspapers to read and made some phone calls. He didn't like leaving Ohio for such an indefinite time. His security blanket were the walks in the fields of Willow Creek and sitting in front of the fireplace with a glass of Port. Now, what was out there ahead of him? He boarded his train to Toledo where he would switch trains for Chicago.

After some hours of studying the reports that Bill had given him, he rose and went to the observation car and sat down in the upper deck. Looking out over the horizon, he wondered how long before the farmland would be gone; houses and factories replacing them. They claimed that in ten years all the land would be gone between Chicago, Illinois and Milwaukee, Wisconsin; in twenty years the land between Columbus and Cincinnati would be the same. The thought of his home being disturbed by other buildings so close that you could see your neighbor bothered him.

As the train drew closer to Chicago, he noted not only an

ecological change, but more important, a sociological change. Houses stood almost on top of each other, people standing around in what looked like rags and groping through trash. Just then he looked up and saw the smokestack that read "Robin's Spices". He knew he was in Chicago, facing unwanted challenges.

About twenty minutes later he heard the conductor call out, "Chicago Union Station, end of the line. He got off the train, found his luggage, and called a cab for the White Birch Inn. As he rode through the city, he was once again shocked at the economic differences, this time between Chicago and Crestline. When the cab stopped before the White Birch Inn, a man in a uniform opened the door. "Welcome to the White Birch Inn, sir." He saluted as Kenneth stepped out of the cab. Kenneth didn't know whether to return the salute or laugh.

"Thank you, James, for the ride, I enjoyed it." Kenneth paid him with a sizable tip. James was a young man about twenty-four, clean-cut, with an aggressive look about him. Kenneth caught his name from the license hanging from the visor. Attached to it hung a graduation tassel with Loyola written on it. "If you're in the area tomorrow morning, I'll need your services again."

"I'd be honored to serve you, sir." James lifted his cap.

"Sir, the White Birch Inn has a limousine service that is the best in town, you don't need taxi service," said the doorman.

"Sir, you, might have the best limo service in town, but I will ride in a cab. Now let me get registered." Turning to James, Kenneth waved and said, "Tomorrow at 10 a.m., James. Don't be late."

The morning was windy with a little moisture mixed in; normal for Chicago he was told. Kenneth went for a walk, not knowing where he was going. The city was just waking up with the rising of the sun. There were few cars and fewer people present until he walked onto Maxwell Street. Suddenly there was excitement in the air. People shouted to each other with the expectation of profit. This was all new to Kenneth, a part of commerce that he only heard of from the older people. Maxwell Street, a place where anything could be bought for the highest offer or sold for the lowest bid. Everything from food to clothing, tools to homeopathic medicines, all available to the public. There were all kinds of people there, florists, retail owners, peddlers, and some plain old bargain hunters.

Slowly he headed back to State Street and the White Birch Inn, thinking of the different ways people choose to make a living. Chicago was a place of opportunity to grow and expand. Yet what he saw in the annual report of Robin's Spices indicated the exact opposite. For five years the sales moved upward; for the same amount of time costs had moved in the same direction, but at a much faster rate. What would the key be to reversing the process? This was Mr. Strowe's first plant purchased; he would take it personally if it had to be closed.

Ten o'clock sharp the cab pulled up in front of the White Birch Inn. James was smiling, the cab clean inside and out. "Well, James, are you ready for a day's work?" Kenneth asked as he got into the back of the cab. "The first place I need to go to is Pioneer Bank on Milwaukee Avenue. I have a ten-thirty appointment and if you don't mind hanging around, I'll need you to take me to three other places."

"Fine, but my meter is running while the clock is ticking, sir. If you need me, I'm yours." James pulled down the meter lever as he pulled out into traffic with a squeal of the tires. "Are all these places close to each other? Maybe you can cut expenses by telling me ahead of time where we're going so I can miss the heavier traffic."

"From the bank I'm going to the Board of Trade and then to University of Chicago. If there's time I'll be going to 111th and Western Avenue for three or four hours. When that's done I'll go back to the White Birch Inn."

"Why would you want to go to 111th and Western Avenue? I mean, I grew up there and, man, that's no place for someone dressed like you. I don't want to tell you your business, but that is the poorest, meanest place in town. Their only jobs are in the spice factory. If you want a job there, you have to be female and willing, if you know what I mean. Well here we are, Pioneer Bank. Do you want to pay me now or should I keep the meter running?" James looked back at Kenneth, wondering *did I cross the line.*

Kenneth must have read James's mind because he handed him his payment plus a tip. "You decide for me, James. I like riding with you, but if you don't want me for a passenger, I understand."

"Man, you are crazy!" James said.

"I know, but it helps keep me from losing my mind. I'll be right back." Kenneth went into the bank and presented his credentials. They gave him the information on the company, cash for his expenses, and he left. There was James, standing outside his cab. "So, you like my money or maybe you wanted to save this poor country boy who's crazy as a loon?"

James laughed. "Your money has a nice sound to it, but I guess I just want to see if you're as crazy as you sound, or crazy like a fox."

"Let's hope I'm crazy like a fox. This trip means a lot too many a person, not only here but where I'm from as well. You said something about growing up in the 111th and Western Avenue area. The bank also painted a poor picture of the area. Do we have time to discuss the situation while we go to the Board of Trade?" asked Kenneth. "What's this 'you have to be female and willing' statement? Is it what it sounds like, or a Chicago lingo I'm not used to?"

James became serious as he thought over his answer. "It isn't strictly a Chicago lingo you see it everywhere there is poverty. So where are you from and why are you interested in Robin's Spices?"

"I'm just a country boy working on a project," Kenneth said. "The university asked me to do research on businesses that are failing. Robins Spices once had a great future but now seems to be on hard times. It's my premise that it's not the economy, but the leadership from the owner down, that's causing the decay. The bank tells me their records show a sixty-percent turnover in all new employees. They said that most of the turnovers are due to maternity leaves. So I said, 'Well, why do they hire young, married women?' The banker looked over his glasses and said, 'They aren't married when they come in or go out.' That's why I asked about the statement you made just before I got out of the cab at the bank. Is it that bad, and if so, where does the problem start? I'm sure the owner, who I understand lives hundreds of miles away, isn't aware of this."

"The question isn't does he know, but shouldn't he know about it? I mean when you own a business isn't it your responsibility to know what's going on? I'm not an Einstein, but one thing I did learn in school is the owner has responsibilities for his employees. It shouldn't stop when a person punches their time card and goes home. My father, mother, brothers and sisters worked in that factory. When I turned sixteen, I got a job sweeping the floor. The pay wasn't much for any of us, but old man Jacobs made us feel like we were part of something. He died and his wife sold it to some money-hungry industrialist out east. He hires all these jerks and wonders what happened."

"My parents were fired because they were too old and couldn't adjust to the changes. My sisters were fired because they wouldn't join in the team concept. What they meant was that they wouldn't go to bed with the bosses. Do you know what it means for a whole family to lose their income in that neighborhood? Death! Oh, it forced me to go to college and get a degree. I should be thankful. I work two jobs to support my parents and my family. That I don't mind, but looking into my parent's eyes and seeing nothing, nothing at all—that hurts."

"Okay, James you're mad at the world because of a few bad breaks, but why do you think it's the owner's fault? He bought it as an investment, not to run. Can you blame him for that?" asked Kenneth.

"When you buy a house for an investment, you keep it up, paint it, and check the electrical wiring, the roof. When you buy a racehorse for an investment you hire the best trainer you can find, feed and care for it so it can run. When you buy a factory do you just toss the keys to someone and say make me money? That's your logic. I might be weird, but I say you're wrong. The owner has a moral responsibility to his employees. So now you're going over there, look at it for a few hours, and then suggest what, that it be torn down?" James asked.

"No, I'm not going to tear it down. I don't have any authority for such a decision. Besides I never even met a Mr. Goebel. Here's the Board of Trade. Let me off, but before you do, can you give me your phone number? I have an idea you might be interested in," Kenneth said.

"You're mad at me. I overstepped the line didn't I?" asked James.

"No and yes, but I am glad you did. We'll do business tomorrow, James." He paid his fare and walked into the Board of Trade. *The only building in the world that has the Angel of Harvest on it,* Kenneth thought. Then he thought of all the James' who would be thankful for just one crust of bread.

Kenneth opened an account for Mr. Strowe with Abram Goldstein for $100,000 with the instructions that no one was to trade but Kenneth.

"Kenneth," said Abram, "we've been friends for three years now. You've always been careful not to put me in an awkward position. But you know the rule—the Exchange will not let someone have an account without a financial statement."

"So a cashier's check for $100,000 isn't enough of a reference? You took me on with nothing but a $2,000 personal check. Okay, okay. I'll have a financial statement in your hands within three days. Just don't do anything with that account until I say so, you hear me?" Kenneth said angrily.

"Yes, Kenneth, I'm only doing my job. Would you like to go out on the town sometime?" asked Abram.

Kenneth just shook his head and left the Board of Trade. *Why is everything complicated?* He wondered. *All I wanted to do was open a simple account, now I have to go to the University of Chicago, and I sent James on his way. He was about to flag a cab down when he saw James standing next to his cab.*

"You forgot the university; I thought I'd stick around just in case."

"I'm sorry James, I just wasn't thinking of my schedule, and I shouldn't have brushed you off like I did."

"That's okay I thought I had better stay around just in case. Let's go, I have two hours before I start my second job. Which university do you want to go to, Loyola, Northwestern or the University of Chicago? Say the word and we are off." James laughed. "Besides, you are one great tipper."

"University of Chicago, Hyde Park, I think it's on 55th Street. I need to go to the School of Business. Do you know where it is?"

"Sure do, but it's not in Hyde Park. They moved last spring. Now they have the school on Lake Shore Drive and Lincoln. I know because I've applied to go there to study for an MBA. They haven't turned me down. They were kind and said, if I could raise the money, I could come and study. That's how the elite keep us poor people in line." James said.

"Well get me there and wait for me. I've come up with a solution to my problem," Kenneth said.

James pulled up to the entrance of the school. "I can't stay here, so I'll just keep an eye out for you over there." He pointed to a side street.

Kenneth went in and received the papers showing that he was doing research and then went to the Registrar's Office. Introducing himself, he asked if a James Huggins had been accepted.

"Yes, he has been for over a year now. As soon as he has the first semester's fee he can start. He must want to come here, he calls at least once a month checking his standing. If he does as well as he did at Loyola, we'll put him on full scholarship." Dr. West said.

"Thanks," Kenneth shook Dr. West's hand, "you'll be seeing him."

He walked out smiling. He not only had his papers, but a plan to find out what was going on in the factory. Now all he had to do was convince James to play along. Looking to the corner, he saw James starting in his direction. *This has been a good day,* he thought. *Joe would be proud of me.*

"So what are you doing tomorrow?" Kenneth asked, expecting to hear, driving the cab.

"Well sir, I can only put so many hours a week on this old girl. My license won't let me drive her tomorrow. So I'll be helping my wife around the house or go over and help Mamma with Pa."

"Can I ask you a personal question?" Kenneth asked.

"Sure, I have nothing to hide," said James.

"How much do you make driving a cab per week? I know it's none of my business, and you have stated that I'm a good tipper, so don't consider my tips. How much?" Asked Kenneth.

"I don't make that much. Most of the time the people I give rides to are those who can hardly afford the fare. But if you want to know, last week I had a good week and made $185.00." James slid down in his driver's seat embarrassed. "But then I have to pay for my gasoline and cab upkeep. Someday I'll be able to afford a full-time license, not just this three day stuff. Then I'll be able to go back to school."

"What was your major?" asked Kenneth.

"I went to the downtown campus of Loyola. It took me six years but I got a B.A. in Business Management," James said proudly. "Not only the first Huggins to go to college but to finish in the upper ten percent."

"This is what I want to ask you: for $100.00 a day will you work for me, not as a cabdriver but as a co-worker? If so, you will meet me at 7:00 a.m. in the White Birch Inn lobby and I'll lay out the plan over breakfast. Are you game?" Kenneth offered James his hand.

"I'll be there to listen, but I won't do anything that is illegal or immoral." James said as he shook Kenneth's hand.

Kenneth worked into the night on both Abram's papers for the Commodity Account and the plan to sell James the idea to help him. Both were important, but then everything is important on this trip. He sat and finished his Port a little after two in the morning, thinking of the girls and their future. And then he thought of his journey to where he was at that point in his life. It seemed almost as if a hand had maneuvered him step-by-step. *What am I here for?* He asked himself as he went to bed. As he slept a dream came to him that he didn't understand. He was saving people in need. He saw James' face, a black man, a young couple holding a baby and others that appeared in more of a vague sense. But he knew he was to save them.

At seven sharp the phone rang in his room. The front desk said a Mr. James Huggins was in the lobby waiting for him. He had James come up. He also asked for a waiter from the restaurant to come up with the breakfast menus and coffee.

James knocked on the door of the room; it was a knock of uncertainty, almost so quiet that Kenneth didn't hear it. Kenneth opened the door with a smile on his face. "Come in, James, welcome to my home away from home."

"You didn't tell me that you had the Penthouse, sir," James said with a great deal of hesitancy. "You aren't part of the Family are you? I don't do business with the Family."

Kenneth laughed. "No, no James I am not part of the Family, nor do I do business with them, knowingly. By the way, what nationality are you? I'm Scottish and Irish. Not that it matters. If you were from Mars and you had the skills I needed, I'd hire you."

"I'm Irish. My grandparents came from Dublin in the midst of the Potato Famine. My wife is Irish and English, but then we can't be perfect can we?" Replied James with a smile.

They talked about their different backgrounds and dreams till breakfast came and they ate.

"Now that breakfast is done we need to get to work. I'll give you your $100.00 now so if there's anything you feel is illegal or immoral and we can't work it out, you can leave. The only thing I ask is that what is said in this room stays in this room. The lives and the future of many are at stake." Kenneth looked closely into James' eyes, trying to see if he could trust him.

"You said that you worked at Robin's Spices. Do you remember after the change of ownership there was a fire? A Family member wanted it but the owner outbid him. His life was threatened and then the building was set on fire, so he fled. That's why he hasn't been around like he should have. They're still looking for him." *And me,* thought Kenneth. "He also changed his name, but kept his former name on the papers of Robin's Spices. So now you know why you're up here instead of in the lobby. We do not want any of this to get out into the public."

"This is what I need from you: I have papers stating that we're working on a project for the University of Chicago to analyze Robin's Spices. I can handle the front office, but I need someone with business and street savvy to work the plant. I'll give you a false name so if someone tips off the Family, you'll be back in your normal life before they can organize. I'd like to get in and out in one day. Then come back here and analyze the information. That's about it, so are you in?" Kenneth asked.

James sat there for a moment playing with the hundred dollar bill, "You make it sound so easy. Do you have any knowledge of what you're getting into there?"

"No, that's why I need you. Are you in or not?" Kenneth asked one more time. "If not, then there's the door. If you are, let's get to work."

"I guess I'm in, may God help us." James sighed and made the sign of the cross for protection.

They worked all-day, writing out questions, looking at the Annual Report, riding out and looking over the neighborhood.

The demographics showed the plant was not only found in the poorest area of the southwest side of Chicago, but there wasn't a way to and from the plant other than to walk or drive. Cabbies didn't want to go there nor did the buses. Driving was out because of the high crime rate, and walking meant six blocks of putting one's life in jeopardy.

Kenneth had invited ten of Mayor Daley's people to come to the hotel and diner at the 95th for input, but only two showed up. Finally James had to go and Kenneth had to do some work on his next project. Just before James left Kenneth said, "We'll use the White Birch Inn's limo tomorrow. I'll be at your door at 7:30 a.m."

After James left, he picked up the phone and dialed the front desk. "I'm going to need a limo in the morning leaving here at 7:00 a.m. Also I'm having dinner at the 95th with two Alderpersons, I'll need an intelligent escort can you help me?"

"Are you going formal sir?" The woman asked.

"Of course and we will be late returning. The dinner is at 7:30 p.m. I'll need a limo for that also. Do not have the young lady come to my room," said Kenneth, "Oh, also make sure she can dance."

"It will be taken care of sir," the voice at the other end of the phone said and hung up.

"Father, you often said they're just a different face, a different body. I hope I don't get caught in that trap." Kenneth said aloud. "I just don't want to be alone tonight."

At 7:10 in the evening the phone rang with the message that his escort and limo were waiting for him. As he came off the elevator, he saw a beautiful young woman with light brown hair in a black velvet dress with a high neck and low back. She gracefully rose as Kenneth approached. He noticed not only her brown eyes and that she stood almost to his shoulders, he felt a leap in his heart as he looked into her eyes.

"Mr. Adams, I'm Julie Cohn, your companion for the evening." She extended her hand to welcome him with a smile.

11

The two alderpersons arrived about ten minutes late at the 95th. The discussion was lively and worthwhile. The meal was excellent and the dancing was heavenly. Julie was like a feather on the dance floor, responding immediately to the slightest pressure of Kenneth's hands. The alderpersons promised to look into getting bus service to and from the area of the factory.

As Kenneth and Julie were going back to The White Birch Inn, Kenneth innocently offered her the opportunity to come up for a nightcap. She accepted.

It was obvious to Julie that he was not happy with the acceptance. "Kenneth, are you okay with me coming up for a nightcap?" She placed a hand on his leg.

Kenneth laughed nervously. "Sure, who wouldn't be happy to have a beautiful young woman in his room at three in the morning?"

"Listen, you are aware of my fee, right? It covers companionship for twelve hours, which includes all types of companionship. If you have any problems with that, you should have notified the front desk when you ordered the service. This is my Profession. You are a businessman; I'm an escort. I'm not ashamed of your profession and you shouldn't be of mine." Julie moved away from Kenneth.

"I'm not ashamed of your profession. I am ashamed of not wording my request properly. I'll have the chauffer take you home. It's been an enjoyable evening and I don't want to ruin it." Kenneth said as they pulled up to the hotel. He tipped the limo driver with instructions to take Julie home and went up to bed. *Was this how his father got caught in the trap that broke his mother's heart?* All-night he tossed and turned, pulled between his animal instinct for Julie, his father's opinion of women, and his mother's comments on morality and an unknown feeling that he couldn't explain.

The next morning the phone rang at 5:30 letting him know it was time to get up. He rose took a shower and shaved, thinking of the opportunity that was ahead of him. If he could get this turned around for Mr. Strowe, then he knew he could make him proud of him. The thought suddenly gripped him—he never cared if his father was ever proud of him. *Was it possible that he wasn't proud of his father?*

He had breakfast with James and then they went to 111th and Western Avenue. He smiled as he watched James trying to adjust to the limousine. They went over their particular roles; he would handle the office and James the plant. They wouldn't talk about anything they found until they got back to the hotel.

As the limo pulled up to the main entrance of Robin's Spices, Kenneth got the feeling of being at a jail or insane asylum. There was a high fence all around the property with razor ribbon on top and bars covered the windows and doors.

They entered the office and introduced themselves. The receptionist almost panicked when Kenneth presented his papers of authority. She excused herself fell over the chair and then a plant trying to get to the president's office. Kenneth noticed that it was a fake plant, like everything else in the room.

Mr. Kinston came out, with his shirt out of his pants and hair messed up. Minutes later Kenneth noticed a young female slipping out of the same office. They went around meeting the office employees and then went out and looked at the plant. There was a sense of concern about their presence. Finally Kenneth asked for two offices in which they could work, he told the personnel man and Mr. Kinston that they were to have the day off. Mr. Kinston protested that he had too much work to do to leave, but Kenneth simply said, "Then take it with you. But you leave in twenty minutes or you will leave permanently." The two men left, leaving numbers where they could be reached.

Kenneth went over the books with the financial officer and discovered that both the president and the vice president had received sizable raises each year over of the last ten years. The other office employees received merely one percent more than the cost of living. He also found a hospital fund that couldn't be explained by the financial officer. Mr. Kinston controlled it, dictating when a check should be sent and for how much.

The financial officer, Jacob Mertz, was a small man, not only in height, but in frame as well. On his desk was a picture of living skeletons standing in front of a fence. *Auschwitz,* Kenneth thought. Holding the picture in his hand he asked, "Was it that bad at Auschwitz?"

"I don't know. I never was there. They sent me somewhere else," replied Jacob, looking over-the-top of his round steel-framed glasses. "And before you ask, no I don't want to discuss it. Our society might have different names and laws, but the depravity of human nature hasn't changed."

"So what you're saying is the immorality of the human mind that existed in Hitler's Germany is here in the United States. You know, that's scary, Jacob." Kenneth placed the picture back down. Seeing the look on Jacob's face, he knew to move on to business. "Let's talk about the profitability of Robin's Spices. The records show that you have stayed above the red line, but you haven't grown. You have a Research and Development Department listed here, but I didn't see one. Is it located elsewhere?"

"You'll have to ask Mr. Kinston about that. I haven't seen one in the twenty years I've been here, but each year twenty percent of the income goes to it." Jacob shrugged, once again playing with his glasses.

"Jacob, you're going to have to get new glasses if you keep rubbing them." Kenneth put his hand on Jacob's arm. "I've been around the block once or twice. If I couldn't be trusted, I wouldn't have been given the authority I've been given. But you either have to answer me directly by telling me the truth, or just say you can't answer the question. I'm not here to cut someone's job. When I leave, my job will be to figure out how we can make this business more profitable."

The two men talked for another hour about profit and loss, the possibility of adding another product line, and lowering expenses. Kenneth was impressed that Jacob understood more than the financial end of the business. Finally he asked, "Jacob, I'm sorry for being rude, but you said you've been here twenty years. That means you where here when Mr. Abrams owned it. Were you always in the financial office?"

"No, Mr. Abrams believed that a good employee should know everything in the factory as well as the office. So if something happened there was always someone here to fill in. He couldn't pay much, but we felt that this was our company. He gave us pride, and since Mr. Goebel bought, that pride has gone."

"Do you know why Mr. Goebel is an absentee owner?" Kenneth asked.

"Oh, yes. Here" Jacob opened his drawer and handed Kenneth a yellowing envelope. In it was a notice that read: $20,000 reward for anyone who gives information that leads to the whereabouts of Mr. William Goebel. "My father was offered a reward, too, in Germany. He wouldn't take it, so they shot him."

"Well maybe it's good that I never met this person," said Kenneth handing back the envelope.

"Listen, James should be ready for a break, let's go out for lunch. It would be good to just laugh and talk." Kenneth watched

James walk a young woman, clearly in her second trimester, back to the plant.

"No thank you. I'm an Orthodox Jew and therefore must decline your generous offer." Jacob rose to walk Kenneth out of his office. "You won't be able to get a cab to come down here, so if you want to eat someplace, you'll have to walk about seven blocks south on Western Avenue. By the way, someone from the office has notified the Family."

James joined them in the open office area as Kenneth was about to ask a question. "I have enough information to digest if you want to go back, Kenneth." He looked exhausted.

"I'll call the limo and we can move on. While we're waiting, do you have a person who can take dictation, Jacob?" Kenneth asked.

As Kenneth called for the limo, Jacob arranged for Shelia to take dictation. Shelia came into Mr. Mertz's office and sat down.

"Shelia, I'm addressing this letter to Mr. Kinston, President of Robin's Spices. You may fill in all that info when you type it up for me to sign. Dear Mr. Kinston, Paragraph, as promised here is a summary of the report I will be sending to Mr. Goebel concerning Robin's Spices. Paragraph, Robin's Spices has the appearance of a company that is barely keeping its head above water. Although there are some financial categories that seem questionable, it appears that Mr. Kinston is continuing to move forward in keeping the company in the black. Paragraph, He should be given more time, money and freedom for research and development to possibly expand the product line. Paragraph, Hope this meets your satisfaction. If not please give me a call and I will discuss it more fully with you. Respectfully, Kenneth E. Adams. I need four copies, one for Mr. Kinston, one for Mr. Mertz, one for Mr. Goebel, and one for me. And Shelia, I need it immediately." Kenneth said.

Looking at her watch Shelia asked. "Yes, sir, can I do it right after lunch?"

"Is after lunch immediate?"

"No, sir," and went off to type the letter. Ten minutes later she came back for Kenneth's signature.

"Thank you, Shelia, I do appreciate you doing this for me," said Kenneth.

"Jacob I want you to witness this," said Kenneth.

"Why?" Jacob asked.

"Two reasons, Mr. Kinston knew that we've been working together this morning. He'll be asking questions. Second, you've been honest with me and deserve to know what's in the letter." Kenneth signed it and put it into the envelope. He handed it to Jacob. "Give this to him when he comes in."

On the way back to the hotel, James was quiet, just looking out the window, playing with his hands. Kenneth knew that he had the hard job—dealing with people was always more of a challenge than financial and production reports. "James, why do you insist on the University of Chicago - School of Business?" Kenneth asked. "It is the best in the nation academically, but you can get into Northwestern or Loyola and Loyola would give you a scholarship. Dr. West told me so."

"It's more than the academic. Maybe not even that," answered James, exhaustion all over his face. "When I was in high school I had an adviser who suggested that I drop out of high school and be a common laborer like my father. I got mad and said I was going to college and get a degree. He laughed and said, 'What college would accept you?' There was a sign behind him with the University of Chicago name on it, so I said, 'I'm going to get a degree from the University of Chicago.' When I finished Loyola, I met him and told him I had graduated and he said, 'Yes but not from the University of Chicago.' So now I will go and get an MBA from the University of Chicago. I love business and my grades are good. I can do it if I have the chance, I know I can."

"Are we going to talk about Robin Spices today?" He asked.

"No, you look exhausted. I know it wasn't easy on you,

emotionally. We'll do it in the morning. By the way I'll need you to bring your driver's license, Social Security card and another photo I.D. tomorrow. I have one more item that needs to be taken care of. The chauffer will take you home, come back for breakfast. Let's say 6:30 a.m.?"

When Kenneth walked into the hotel, the woman behind the front desk handed him a list of messages. One was from Julie. "I'm sorry for the way we parted last night. It was unprofessional of me. May we talk? Julie." Turning to the woman behind the desk he asked, "Do you have Julie's telephone number?"

"Yes, Mr. Adams, but I'll have to make the call, hotel policy you know," she said with a smile.

"Give me a moment to get upstairs and then call her," Kenneth said, shaking his head. Arriving in the room he put his briefcase down and started to go over his messages when the phone rang. "Mr. Adams your call has gone through would you like me to connect you?"

"Yes, please," said Kenneth. "Hello, this Mr. Adams speaking."

"Kenneth, this is Julie, did I catch you at bad time? I can call later." Julie said hesitantly.

"No, no Julie, I'm glad you called. It has been a busy morning. What can I do for you?" He asked, as if he didn't know. *She's trying to get me in bed with her,* he thought.

"I just felt that I should have been more gracious last night. I just was shocked that I was being turned down," Julie said. "I mean, that is usually what I'm being hired for, and you were just trying to be gracious, inviting me up for a nightcap. I'm sorry for my reaction. As a professional, I should have followed your lead."

"It's okay. If you want to see me again just say so. If not, then your apology is accepted and thank you for calling," Kenneth said curtly.

"So you are mad. I'm not saying I don't want to see you again, but in my business you have to ask for me. I'm sorry if I came across as trying to drum up business. I don't do that. I work for The White Birch Inn as a public relations specialist. And I don't feel that I have to explain it to you or anyone else." Her voice broke, "Listen, if you want to use my services again, just ask for me. I hope you're having a good time in Chicago. Good-bye Mr. Adams." She hung up the phone with some force.

Kenneth sat and thought for a longtime of his fears, need for women and this yearning for Julie. He picked up the phone and called the desk, "Can you get me two opera tickets? If not, then symphony tickets, please. When you have that done, call Julie and see which one she would prefer and call me back. Thank you." He was going to face this monster.

The phone rang sometime later. "We can get box seats at the opera. Its opening night for the opera *Carman* and you can get into the Green Room for dinner after the performance, Mr. Adams. Julie will be here at six and the limousine will leave here at ten after seven. Is that acceptable, sir?"

"Yes, and when Julie comes, have her come up. I know it isn't proper, but we need to talk first," said Kenneth.

"Yes, sir, that is exactly what she said," came the reply.

He called down for a chilled bottle of Dom Pe'rignon and some caviar canapés to be brought up at six sharp. At six there was a knock at the door. Kenneth opened it to find the wine steward and Julie standing there. "Talk about being punctual, you are good." Kenneth laughed nervously. They came in and the wine steward poured the champagne. Kenneth signed the check and let the man out, leaving him alone with Julie, who was radiating with a quiet beauty and charm.

"Will you join me," Asked Kenneth as the scent of her perfume filled the room.

"Not until I have my say," she responded with the same hostility he had heard on the phone.

"I think you have something backwards, Julie. You made it clear that I was the employer, you the employee. I get to tell you what to do. Join me, please." Kenneth responded in a way that even shocked him. "I realize you're a beautiful whore, and possibly a damn good one or you wouldn't be working here. But I'm having a problem with the whole idea of paying for sexual pleasures. I never had to, and now suddenly I'm becoming what my father was," he blurted. "The reason I asked for an escort was because I wanted companionship at dinner and maybe conversation alone after dinner. I know, psychologically, I may have been asking for more, but it wasn't consciously."

Julie's eyes filled with tears as she looked at him. *Why doesn't she respond*, he thought.

Finally, she got up and walked to him. "I'll probably get fired for this, but I don't give a damn." She slapped his face as hard as she could. "No one calls me a whore. I might be one, but no one calls me one, do you understand?" She put the glass down and started for the door.

"Whoa, I didn't see that one coming." Wiping the spilled champagne off his hands, "Julie, *Julie* come back and sit down, please. We need to get this settled before it gets out of hand."

"I think it has already has gotten out of hand," Julie snapped. "I'll be your escort tonight, but I will refuse to be employed by you ever again." She looked at Kenneth standing there with the handprint on his cheek turning red. She started laughing. "I am so sorry, Kenneth. I shouldn't have lost my temper, but being Irish, is a weakness. Come on let's see if we can get the redness down before we have to leave for the opera."

Skillfully Julie wrapped ice in a towel, holding it gently against his face. This soon reduced the mark so no one could see the shape of a hand. She tenderly kissed it, took another drink from her glass and said, "Let's have a good time tonight."

"It sure isn't boring around you, is it?" Kenneth offered her his arm.

As expected, the opera was excellent. The Green Room, however, was an experience. Neither had ever been invited to the Green Room, so they didn't know what to expect. The Green Room was just that, a room decorated in a light shade of green, where the patrons of the arts were invited on opening night to meet the stars and dine. They were served what Kenneth called a "light dinner" of finger sandwiches and wine. Julie enjoyed it and was the main attraction as far as the men were concerned. Kenneth enjoyed watching her work the crowd; always sure he wasn't excluded from the conversations. Everyone knew by the end of the night she was with him, but she was also available.

As they were about to get into the limousine, Kenneth asked, "Are you as hungry as I am?"

"I don't know, but I am famished," she said with a flirting smile. "You are talking about real food, right?"

"For right now I am." He laughed nervously, face turning red.

They ordered sandwiches from the main dining room of the hotel on the way back to the room. A new bottle of champagne was on ice, the music playing quietly, as they came into the room. Julie turned to Kenneth and asked, "Shall we dance, my friend?" They danced, drank, ate, talked and laughed until the sun started to break the horizon. Then they made love.

Kenneth had just stepped out of the shower thinking he could get a little sleep when the phone rang. It was his wake-up call.

Turning to Julie who was lying with just the sheet covering her midriff he asked, "What do we do now? I have a gentleman coming in a half hour for breakfast. The room is a mess and you're naked."

"I've been in worse situations. Just call room service and tell them they have a half hour to straighten the living area. Put a do-not-disturb sign on this bedroom door. And, if the gentleman needs to use the powder room, have him use the one in the other bedroom. I will go to sleep for a little while and then leave through the secret door." Julie pointed to a narrow door inside the wall closet.

Kenneth did what he was told and got dressed. "It was much more pleasant last night, Julie. Thanks for helping me work through my fears. Too bad I'm leaving town late this afternoon." He turned and looked for a reaction, but Julie was already asleep.

James came as the cleaning crew was leaving, "Good morning, Kenneth busy night last night?" James laughed and then became suddenly serious. "I could hardly sleep last night. What I found out made me so mad I could have killed Kinston. Did you know how you get raises there? Why it's nothing more than a private whorehouse."

"Let's keep it down, James. Yes it was a rough night last night, and yes, I expected the same when I found secret accounts for private medical care and an R&D account with no R&D department. But before we do that, let's order some breakfast. I need coffee."

The waiter came up with a pot of coffee and took their orders. Sitting back in his chair, Kenneth looked out the window and spoke more to himself than to James. "Why does a man work day in and day out ten to twelve hours a day? So someone else can get rich? It isn't for the betterment of mankind. Just look out there, everyone is rushing to get nowhere fast. God, I miss Willow Creek. When I was young I could just jump on old Sage and ride the countryside, but he's gone now and so is my innocence." He paused and then said "let's get to work before I turn into a sentimental fool. What changes do you see that are needed to turn this company around?"

"Besides firing all management personnel, or maybe castrating them, I would say have all the women that are hired be over sixty. I knew it was bad, it was when my sister and mother worked there, but now everything hinges on sexual output." James sighed.

"I know Jacob said it was just a different form of Hitler's Germany. What about production layout in the plant? Is there anything that can be automated or moved to increase production without increasing the load on the employees?" Kenneth asked.

"Yes, conveyors can be put in so the containers don't have

to be manually moved. Also all sealing of packages is done by hand. You can buy a sealing machine, but that would put three people out of work. There are also safety hazards everywhere. If that new government program called OSHA comes in, we will be screwed royally." James stood in front of the window watching the traffic move up State Street, thinking of his great city. "The other is the pay, it is just enough to keep the employees off ADC, but not enough to allow them to get ahead. Can anything be done about that?"

"What would it take for you to step into a leadership role at Robin's Spices?" Kenneth rubbed his chin thoughtfully.

"I don't have the experience or the expertise," said James. "And I would be constantly causing trouble for those who forced the women to have sex with them."

"Let's talk about experience. I have learned the only way you can have experience is by someone hiring you and letting you make mistakes at their expense. Now the training, you're getting training from your full-time job and the way you handle people in your cab business. What other training do you need? Surely not an MBA, I have one and watching you yesterday, I have to admit you're better than I am at handling people," Kenneth said.

"No, I want my MBA and I don't want to work at Robin's Spices." James said flatly.

"Then the issue is the MBA, and it has to be from University of Chicago. So what's stopping you?" asked Kenneth.

"Money, I'm still $3,000 short to start there. They said if I can pay my first semester and get good grades, then I can get a scholarship for the rest. At the rate I'm working and saving that will be in eighteen months," replied James, "unless I can keep you here at $100 a day."

"No, I'm leaving this afternoon, so let me lay out another plan before you. We go down to University of Chicago and pay for the first semester. You start in two months. How long before you're done, five or six years part-time?" Kenneth handed him the $200.00 owed him. "And don't count on promises. The school can only give scholarships if the donors give money to the school."

"Why would you do that?" James asked, shocked.

"Because I was in your shoes five years ago and someone helped me. Now let's go and register you for the fall." Kenneth laughed "Oh, I need to leave a note for the cleaning people. I'll be right back." He went into his bedroom hoping Julie was still there. She was asleep. He wrote a short note telling her if she needed anything to call him, leaving his personal telephone number.

After getting all the paperwork in order and making sure James was registered for the fall semester, Kenneth dropped him off at his home and went back to the hotel. Things were falling in place, he could save the plant, help James in school, and he found a new relationship in his life. Yet he somehow wished it was more than professional.

As he walked into the penthouse suite, he could hear Julie moving around. *Good she isn't gone yet,* he thought. Knocking on the bedroom door, he heard "Just a minute," and then "Come in." There she stood with her hair wet from the shower, the hotel robe draped over her body.

"Should I order lunch?" He asked. She shook her head with a sad smile. *She saw my note*, he thought.

"How much time do you have?" She asked.

"About four hours before I have to be at the station. My tickets are bought; the luggage is ready for the bellboy to come and get it, so I would say four hours. What do you have in mind?"

"Le Parakeet," said Julie. "It's a little restaurant on Oakton Street up by the Drake Hotel. It specializes in a lunch menu. Can we go there? My treat, you can check out, and then all you have to do is show up on time at the train station. Come on, say yes."

"No, I will not have you pay. Yes let's go." Kenneth laughed, relieved that she wasn't asking for another lovemaking session. He hadn't recovered from this morning, although he wouldn't say no if she suggested it.

He called down and told them that he needed a limousine and that he wanted to check out. He left tips for the maid service and they went downstairs. "Still working, Julie?" the woman behind the desk asked with a dirty look.

"You know me, I'm always working, either on my feet or on my back," replied Julie giving the same dirty look back. "I have to change. Be right back," she whispered, and was gone.

Kenneth finished the paperwork for checking out; The White Birch Inn was going to send the bill to Mr. Strowe's P.O. Box. He left a tip in cash for the bellboy and the other staff, except for the maid service. He noticed a line for Escort Service: $2,400.00. "Can I pay for this out of my pocket," he asked.

"Sure, if you don't want your wife to find out or you need to cover your dirty tracks. Here" She handed him a separate bill.

"Can I see the manager?" Kenneth demanded.

A man's voice from behind him said, "I'm the manager and I heard what she said. It was uncalled for and it is not the hotel's policy to judge people, is it, Jane?" Taking the bill from Kenneth he looked over it as if he was adding it up in his mind. "It looks like you have been overcharged for the champagne, Mr. Adams. Take it off, Jane." He handed it back to her.

"Three hundred dollars won't break me," said Kenneth. "I just wanted you to be aware of what she said. Other than that my stay has been superb. Here is the $2,400 for the escort service. By the way, I don't have a wife or a girlfriend."

Julie showed up in a summer frock, hair pulled back in a French twist. Her makeup artistically detailed her beautiful face. "Hi, shall we go for lunch?" Taking his arm she marched him out of the lobby. "Jane is such a jerk! I hope she didn't embarrass you. She used to work for the public relations department, but her mouth kept going even though her brain had stopped."

"No, the manager heard what she said and took care of it,"

said Kenneth as Julie got into the limousine. "How much of the twenty-four hundred do you get? I'm sorry it is none my business." He asked, wishing he hadn't said anything.

"It's a three-one ratio. For every three dollars I receive, they get one. And no, it isn't any of your business. I thought we settled that issue when I slapped your face, or am I going to have to do that again?" Julie teased.

"Le Parakeet, what kind of a restaurant is it? Do they serve parakeets there?" Kenneth laughed, willing to just let the matter drop.

"It's pronounced 'kaa' and no they don't serve parakeets there. It's a French restaurant that caters to upper-class businesspeople. I've never been there, so I can't tell you what to expect, other than it will be expensive. You must have a business card to get in. They don't give you a check when you're done eating. You just get up and leave. They'll send the bill to your business address. So if you want me to pay for lunch, I will offer my White Birch Inn card."

Kenneth almost made a crude remark of her profession and then thought differently, "No, I would be honored to buy you lunch, if there are no strings attached."

"What about the note" asked Julie?

"The note stands. Any place, any time, if you need me, call," Kenneth said, "No strings attached. What you did for me, only a caring, sensitive friend could do."

The restaurant was on the second floor of a small house on Oakton Street. The entrance was an elevator going directly to the dining area and the room was just a plain off-white color with parrots painted on the walls. The waiters wore tuxedos and white gloves. The room was full but quiet. Kenneth handed the maitre d' his business card and they were seated. The food was excellent, truly French, a pleasant blend of intriguing flavors and textures, delicately accented with a fine French wine sauce. Kenneth felt a sense of power within the room, and yet couldn't put his finger on where it came from.

At one point he looked up, there sat the two Alderpersons who met with him dining with what looked like Mayor Richard Daley. He mentioned it to Julie, who just smiled and said, "Yes, they dined with us at the 95th remember?" She nodded toward them and smiled. When she did, their waiter suddenly came over and asked if they would like to join the mayor and his party.

Kenneth smiled and said, "Tell the Honorable Mayor no thank you, we are almost finished, but I'll stop by on my way out and greet him."

They finished with about an hour to spare. Then they rose and went over to the mayor's table. Michael Belinda introduced them to the mayor and the rest of the party. Mayor Daley made some light talk about the 111th and Western Avenue area, as if the Alderpersons had kept their word to discuss the problem with him. That issue settled they excused themselves and left the building. Julie hung on tightly to Kenneth as if he was nothing more than a dream and she didn't want it to end.

Kenneth had the doorman call two cabs. He gave the first one to Julie, kissed her, handed her an envelope and whispered in her ear, "It's been fun, thanks." He paid the cabby to take her anywhere she wanted to go. Getting into his cab he told the driver with a sigh, "Union Station, please." He suddenly felt bone tired.

The trip to Cleveland and then Philadelphia was uneventful. The companies needed no real changes. The reports Kenneth had showed everything that appeared at the factories. The management of each company had an expertise about them that wasn't there at Robin's Spices. Kenneth asked them to write out one-, five-, and ten-year plans showing what needed to be done, how much it would cost and send it to him in a month. He would go over them with the owner and get back to them. One of the things that surprised Kenneth was the owner's name was never the same, nor was it ever Mr. Strowe's name. What was he hiding or hiding from? The next place on the list was Hoboken, New Jersey, a little soup company that had its second year in a row of red ink. It specialized in dehydrated products. "Just Add Water" was its motto, run by a woman about sixty-years-old.

The employees called her Ma Parks and in many ways she appeared the caring type, but she was all business with Kenneth. The company had been in her family for forty-three years. A Mr. Milner bought it out after the war and let her run it as a favor to her late father. Although the buildings and the interior looked worn, they were clean and well-kept, as if she loved it.

She looked at Kenneth as the enemy trying to steal her baby away. Using all the skills he had with great patience, Kenneth gained enough trust to get the information he needed to make a competent suggestion. In Kenneth's eyes, if Parks could get product from Kinston in Chicago, they both would benefit.

The last stop was New York City. Kenneth wasn't excited about this stop. Like Chicago, he had heard things about it that scared him. The city was so big that people would just disappear. His father would say as he was growing up, "They find more bodies in the Hudson River than in the cemeteries." The factory was fairly well run. They tried to Unionize it three years earlier, it was clean, and the people seemed content.

One afternoon Kenneth reached into his wallet and pulled out the address that his mother had given him. He called a cab, went to his grandparents' apartment, rang the doorbell and waited. A woman about five years older than Kenneth's late mother looked through the window of the door. "Alice McGee?" He asked.

"I'm sorry she died about six months ago. I'm Joyce," she said.

"Is your father and mother here?" asked Kenneth.

"My mother is. Would you like me to call her?"

"Yes, tell her that her grandson, Kenneth, is here to see her. Sarah was my mother," Kenneth said.

Suddenly Joyce turned white as a sheet and fell to the floor. "Somebody help me," Kenneth yelled as he kicked the door open and knelt beside Joyce. *Boy, she sure isn't like her sister,* he thought.

An old woman with a walking stick came around the corner and saw Kenneth kneeling over Joyce. "Leave my daughter alone, you bastard," she screeched.

Looking up Kenneth saw the walking stick coming, but couldn't move. He woke up, lying on the floor looking at Joyce and his grandmother's face. The look on their faces caused him to break out laughing. He sat up and reached out to the old woman. "You must be Grandma. I'm your daughter's son, Kenneth. Mother told me about you just before she died."

"She is dead then. May God have mercy on her soul," the old woman made the sign of the cross. "Come on get up, what kind of a grandson are you, lying on my clean floor?"

"Tell me about Sarah. We haven't heard from her for over thirty years," said Joyce.

"Well, she moved to central Ohio, met my father and fell in love," said Kenneth.

"Were you conceived out of wedlock?" Grandma shook her finger at him.

"No, I wa-" Jonathan was once again interrupted.

"Ah, the Saints be praised. She was a good girl then. Well, go on lad." Grandma poked him with her walking stick.

"She had two boys and two girls, none of them out of wedlock."

"Of course not, I didn't raise her to be that way, what kind of a mother do you think I am?" She furiously shook her fist at him.

"Anyway, Father died in a hunting accident and Mother died of a broken heart sometime later. But before she died she told me of her two wonderful sisters and Saintly mother."

"So she died a Christian then?" Grandma asked.

"She was married in the Church, had all of her children baptized in the Church and she and Father were buried by the

Church," Kenneth said. "Now is my grandpa still alive and, if so, where can I find him?"

"Ah, that black-hearted man, yes he is alive. He's working for that man Frankie, the one that started all this violence. You better not talk to him. He'll tell Frankie and then I'll lose you, too." Grandma had put on a pot of water for tea. "He won't be back for another two hours so sit down and sup with us, Kenneth."

Kenneth made an excuse that he could only stay for a short period of time, but joined them for tea. Grandma was moving around without her walking stick, laughing and crying at the same time. They spoke of Sarah's childhood as well as her life at the Estate. Kenneth was careful not to tell them where in Ohio it was, but did paint a picture of his mother's life. He made it sound as if she lived in the main house rather than the three bedroom home that meant so much to her. He said his good-byes and left, wondering what was on his mother's heart when she left her home for good.

Kenneth flagged a cab and asked to be driven around the neighborhood; he saw Saint Anthony's, the pawnshop and Frankie's. There was an old man sweeping the sidewalk, he assumed it was his grandfather. The café was now a large restaurant. He had no need to go in or to talk to the old man. He directed the cabdriver to take him to the hotel and then to the Grand Central Terminal. His trip back to the Estate was quiet and uneventful, almost as if he left one world and entered another. He was looking forward to seeing his sisters and talking with Mr. Strowe.

The first thing Kenneth did when he arrived at the Willow Creek Estate was to see his sisters and give them gifts from his trip. When he saw them, a sense of pride welled up within him. They were his and nobody could take that away from him. Oh, someday soon some boy would come calling, but they would still be his girls. As he watched them open their presents, he was amazed by how much they had grown in the two months he was gone, or was it that by being gone, he suddenly realized that they were growing up?

From there he went to sit on the bench his father had built for Naomi. It was there that she had buried his father and Kenneth had buried his mother. He sat there for hours, telling them of the changes that had taken place, the changes that he saw in the girls when he came back and what he learned from his trip. Finally, as the sun was setting, he got up and went to the main house to face Mr. Strowe, hoping he could hold off until morning, to discuss the ideas that he had for the future of the five companies. As he entered the house he heard Mr. Strowe coming from his office.

"Kenneth, I mean Ken, my boy. Come on in and tell me

about your trip. Let me pour you a glass of wine. Sit down, sit down. So how was it? Did you have a good trip? What did you discover about the businesses?" Bill asked with great excitement.

Ken noticed his hands were shaking as he poured the wine. "Here let me do that, Bill. We need to talk in great depth about these five businesses, and I don't intend to do it tonight. I haven't had a good night's sleep since I left here and my bed is calling. So I will sit down, give you a thumbnail sketch of my trip and then I'm going to bed. But first let me say that it is good to see you again. I missed you. Do you mind if I give you a hug?"

Bill's face went red and for a moment he was speechless, "I ... I guess not, I never thought of it. *YES*, you may hug me!"

Ken went around the desk and gave Mr. Strowe a big hug. "I guess I didn't realize until I left what you meant to me, Bill. You going out on the limb for Mother and Father, and then putting your trust in me on this trip. Thank you. You won't be sorry."

They talked about the trip in general for an hour or two, and then Ken got up, excused himself and went home to sleep in his own bed. That night he had dreams of the people he had to deal with on his trip, especially Julie. He kept seeing her laughing as someone was executing him. As the sun broke the horizon he woke up and went to the top of the hill.

There in their usual place sat Joe, an empty pipe in the corner of his mouth, just waiting for him. They embraced as if they were family and then Joe started to ask questions of the trip. They sat there laughing and telling stories of that had happened while they were apart.

Finally Joe said, "Strowe made a decision, Kenneth, and you won't like it. The horses are going. He asked me, 'What is the least profitable part of the farm?' I had to be honest, so I said the equestrian. Last month he came to me and ordered me to sell the broodmares and yearlings. We're planning a sale sometime in October. He's debating on including the stallions. I know how much you loved the horses, but I had to be honest." Joe shook out his pipe like he had it full of ashes, not daring to raise his eyes into Kenneth's.

"When Mr. Strowe told me of some of the challenges that were rising here at Willow Creek, I told him that he should listen and trust you more. After I said it, it occurred to me that I might lose my horses. You did right. They are the millstone around our neck, and they have to go. So what is he going to do in place of the horses?" Kenneth played with his thinking stone.

Joe sighed. "He's leaning toward just turning the soil over and raising grain."

"Listen Joe, I have to talk to Mr. Strowe today about my trip. Why don't you and your Mrs. have dinner at my house tonight and we can discuss an alternative," Kenneth said as they rose to get a start on the day's work.

"The Mrs. will not hear of it, Kenny boy. You and the girls come to our house. Tell the girls to make your mother's strawberry pie, or better yet make two of them and leave one just for me." Joe headed to his home to eat breakfast.

Kenneth went home, woke up the girls, told them of the pies and headed for the main house with his papers. He knew what had to be done to save Mr. Strowe, but would he let him do it? The choices for one was profitable, the other four questionable. But if something wasn't done soon Mr. Strowe could lose everything that he had worked so hard for.

"Am I too late for breakfast?" Kenneth called as he walked into the dining room. Suddenly everything became quiet. Everyone just sat there looking at him as if he was either a ghost or a stranger. "Maybe I should introduce myself." Kenneth laughed as he pulled out a chair. "I am Kenneth Adams, your worst nightmare. I have come back from a two-month trip hungry. If you don't finish your plates, I will finish them for you."

They went back to eating, but were still quiet. Jill, one of the domestic helpers spoke up, "Kenneth, we heard that you went on this trip to find a way to get rid of Willow Creek and us. So when and where are we going?"

"Part of the rumor is true, but the problem with grapevine gossip is that all you get is bad wine. I went out to look at a few companies to see if they can improve production so we'll have more money to live on. The answer is a strong yes if we do it right. And unless Mr. Strowe says different, I would expect to live here a longtime. Remember, if you go, I go, and I have nowhere to go. Like each of you I have my shadows chasing me, plus my parents'. Now what do we have left to eat?"

The cook came in with more eggs, bacon and pancakes. Kenneth told stories between bites of food. Soon the atmosphere changed to laughter and joy. Mr. Strowe came in and said, "I see the prodigal has come home and is filling you with all kinds of corruption. Well I need him now, so if you will excuse him, he will be back later to tell you more lies."

Kenneth picked up his coffee cup, turned to Joanie the cook and whispered, "Bring me a pot in fifteen minutes."

They went into the office. Bill closed the door and said, "Which ones do we have to close or sell?"

"Personally I wouldn't close any of them. You've made some bad business decisions, but none that can't be saved. I would sell one immediately, the steel plant in Cleveland," Ken replied.

"But that's the most profitable, why would you want to sell that one?" Bill asked as a knock came from the door and Joanie came in with fresh coffee. "Thank you Joanie, I'll need another one in about an hour."

"Because that plant is unionized, they have two years left on their contract. To make it more profitable we'll have to come in and automate some of the jobs. The union will cry foul and you'll have a labor dispute on your hands. Then no one will want to buy it. No, now is the time. Their workload is running behind, meaning there's a backlog of income waiting for the new owners to harvest. We can get top dollar and hand the headaches over to the new owners," Ken explained. "The management team is solid and is recognized nationwide. If they aren't kept on, they won't have any trouble getting jobs equal to, if not better than, what they have now.

"The two plants in New York City—either combine them or sell them. The managements of both plants are nothing more than parasites. They are cannibalizing each other to death, they have related products, and the union was voted down by less than ten votes. This means in a year they can call for a revote. Believe me they will, and you will have another labor dispute. I understand the strike in Cleveland lasted over a year. Can you afford that? My suggestion is this: offer the two plants in a joint package. If someone bites, get rid of them, if not; raise the price for each by twenty percent."

Bill sat at his desk with his head in his hands. "God and this is the good news. What are you going to say about Chicago and Hoboken?"

"That they both are Mom and Pop businesses and you can't sell either one for a profit. In the present condition you will have to close one, if not both, within two years. Your dehydrated soup company—great idea but no opportunity to expand. I would say, unless you move it or make major changes, it will be the first to close. This is why: Hoboken, New Jersey is a small town that has its youth leaving for the Big Apple to make living wages. Ma Parks, as they call her, has been giving her pay increases to her factory employees just to keep them around for another year. The humidity in that area has a yearly average of eighty-three percent and you're trying to dehydrate goods. The herbs and spices that you need don't grow on the East Coast but in the Midwest. The company that should be supplying her product refuses to deal with her. Who is this company? None other than Robin's Spices, and why won't they deal with Ma Parks, because seventeen years ago Kinston had a falling-out with her father over one order."

Another pot of coffee came in, this time with fresh sweet rolls. Ken was about to go on when Joanie announced. "The noon meal will be ready in an hour gentlemen. Should I prepare a place for you at the table, or should I have it brought here?"

"Have it brought in here, Joanie," said Kenneth. "We still have a lot of work to do."

"No, we'll eat with the others. Our young friend here might have a cast-iron constitution, but I don't. I need to move around for a few minutes. Thank you Joanie and please, no more coffee," Mr. Strowe replied and turned to Kenneth. "You've been ignoring Chicago. Why?"

"Because you have major problems there and they are not all economic. If you don't mind, let's leave that for last," Ken answered.

"What do you think we can sell these companies for?" Bill asked hesitantly.

"I asked around and with the condition of Cleveland, the steel market, we can ask for thirty-five and settle for twenty-nine or thirty million. The New York plants, as a joint deal with closing cost, twenty-five and separately fifteen million. As I said, I don't think the other two can be sold at a profit now. That would give you a cash reserve after taxes, commissions, of about $35,000,000.00. If you hang onto them you will have to put $450,000 to $500,000 into each of them. You can lose up to $40,000,000 in strikes, legal fees and lawsuits." Ken said, as if it was nonnegotiable. "And if you wanted to hold onto Chicago and Hoboken, you'll have money to pour into them. It isn't rocket science, Bill. It's business."

"Yes, but it is part of my past and that's disappearing so fast it scares me," said Bill. "By the way, I just received a notice from the Chicago Board of Trade that I had deposited $100,000 to open an account. Do you know anything about that?"

"Yes, and as of this morning it's worth $275,000. Now, don't get excited. Until it's transferred into your bank, you can't say you have it. The market swings on a moment's notice so don't spend it yet," Ken replied. "Now, can we get back to Hoboken, New Jersey?"

There was a knock on the office door. "Come in," Bill called.

It was Mercy, out of breath. "This man called and said he had to have an answer immediately." She handed Kenneth a message.

"Thanks Mercy, I'll take care of it immediately," Kenneth said and she left. "Great kid, God blessed us when he sent her to the Adams' household. You know she wants to meet her real mother don't you? By the way, this note has raised your account by $45,000. Can I use your phone?"

"Ah, yes, of course, sit down at my desk. Do anything you like," Bill said.

Ken called Abram and told him to get out of the position, and twenty minutes after open in the morning reverse the position. He hung up and looked at Bill who just stood there with his mouth open. "That's it? Twenty seconds on the phone and the deal is done?"

"No, now I have to sit down and figure out, if I'm wrong, how much I'm willing to lose. That's the biggest part of the trade. Anyone can place a trade, but to do it profitably forty percent of the time is the trick. Now let's get back to Hoboken, or stop for lunch?"

They went into the staff dining room and sat down to eat. "Ken, you are a God sent," whispered Mr. Strowe.

Kenneth laughed. "Let's see if you say that after this afternoon."

They ate. Mr. Strowe went for his afternoon nap, and Kenneth went riding with the girls. While out riding, Mercy once again brought up the subject of her real mother. At first Kenneth pretended he didn't hear her, but she kept after it. "What difference does it make what your real mother looks like or what she does for a living, Mercy? Isn't it enough that you had a mother and father who loved you and raised you to the best of their ability?" Kenneth asked.

"So you know who she is and where she lives?" asked Mercy

excitedly. "Have you seen her, talked to her? What's she like? Tell me, please tell me."

"You know Mercy, Sarah and I love you, isn't that enough?" Kenneth asked.

"Yes, that is enough," Sarah said, "but Mercy has the right to know and meet her real mother. I mean if the tables were turned and I was Mercy I'd want to meet her, so what is the big deal?"

"The big deal is that I couldn't get her to say yes, and I feel like I failed you for not doing that," Kenneth lied.

"Oh, Kenneth, you could never fail me," Mercy said as she spurred her horse and called out, "Race you to the barn."

Kenneth called Sarah's name just before she could spur her horse into a gallop. "Sarah, there's more. I don't want to hurt her, but her mother is not what she dreams of her as. She is a worn out old woman who hates the world. I just don't want Mercy hurt."

"You'll hurt her more by hiding that from her." Sarah took off in Mercy's direction.

They cooled down their horses and Kenneth had the girls brush his because he had to get back to Mr. Strowe's meeting. The girls had promised to finish the pies and have the house clean before he got back. He promised not to make them stay at Joe's house more than a half hour past dessert.

Kenneth entered Mr. Strowe's office ready for battle over the two remaining businesses. "Can we finish with Hoboken, sir? The product line is old, but people are not grasping the idea of just adding water. What we need is maybe a $250,000 line in the budget for an advertising campaign." Looking for some reaction from Bill, he went on, "We pull the dehydration department and ship that to Chicago and increase the packaging by automation. Then we **order** Kinston to do business with Parks at a reasonable rate."

"And if he doesn't?" Asked Bill.

"Then we ask the basic question that should have been asked ten years ago." Ken put his hands on the desk, looking Bill in the eyes. "Who is the boss? If you knew what has been going on in the Robin's Spice Company for the last ten years, you would be horrified. Did you know that Mr. Mertz compared you to Adolf Hitler? That's right Adolf Hitler, because you can't get a job there unless you are, one, female; two, willing to spread your legs at the boss's whim. There, I said it. That is the main problem of Robin's Spices. Did you know the Research & Development Department covers the same things the Medical Emergency Fund does? Abortions, that's right illegal abortions! I had to sit there and pretend to be a part of that debauchery. And before you deny it, I have proof right here from hospital bills and check receipts stating that these women had work related surgery."

"So did you let them go?" Bill asked, the horror of financing abortions was written all over his face. "After all, we can't have that going on for any reason."

"No, and I will tell you why," replied Ken. "We don't have anyone to step into the leadership role. The closest one is Jacob Mertz. He has the education and he worked from floor sweeper to his present job. But to fire the supervisor, the vice president of personnel, the vice president and the president would send the message that we're in trouble. This is what I would propose to do: first notify them that all senior office employees will have to take a ten percent cut in pay starting next month. If they don't quit on you, then start taking authority away. At the same time bring in new employees that we can trust. Then notify finance that all checks must be signed by an outside party, such as the bank or a CPA. Believe me when the word gets out the rats will flee the sinking ship."

"Is it that bad?" Bill asked.

"Let's put it this way, since you took over there have been ninety-seven company paid work related surgeries, which includes seven deaths because of these surgeries. They weren't listed as abortions in the hospital but that is what they were. Yes, Bill, it is that bad."

Bill sighed. "Let me sleep on it."

"Then that's about it, except I did enjoy myself. Thanks for the honor of letting me represent you," Ken said. "By the way, can I buy three horses from you before you post the auction?"

"Just take them, Ken. You can have them. I don't care." Bill's shoulders slumped.

"No, this is business." Ken smiled as he left for the day, leaving the important papers with Mr. Strowe to review.

Kenneth always enjoyed going to the Murphy's. It reminded him of his home when Naomi was alive. Molly standing over the wood burning stove stirring the pots. The smell of fresh bread in the oven, the smell of herbs and spices floated throughout the house. The furniture was old, but loved. Like his home, Molly and Joe had to use the old unwanted furniture from the main house.

That night they had an Irish stew that only Molly Murphy could make. The stories of the old country and the laughter of Kenneth's experiences rang throughout the house. Finally the strawberry pie was eaten and the girls left for the night. "I asked them not to stay," said Kenneth, "because what we have to talk about is none of their business."

"Do you want me to leave too?" Asked Molly.

"No woman, we can talk treason with you present, it won't go anywhere." Joe laughed.

"I don't know if it will be treason, but I want this to be your idea, Joe. You are the cattle expert. Now Molly, in the old country didn't you say that you handled your father's cattle?" Kenneth asked.

"No, the lads took care of the cattle. I took care of the weanlings," she answered.

"So you have knowledge of cattle care right?" Kenneth asked.

"Ah, lad she has forgotten more than I can remember," Joe said. "Why when we were just wee kids she taught me more about life than she would admit." He watched his wife's face turn beet red. "But what does that have to do with the Estate and us?"

"While I was in the cities I asked questions about business and agricultural products. Did you know there are elite restaurants that serve what they call grain-fed beef? They pay a premium for beef cattle that are fattened only on grain and alfalfa and the good news is, if the cattle are Angus, they pay a premium on top of that premium. Now, we have one of the best Angus herds in the state. The price of grain is about to go down, and Mr. Strowe wants to move from the equestrian program to something more profitable. If we can corner that market here in Ohio, it will give us an edge on the future market as well."

"But will they buy all our cattle, or will they just come and choose which ones they want," asked Molly.

"Until we get our reputation proved, they will want the right to inspect our herd. But if they don't buy all of them then we will still sell them at premium by the lot." Kenneth said. "What the restaurants do in Chicago and New York is they tell the cattle producers about how many head they will need and when. That's why they're willing to pay the premium."

"Yes but it takes from thirty to thirty-six months from the time the calf hits the ground to slaughter. How do we sell that to Mr. Strowe?" Joe asked.

"Easy, we sell him on the idea with the understanding that we will slowly change the production program," explained Kenneth, "You both know that he doesn't like radical change, so use that as a selling point. What I need you to do, Joe, is to go to him with the idea, ask him for permission to explore it, and then give him a sales pitch. I promise you that I will work with you on the side, but it's your idea." Kenneth said excitedly.

"What profit are we talking about Kenneth?" asked Molly. "You know Joe is on a share program here. We'd like to have an idea of the gamble."

"I don't know. What you two will have to do is figure out what the difference will be in cost and I'll get the difference in sale price," said Kenneth. "Now I need to get home. My bed is calling. I didn't think I'd miss it so much."

"Don't forget your extra pie, Kenneth," said Molly.

"Now woman, don't you go showing your black heart by insulting Kenneth with that pie." Joe gave Kenneth a wink.

"That's right Molly; I'd take it bad if you didn't keep it. If you didn't like it, give to Joe. He'll eat anything."

"Ah, you are a true friend. May the wind always be at your back, Kenneth," she said quietly, kissing him on the cheek.

The next morning Kenneth waited to go up to the house, knowing that Bill had to have time to put his questions in order. He took out his fishing pole and went to the lake and threw in his line. After about two hours he heard someone approaching. Turning, he saw Bill.

"I thought we had issues to discuss," said Bill with a mock frown. "Is this the new executive's life, shoes off, feet in the water, holding onto a fishing pole that if I know you has no hook on the end of the line?"

"Quiet, I think I have a bite," Kenneth laughed pulling in his hook less line. "I just don't like cleaning them. So if you want to clean them I will be more than happy to eat them."

"Well, I had time to think," said Bill sitting next to Ken. "You make sense about selling those three plants. But I have trouble with the other two. I'd like to kill Kinston and his associates. I never thought such things could go on nowadays. I'm indebted to Ma Parks. It was her father that lent me the money to set up the Willow Creek Estate. I couldn't go to a bank because the Family would find me. Therefore, the sale had to be cash. So in a way you, too, are indebted to her."

"That might be so, sir, but the facts are clear. You can't dehydrate with the humidity as high as it is in Hoboken. Plus, shipping fresh herbs and spices from the Midwest to be dehydrated is poor business. You're going to have to decide."

"I have," Bill sighed "I'm too old for this, so I'm going to turn everything over to you."

"No, no you are not! You have the responsibility to make a statement to Parks and the people of Robin's Spices. You can say, 'Ma Parks, because of your father I will stand with you and turn this company around.' And to the employees of Robin's Spices you need to say 'Enough is enough. I didn't know of this corruption and I'm putting a stop to it now.'" Ken said. "Then if you want me to take over, fine. I'll do my best. Now if that's okay with you, let's plan to see Ma Parks as soon as possible. How about leaving on Saturday? We'll be there on Monday when the plant opens."

"What would you do with that plant if it was yours, Ken?" Bill asked.

"Knowing what I know now about her father, I'd get it on its feet and hand her the keys. But then I'm not you. And before you ask, I would make Mertz the president of Robin Spices. Then hire all new leadership, the company still has potential, but the present administration is bleeding you dry."

"I sent Kinston a telegram asking for the latest wholesale price list, needing it in three days. I should have it in time for the trip. Get things in order so we can go." Suddenly Bill looked tired as he got up. "I have a meeting with Joe tomorrow morning at 8:00. I think he will be leaving us because of that equestrian decision. Lord, when will this all end? Thanks for helping. I could use some help tomorrow with Joe. We do need him here, no matter what I say. He's far more than a dumb Irishman. Clumsy, uneducated yes, but I'd match him with any graduate student when it comes to animal husbandry. And people skills. I think he could talk the good Lord into running ice water down to the devil."

Kenneth sat by the lake for a while, thinking of his friend Joe, Julie, the girls and, for some reason, his late brother Henry. If Henry had lived would he be in Kenneth's shoes right now? And if so, what would he do differently? Could they have worked as a team? Some families just can't work together, he was told, what about Henry? Suddenly he felt alone and cold, wondering what purpose there was for him to be part of this organization. He wrapped himself in his arms and cried quietly for a while. Suddenly he smelled his father's tobacco and felt a soft hand on his face. Looking up to the sky, he smiled and knew they were there with him.

13

In the morning while the sun was rising, Kenneth headed to the hilltop. He hoped that Joe would have a solid sales plan to present to Mr. Strowe. Joe never arrived. Looking out over the Estate with a bright reddish yellow sun coming over the horizon, he saw what looked like a small thin film hanging over the dairy barn.

Not sure what it was, he closed his eyes and saw himself in the barn, smelling the cattle and looking for problems. Suddenly he came on a cow with a 316 tag on her ear and a foul smell. Going farther into the herd he found 422 and 291 walking in a jerky motion with the same odor.

Rising from his favorite spot, he rushed down to Joe's house and banged on the door. Molly answered the knock with a few Gallic terms that Kenneth didn't understand but he did understand the tone. "Molly, I need Joe immediately at the dairy barn. I'm not sure what we'll find, but I need him. Is he here?

"No, he said something about getting up early and practicing his speech. Can I help?" Molly offered.

"Yes, get to the loafing barn immediately and check it. If you see him, tell him to come, too," Kenneth shouted, as he left on a run for the barn.

When he got there, he found the milkers just finishing the morning milking. Waiting for the last cow to leave the parlor, he asked the milkers to take a short break. After they left, he began his inspection. The milk filter was extra dirty, and there were dark, tar-like feces with blood clots mixed in on the floor. Old whitewash was peeling off the walls and ceiling of the parlor. Joe and Molly walked into the parlor with the same story about the loafing barn, plus the bulk feed trough had old feed in it.

"Joe, when I left the leadership role who was put into my place of the dairy production? Kenneth asked.

"To my knowledge no one is in charge. I've been trying to keep an eye on the livestock, but I guess I have failed." Joe kicked the dirt with his toe like a boy about to be scolded.

"I want 291, 316 and 422 pulled out and sent to the slaughterhouse immediately. I don't mean tomorrow or this afternoon, I mean immediately. Even if we have to ship them ourselves," Kenneth said to the milk hands.

"But we don't have permission to do that. Why don't we just call the vet and have him look them over first," said Bob, the head dairy herdsman.

"First those cows will be dead in five hours, so we don't have the time to waste waiting for vets. Second, I'm giving you a direct order. Ship them, end of conversation. Molly, thank you for helping, Joe let's go up and talk to Mr. Strowe," Kenneth said "Do you have someone you can count on to ship those cows?"

Joe sighed. "Ah, laddie, but the dairy barn doesn't like it when we get involved with their problems."

"Go back there and try to help them. Suggest that you have a truck coming. If they protest, pull rank and tell them their jobs are on the line because these diseases are caused by poor sanitary conditions. Do whatever it takes, but get them out of here, now. I'll go up and delay Strowe's and your meeting." Kenneth laughed. "Oh by the way, he thinks you're going to tell him that you're leaving the Estate. Play it up and you'll come out of this smelling like a rose."

Kenneth walked into Mr. Strowe's office expecting to find him reading his ticker tape. But instead he was reading a copy of the *Commodity Prospective* with confusion written all over his face. "Come in Ken, I'm glad to see you. I can't make heads or tails of this thing called commodity trading. We have thirty minutes before Joe comes, can you help me?" Bill asked.

"In one word, no, Bill! Not because I don't want to, or I don't know how, but because you have more pressing problems. You are about to lose your whole herd of dairy cows, because of clostridium. It's a classification that three bovine diseases fall into and they can wipe out a herd in three days. We're shipping three cows this morning because of these diseases. Why haven't you replaced Schmidt? Do you realize that if these three are the only ones infected, you will lose ten to fifteen thousand dollars, in production? If it wasn't for Joe noticing the signs, we would be in trouble."

"What does Joe know about dairy? Why, he's just an uneducated beef man," Bill said.

"Uneducated, yes, but you know as well as I do that all the graduates that come out of OSU can't hold a candle to Joe and his 'uneducated wisdom'. Between him and Molly you are running in the black while all the other beef farmers are going broke. He can pat the hind end of a steer and it gains ten pounds. And what does he know about dairy? The same principles that exist in beef exist in dairy because they both are bovines. You'd do yourself a favor and keep him around by promoting him to Head of Animal Husbandry. Hire those who think they know what they're doing to feed and work the cattle. Let him supervise the whole livestock part of the business."

"And what would that cost?" Bill asked.

"$30,000 plus room and board for someone at the entry-level, and believe me when I say he is worth every penny of it," Ken answered.

"$30,000! That's three times what I'm paying him now. I can't afford to pay that."

"Then offer him $20,000 and some of the profits from that part of the Estate. You will have a proven employee who has an extreme gift working with you for profitability," Ken explained.

"It won't do any good. He's going to be here in a few minutes to give his notice, God what am I going to do? I'm getting too old for this. When I started the Willow Creek, all I wanted to do was protect the innocent. What am I going to do?" Bill ran his fingers through his hair, shaking his head. "Can you help me?"

"The first thing you're going to do is go and rinse your face with cold water. Then when Joe comes in, you're going to face him like the man you are—in charge, not fearing anything. If he leaves, then he leaves. We'll hire someone in the $30,000 bracket, experience losses for a few years, but we will survive. If he stays, we'll be far better off with the man leading your livestock program. Now go before he sees you this way. If he comes in before you get back, I'll talk with him."

Throwing a questioning glance at Ken, Bill quickly left to do as he suggested.

Joe and Mr. Strowe walked into the office together, both laughing. "Well, Kenneth, that issue's settled," Mr. Strowe said. "Joe has agreed to stay on with a pay increase and some profits. Boy was I a fool worrying about losing him; all I had to do was give him a raise."

"I think you missed the point, Mr. Strowe. I accepted the raise, but staying on had nothing to do with the raise. And if you think it was, then you better continue worrying." Joe said.

"What do you mean? I thought we had a deal." Mr. Strowe looked scared.

"Ha, I'm accepting the $22,500 base plus five percent of the profits, but the reason you're keeping me isn't because of that. I was offered $35,000 plus ten percent of the profits just down the road at O'Dondall's. I'm staying because finally, after all these years, you spoke to me as a man, asking me to be part of something that is bigger than we are. Something we both believe in—helping to protect the innocent," Joe said. "But now we must talk about something far greater than my pay. What I saw today is a combination of bloody gut, red water, and tetanus. I know Kenneth here has the scientific name, but these three diseases can wipe out a herd in matter of a couple of days. There is no cure that we know of, but it can be stopped. What I suggest is that you, Mr. Strowe, tell all concerned about my authority so it won't be questioned. Second, we free up the equipment and personnel for two days to clean and whitewash the interior of the barn, milk parlor, and milk house. And then third, we set up a schedule to keep the bacteria under control so we don't have to lose anymore cows."

"I'll get the word out this afternoon. You and Molly will be invited with Kenneth here for monthly dinners to talk over the next month's plans. The next one scheduled will be two weeks from tonight. Your pay increase will be dated back to the first of this month. Is there anything else that needs to be discussed before we move to the next issue?" Mr. Strowe asked.

"No sir, and thank you for this opportunity," said Joe.

"Now Kenneth, we need to make you part of the decision-making of the Estate. I've spoken to my lawyer and he drew up these papers. Also, you will be the executor of the estate at my death. Joe, you will be moved up to second in command and that is why I want you present on all decisions from now on. Is that understood?"

"Yes sir," they replied.

"Then let's get down to the barn and handle that issue. What I want you to do is show me why you think this could have been prevented and what we can do about it," Mr. Strowe said.

"Mr. Strowe, I don't want to point fingers," Joe said, "but Bob isn't a trained husbandry man. If anything, you are at fault rather than Bob. You didn't hire a replacement for Schmidt."

"Joe, it isn't the best idea to accuse your boss after he has given you a raise and a promotion, but yes it is my fault," Mr. Strowe said.

They started at the milk house and saw the poor condition of the building, dirty containers and broken sinks. From there they went into the parlor and saw the poor whitewash, the broken boards and dirty milking equipment. Finally they went into the loafing barn. Kenneth was shocked at the conditions the cattle had to live in. Manure was up to their knees, the feed trough was filled with moldy silage, and rats were feeding in it.

Mr. Strowe called all the dairy people together and announced Joe's position with the Estate. Then he turned to Joe and said, "In three days I expect a summary of what has to be done to turn this around. When William was alive this was a showplace. I want it that way again." He walked out, leaving Joe and Kenneth knee-deep in problems.

"So where do we start?" Kenneth asked.

"Let me get the tractors and spreaders from the horse barn and beef barn. The hay needs to be baled today, but we can leave it on the ground once it's baled for up to a week. The personnel we have for haying we can move here and get the barn and feed troughs done first. I'm not sure what he meant when he said, a summary, but we can figure that out after the men get going on the main problem. I am not sure he'd want you involved in the dirty work but I do appreciate all that you've already done." Joe played with his pipe.

"I didn't do anything, Joe. Remember, you're good at what you do. You might not know the scientific terms or the advance formulas for feed production, but I'll match you up to anyone for the finished product. And that's what matters. Education can come if you want it, just let me know and we'll work it out. Now do you want me to get my work clothes on or do you want me to make phone calls to have the buildings whitewashed or what?" Kenneth asked.

"You line up the whitewashing while I get the men working in the loafing barn. Then I need your help with the milking parlor and milk house." Joe headed out to get the men and equipment together for the day's project.

Kenneth went home and started making the phone calls, not

only for the whitewashing, but trying to find out who could do the building repairs. There were several private contractors who claimed that they could do it, but every time he closed his eyes and visualized, he saw problems. Finally he came across a name: Arnold May Builders. *That's the one,* he thought as he picked up the phone to call. He got a Mr. Braumnsfelt who assured him that Mr. May would be out in the morning to talk to him.

As Kenneth was getting ready to go up to the house and present some ideas to Bill he heard a knock on the door. Going to the door, he found Bob and Joe standing there with a looks of hatred for each other all over their faces. He laughed. "Come in gentlemen. I see you have already decided to disagree."

"You knew this was going to happen?" asked Joe.

"Oh, yes, anytime you have two people with your abilities for improving the business, you're going to have disagreements. That's what makes the potboil. As long as you two can agree to disagree, it will work out fine. Now what's the challenge before us?"

"Well, laddie, it's twofold. First, who is in charge of the dairy, and second, who has the authority to fire and hire?" Joe asked.

"Well, before those buttons start popping of your shirt, Joe, you've been given the authority to hire and fire. However, if you think you're going to be in charge of the day-to-day operations of the dairy, you are mistaken. Bob here has done an excellent job with what he had to work with. You take that away and you'll be doing all the work yourself, because the men won't follow you. Besides, you have the challenges of all animal husbandry programs on the Estate you don't have time for the day-to-day operations. Now Bob what's on your mind?" Kenneth asked, as if Joe were no longer there.

"Now laddie, don't you push me aside as if I don't matter. I'm not done yet with you." Joe shook his pipe in Kenneth's face.

"I know you're not done, Joe, but I'm done with you. Bob

here has men working their tails off trying to meet a deadline and you want to argue power. It won't happen, Joe, not today, tomorrow, or forevermore. If you have to demand power or respect, you won't get it." Kenneth snapped.

"Now Bob, what's on your mind?" Kenneth asked once again.

"Well sir most of the questions are answered, but why did you remove those cows so quickly yesterday? We could have saved them if we had called a vet. Those cows were valuable cattle maybe $2,500 or $3,000 each." Bob said.

"You see Kenneth, he don't know anything about cattle," Joe cut in, poking Bob in the chest with his pipe.

"The word is doesn't, not don't Joe, and stop using that pipe as a weapon. Bob do you know what HBS is, or have you heard of the term HBS?" asked Kenneth.

"I've heard the term. It's a disease that sweeps through a herd and can destroy a herd in days," Bob answered, "but I never have seen it."

"Well now you have, laddie," said Joe, about to poke him with his pipe again.

"Joe, I'm going to take that pipe away from you if you don't stop it, until yesterday Joe didn't know the term HBS either, Bob. He knew the symptoms as bloody gut, red water and tetanus. Joe has the capacity to see symptoms long before they become fatal. That's one reason he was put over all the livestock. The other reason is he knows what causes these diseases, so you need to listen to him. Dirty milk parlors, poor hygiene in the loafing barns, moldy silage, all cause these diseases and you had all three going against you. I know you've asked for improvements and have been ignored. Joe has orders to change that for the betterment of the dairy production. Some will be slow, but they will come. Now, is there anything else before I go see Mr. Strowe about something that *IS* important?" Kenneth headed toward the door.

"And this isn't important?" asked Joe.

"Yes, but did you know that we're dumping over a hundred pounds of milk a day because we don't have holding capacity for what we produce? And that is called, dumping profits. In that both of you are on profit sharing, I would say it is important. Now both of you grow up and start working together. I think we can double our production if we do. And that will equal to $2000 to $3,000 more in your pockets each year. By the way tomorrow at 10:00 a.m. an Arnold May will be here to discuss repairs and additions. Both of you be at the milk house on time."

Kenneth went up to the house to discuss the challenges of Bill's announcement. Then they moved to the trip that was before them to New York and then Chicago. Bill asked if Ken could handle Chicago alone, but he refused. Stating, there was too much riding on Robin's Spices not to have the owner present. And finally, they worked on the formula for trading commodities and stocks. Ken was disappointed at the slowness of Bill grasping the principles of the formula. Finally, Bill threw up his hands and said, "Ken, I trust you, you handle it."

"Sir, you've given enough authority already, that I can sell everything and keep all proceeds for myself. Don't you think that's a little dangerous?" Ken asked.

"Only if it wasn't you, Ken. Besides, I don't have that long to live. My doctors say that my heart can give out anytime. And you will be the executor of the Estate anyway. So who better is there to handle the day-to-day operations?" asked Bill.

"Millions of dollars is not day-to-day operations. You need a check and balance system to protect yourself. Do you have a CPA and a lawyer that can work on your behalf?"

"Yes, and they will make a mess of everything and you will have to straighten it all out anyway. So I'm just bypassing them by putting you in complete charge." Bill handed him papers authorizing complete control of the estate. "From now on if anyone has a question about the operation of this corporation, they will have to come to you. I am just your advisor."

Bill felt that they should fly to New York, in that neither he nor Ken had ever flown. Although it was faster, Ken felt that they could have more time to work out issues traveling by train. But Bill prevailed and so early in the morning of July 7th they boarded the plane to New York, neither wanting to admit the fear of being off the ground, and the excitement of traveling in the air. They landed at LaGuardia Airport and called for a limousine.

They met with the realtor and her lawyer to close the sale of the two plants. The Conglomerate showed an interest in the Cleveland steel plant. On the way to the hotel Ken said, "We're moving too fast. Maybe we aren't asking enough for these properties."

"Or maybe the Master has a plan that is falling into place and He doesn't feel that He needs to confide in us," Bill said.

"Now that's a first." Kenneth laughed. "I never heard you speak of the Divine. You aren't getting religious in your old age, are you?"

"I've always been religious. Like you, I pray regularly, worship regularly, and I live out that faith every possible moment of the day. I don't preach my faith like some do and I surely don't judge people because they agree or disagree with me. But I do believe in the Almighty and that as a human I can't please him. All I can do is say, 'Hey I messed up, forgive me,' and then keep going. You might think that isn't enough or maybe too much, but I say it works for me and that is enough. Now, that's more on the subject than I care to speak of, so let's change the subject."

"No, I have questions that need to be answered," Ken replied.

"Make it fast. I'm tired," Bill said.

"How did you know Mother was coming? She told me you knew her before she got here. And how did you know my father was trying to hide from the governor and his secret police? And how—"

Bill cut him off. "And how do you know that a field needs to be fertilized by just looking above the field's plain? And how does Joe know there are sick animals in a building a half mile away? It's a gift from the Master. We all have it, but most of us don't have the discipline to exercise it. Then there are those of us who are here on a mission. To those He has given extra gifts, like seeing the needy or the lonely, looking at a formula that makes no sense at all to the world, but can turn $100,000.00 into a million and a half in three weeks. The question always is: how is this gift being used? That's where we'll hear or not hear 'Well done thou good and faithful servant.'"

"But you asked about your mother and father. I'll make it simple. You told me. Now you figure it out. I'm going to take a nap." He leaned back and went to sleep.

Kenneth called his grandmother to see if she was okay. Joyce answered crying. "What's wrong Joyce? This is Kenneth. Is it Grandmother?"

"It's Papa. He was killed last night at the restaurant," cried Joyce, "and Mother is getting ready to go down and kill Frankie for it."

"Can you get her on the phone? Wait a minute Joyce let me ask you a question. Do you think Frankie did it?"

"Oh, yes, he was killed with a stiletto. He did what he promised he would do," Joyce answered. "I'll get mother."

Kenneth could hear the cane thumping as Grandma came to the phone. It brought back memories of the first time he saw her looking down at him after knocking him out. He couldn't help but laugh at the thought of Frankie facing this little woman so full of anger.

"Is this Kenneth?" came the voice-over the phone. "Kenneth is this you?" She sounded as if she was crying.

This is good, Kenneth thought. "Yes, Grandma, it's Kenneth. I'm so sorry about Grandpa. I know you'll miss him," replied Kenneth trying to think of what to say.

"Miss him, miss him, his black heart is where it belongs, but what about Joyce and me? He has spent every dime we had looking for Sarah, and now her enemy has killed him. I will stop this though. It will not go any farther. The Saints are with me Kenneth, I will kill that black-hearted snake," Grandmother cried.

"Grandma, Grandma, sit down and take a breath. You know you can't kill Frankie. He'll have people all around him. Mother said you could always tell when he killed someone because of the thugs that would appear. What you need to do is treat him like a snake. Wait for the opportunity, when you have the advantage. Meantime you need to prepare the funeral service, do you have money for that?"

"Ah, Kenneth, we are poor as church mice since your mother had to flee this snake. I guess they'll have to bury him in the Potter's Field," she replied.

"No, no, Grandma, no grandfather of mine will be buried in the Potter's Field. I'll get money to you. You know I can't come, don't you? But you will be taken care of. I'll send some extra money so you can live till we get this sorted out. Now swear by the Blessed Mother that you won't do anything to or threaten Frankie until we talk," Kenneth said.

"I do not swear by the Blessed Mother, Kenneth, and

you shouldn't either. You know that's blasphemy. But I will promise by all that is Holy. And thank you." He could hear his grandmother blowing her nose as she hung up the phone.

Kenneth went to one of Mr. Strowe's banks and had the money delivered to his grandmother. He made sure that it was done in cash with no receipt so Frankie couldn't track him or Bill down. He paid extra so it would be delivered immediately and then ordered flowers with his mother's birth name on them and Naomi's stiletto that he always carried, to give Frankie a message.

Back at the hotel he found Bill up and about, reading papers about Ma Parks and making plans.

"Listen, Ken, from here we'll go to Hoboken and then Cleveland. I'll go home after Cleveland while you go on to Chicago. I think I have Ma Park's proposal set, so maybe we should go over that on the train. It's important that we leave New York tonight." Bill started to pack.

"I thought we had another night here in New York," said Kenneth.

"Not after that messenger delivers the money to your grandmother. And when Frankie sees the flowers with your mother's birth name on them, all hell is going to break loose. Frankie is going to send out all his contacts to trace it down. You did right my boy, but you have no idea the impact it will have on this town." Bill laughed. "Now when we leave, we're going to give a Bronx address to the taxi driver. We'll get out there and you can call your grandmother to say good-bye. Then we'll call a cab and go to the Grand Central Terminal for our train. Now, let's hurry."

Kenneth looked at his friend and could tell there was more than his safety at stake. "They're after you too, aren't they Bill?"

"Never mind me, Ken. I've lived with this all my life. It's you I'm concerned about. You still have work to do here. Now let's get out of here," Bill insisted.

Kenneth hurried his packing. Bill went down to take care

of the bill and call a cab. Suddenly Kenneth felt like his world was closing in on him. For the first time in his life, he feared the unknown. As he closed his last suitcase he thought of his mother. *How, did she handle it*, he wondered. *What's going to happen to Grandmother and Joyce or even Mercy and Sarah if they find me? How could he have been so stupid to put Bill into a life and death situation?"* There was a knock on the door and he jumped. "Come in," he said. It was the bellboy coming for the luggage.

They went to the Bronx and Kenneth called his grandmother. Once again Joyce answered the phone. Grandmother was sleeping, and Joyce thanked him for the money. Kenneth explained the flowers and asked that she watch to see the reaction to the stiletto. Promising that they would be taken care of, he hung up. Bill called another cab and they rode quietly to the train station.

Kenneth thoughts were of his family and what price was paid for him to be born into this world. *"I wonder what's it's all about. When it's all sorted out, will it make any sense?"* Kenneth asked himself out loud. Bill just looked at him and smiled his knowing smile. *How can he be at such peace?* Kenneth wondered.

They arrived at Grand Central Terminal and bought their tickets. They only had enough time to get to the train so they had to hurry. Bill looked out of breath as they walked, "We can sit down and rest Bill," said Kenneth.

"No, we're almost there. Let's just keep moving. I'm looking forward to this trip. I should have done it years ago." Bill smiled as he caught his breath, but his complexion was pale.

They boarded their train and found seats together. The train was full of commuters. Bill sat back and sighed, "We're safe."

"How do you know?" Kenneth asked.

"Close your eyes and breathe, Ken. Do you smell death around, or feel the spirit of murder? No we are safe. They're looking in all the wrong places. Now let me take a nap for fifteen minutes and then we have to talk about Ma Parks and our partnership." Almost instantly Bill was in a peaceful sleep, his essence slowly changing from a tired old man to one who could still take on the world.

What made him so vulnerable, wondered Kenneth as he sat and watched him.

The conductor came by and Kenneth handed him their tickets and asked him how long to Hoboken. He laughed and said, "One hour and fifteen minutes."

"What's so funny?" asked Kenneth.

"You aren't from around here, are you? You pronounced it Hu book' en, it's Ho' bo' kin, long o's. We always can tell when someone opens their mouth and pronounce that town if they are true easterners." The conductor smiled. "Let's see your accent, Illinois or eastern Indiana?"

"That's close," said Kenneth. "Try central—"

"I should have known, central Indiana. You know I've been doing this a long time, but the Indiana accents still give me trouble." The conductor laughed and moved on to the next row of seats.

Bill stirred, so Kenneth pulled out the papers for the soup plant in Hoboken. Quickly going over them, he noticed that Ma Parks was not who he thought her to be, but a descendent of a Mertz. That was the same name as the financial person of Robin's Spices. *I wonder*, thought Kenneth.

"Stop wondering, Ken. Yes, he is her brother. My father sponsored their father and mother after the war. They were prisoners in one of the concentration camps. That's why their father helped me, and why they're important to the Estate. And why they are so fearful of strangers. I hope this trip will ease Mae's fears. She'll be calling me Poops, because that was what she called me when we were young and foolish. I wanted to marry her, but they are Orthodox Jews, and I am a homosexual. She married ten years later, two years after they married her husband died. I tried to be heterosexual but it just didn't work. Now you know, although I think you always knew. Maybe down deep I always was one. I don't know, but you're the first I've admitted it to. Now about Mae Parks," Bill reached over to get the papers, "what I'm proposing is that they shut down the dehydrators. The three that work that line should be moved to the processing department and cut the workweek down to thirty-two hours until the production line can be expanded."

"Are you listening to yourself, Bill?" Ken asked. "A week ago you were talking of giving this company over to her, and now you want to control it. I say, we sit her down in a place where there are no distractions and set forth your plans. She might not want the company, or she might want to expand it in a different product line."

"No, she wouldn't want to sell it. When her father was about to lose it, she came to me for help. She didn't want her father or brother to know the trouble the company was in. No, she wouldn't want to sell it. But you're right; we should let her decide the future. But what would it cost to turn it around?"

"Two, three hundred thousand, I don't know. She wouldn't let me get the information I needed to give a satisfactory answer," Kenneth replied. "My gut feeling is that she won't understand my help, either. So it will be up to you. For once I get to see you work."

It was dark when the train pulled into Hoboken. They got off and Bill made a phone call. Coming back he said, "She'll be here in fifteen minutes to pick us up."

"Who will pick us up?" Kenneth asked.

"Mae of course, I just called her. We're going out for dinner and we'll stay at her house. I thought you understood that. Don't you use your gifts for everyday needs?" Bill asked.

"I didn't think of having gifts until you mentioned them in New York. How do you discover them and can you use them for your own good?" Kenneth asked.

Bill sighed. *Had he failed Kenneth's spiritual training? Was it too late to train him? He just didn't know.* "When we get back to the Estate, I'll give you a crash course so just push those that you know you have to the limit. And yes you can use them for your personal good *IF* it doesn't hurt someone else."

A car pulled up and Mae Parks got out. Running to Mr. Strowe, she threw her arms around him and kissed him. "Poops. Poops! God it's been a longtime. I missed you so much. When you sent your man, I thought the worst. Are you okay? Come on let's get you out of the weather."

She's crying, Kenneth thought. *There's more here than a casual friendship.* They got in the car and traveled for about twenty minutes and then pulled into 'The Steak House.'

"I know how much you love a good steak, Poops, this is the best in the county." Mae said. "So tell me, are you still running from the Family? They haven't sent anyone for almost three years asking about you."

They were seated before Mr. Strowe answered the question. "Oh, they never give up, Mae. They'd go after the third generation if I had any children. One thing you can say about them, they are consistently vigilant. The only way to get out of a contract is by dying or marrying one of the Family. But tell me what's been going on in your life."

As they spoke of the past, Kenneth looked around the restaurant, studying the people. At first everything looked to be peaceful. Then he took a deep breath and let it out slowly. A light cloud moved over the heads of those who were in the building. Some had a lighter color than others. One young couple sat in the corner with a dark cloud over them. Kenneth studied them for about five minutes and then he started to get impressions, the sound of a baby crying and the smell of smoke. "Excuse me, Mae, but do you know that couple in the corner?" he asked.

"I know their name is Gustafson. They had a fire in their business yesterday, and they lost everything. The rumor is that someone tried to buy it from them. They refused to sell. You know what that's like Poops." Mae reached over the table and put her hand on Mr. Strowe's.

"I'll be right back," said Kenneth as he rose to talk to them.

"Be careful, Kenneth," said Mae.

"He'll be okay, Mae. He has to do what he does best." Bill smiled. "Kenneth, no more than a hundred grand, no strings attached, no trace of the money, we're too close to the final page to get caught up in a 'Family' feud."

Kenneth went over to the table and introduced himself under an assumed name. Why, he didn't know, it just came out that way. Suggesting that Mae Parks mentioned their fire, he started asking questions. He learned that they had been married for two years and had a two-month-old at Grandma's. The property where they lived was used as collateral for the loan on the business. Now the business was gone and it had been arson. They didn't know what to do. The business was printing and advertising, annual sales of $350,000 with overhead of about $300,000. Why someone would want to buy the property but not the business was beyond their thinking, the land and building weren't worth more than $100,000.

"So what do you plan on doing?" Kenneth asked.

"Part of me wants to rebuild on the lot, another part of me wants to just do advertising through the house and sell the lot. If we go into printing again, we'll need a loan for the equipment and I'm not sure there's that much money in it anymore. Besides, I can farm out the little printing that I have to my brother in Pennsylvania and still make a little profit. The problem is the cash flow in advertising can be slow. My clients pay but sometimes it's two or three months before we receive the money. If we sell this property, we will still owe $30,000 on the loan and without a steady income we don't think the bank will hold the paper," Mr. Gustafson said.

"I guess we're just cursed." Mrs. Gustafson sighed, trying to hold back the tears. "With little Allen and another baby on the way, we just don't know what to do."

"Boy, do I know what that feels like." Kenneth laughed. His laugh was the laugh that Mr. Strowe had when he laughed at the Estate. It surprised not only the Gustafson's, but Kenneth and the rest of the restaurant as well. He looked at Bill and saw him smiling from ear to ear looking back. "I'll be in town for a few days. Let's get together tomorrow about 12:30 at this address," he handed them a business card, "and finish this conversation. Maybe I can help you. What I need from you though is honesty. By the way, you can bring your son." Kenneth got up and went back to his table.

"So did you save the world?" Mae asked.

"No, but maybe I can help save a small sliver of it." Kenneth smiled back. "By the way I'll need an office for about an hour tomorrow at 12:30. Have you two talked about our future, the three of us?"

"What future?" Mae snapped. "You came here to get even, didn't you. It's not enough that you broke my heart forty-three years ago. Now you want to break me!"

"Now Mae, we aren't here to break you. It was my choice to leave so there's nothing to get even for. Kenneth here has an idea that I think is worth listening to, so please calm down," Bill said. "Go ahead Kenneth."

"Never mind, Kenneth, Poops can speak for himself. Nothing personal, but I don't know you from Adam. If you have anything to say, Poops, say it, then we'll have it out." It was obvious that Mae was upset.

"Bill, go ahead, I have some Shalom to bring in." Kenneth sat back and sent peaceful energy to Mae as Bill explained the choices that he saw for her business. She could sell to him and he would transfer everything to Chicago. She could buy him out and then do whatever she wanted to with the business or the third was she could listen to Kenneth.

Kenneth was caught off guard by Bill's statement. "Well Mae, it was supposed to be Bill's idea." Kenneth glared at Bill, who was now sitting back chuckling. "First off you need to get rid of the dehydrators. They're sucking out your profits. Second, and we can help here, you need to increase your advertising and your product line. Third, you need to increase the pay scale of your employees. Right now they're just above poverty, and if Bill and I are going to be involved, they need a better package."

"Well, as you probably already know, Robin's Spices has agreed in principle to supply my herbs and spices dried. Secondly the advertising and product expansion, I would need a Research and Development Department and I can't afford that. Thirdly, I can't afford to give any more money to my employees. So college boy, go back home and analyze that." Mae got up to leave.

"Sit down," said Bill. "I'm not done. Kenneth didn't know about your brother. I kept him out of that conversation. Second, he is my voice in all business matters, so treat him with respect, and third, I have an idea. How much would it cost to get this business in the black, Kenneth?"

"I don't know. She wouldn't let me see the books, but I'd say, if her books are anything like what I did see, maybe $500,000 or a little more," Kenneth answered, not knowing where Bill was going with this.

"So let me put a million into the business for say ten percent of the stock. In nine months you buy me out for a dollar," said Bill.

Mae laughed. "Say that again. You give me a million, I give you a dollar, are you crazy?"

"No. I just sold two plants in New York and am about to sell another in Cleveland. Kenneth here is making money faster than I can spend it in the market. My CPA says I need tax deductions, so let me help someone whose father helped me. Besides, my end is coming and you'll be getting five percent of the Estate in my will, so why not let me see you get it early. I'll be giving Jacob the same choice," Mr. Strowe replied.

"Oh, Poops, how could I have ever doubted you? Forgive me." Mae threw herself into Bill's arms.

"I'll write the check." Kenneth grinned as the couple kissed.

He wrote the check and then called the waiter over and asked for the bill. "I guess you two won't mind if I buy tonight. I might as well talk to myself. You two can't hear anything, anyway."

The next morning Kenneth was busy getting Mae's books in order to move ten percent of the company into Mr. Strowe's control. He was surprised at what he found. Money being transferred into the account from a mysterious account that he recognized over the past twenty years, four and half million and yet no record of whom the benefactor was. Mae walked into the office as he was finishing.

"Mae, where did this four and half million come from in the last twenty years?" Kenneth asked.

"Oh, I think that was from my brother. He didn't want me to know, but I can't think who else would do that for me," she replied.

Kenneth was about to reply when he saw Bill holding his finger to his lips.

"What about taxes, have you paid taxes on it?" Kenneth asked.

"My CPA has put it in as miscellaneous income. You'll find it on the last line of income page. So yes, taxes have been paid." Mae smiled.

The receptionist came in and announced the Gustafson's were there for their 12:30 appointment. Quickly Mae and Bill stepped out of the room while Kenneth put the company's paperwork away. Walking into the lobby, he greeted the Gustafsons, "Good afternoon, I'm glad you came. Have you thought over last night's conversation?"

"Yes, and we have some questions. Who are you and what do you want out of this?" Mr. Gustafson asked.

"I don't want anything out of this transaction. I'm Kenneth, someone who has paid a dear price for being forced into a situation that wasn't fair. And although you can never defeat the Family, there are those who will come and help you in some strange and mysterious ways. I'm one of those people," Kenneth replied with a smile. *God this is fun,* he thought. "Now what do you need and for what?"

The Gustafson's took out a worn file and laid out their plan. If they farmed out their printing work to his brother and did the advertising business in the house, they could make it on $30,000 a year. The land would be sold; the business would be incorporated.

"Now, you won't understand what I'm about to do." Kenneth reached into his briefcase for the money. "You will never see me again. No strings attached, no control, all I ask is that you find someone else to help when you're on your feet. Here is $100,000.00 in cash. I got it this morning from the bank. If you take it, you can never even mention my first name. Also, you cannot tell anyone of this day, anyone except your son, so he can pass it on also if he wants to. As your first client I would like to introduce you to Mae Parks. Mae come in here I know you're listening."

Mae and Mr. Strowe walked into the room from the side door.

"Mae Parks, the Gustafson Advertising Agency, if you have any need for advertising, I recommend them."

"Well Mr. Strowe, don't we have a train to catch?" Kenneth picked up his briefcase. It was obvious that his work was done there, but not for Mr. Strowe.

"Kenneth, we'll take you to the train station, but I want to spend a little time here. You go get things lined up and I'll come, probably on Monday, for Tuesday appointments. You understand don't you?" He asked like a little boy just wanted to be with his best friend.

They took him to the station, but they didn't hear a word he said to them. As he boarded the train, Mae came up to him and kissed him with tears in her eyes. "Thank you for bringing my Poops back to me. May God bless you, my son."

He left the two friends walking arm in arm back to her car.

He took the train to Cleveland where he received word of Mr. Strowe's illness. The night that Kenneth left, Mr. Strowe had a massive heart attack. The telegram read: "Dad' had a heart attack, is in hospital resting comfortably. Will send him home when it is safe, continue with business as if he were there. Love, Mae"

Kenneth called home immediately. Mercy and Sarah hadn't heard anything. He directed them to go over to Joe's house immediately and tell him to stay close to a phone.

Finally, he went to a Catholic Church and for the first time in his life, he sincerely prayed to the Blessed Mother.

The next morning he called for a meeting on the sale of the steel plant. The conglomerate made a low offer and Kenneth accepted it. He signed the papers and left instructions for the transfer of funds to Pioneer Bank in Chicago, Illinois within forty-eight hours or the deal would be canceled. He didn't want anyone to hear of Mr. Strowe's illness or possible death.

Giving the front desk an order for an early wake-up call, Kenneth went to sleep. He kept moving in and out of different dreams. In one, he saw Julie in black holding a gun on him, another, his grandmother sheltering his aunt and sisters from vicious dogs. Faces of those who needed help, finally, his mother standing with an angel, calling him and saying that everything would be okay, just let go. Suddenly the phone rang. It was his wake-up call. Asking that his bill be ready for him, he prepared to leave.

As Kenneth walked up to the front desk, an old woman was standing there asking how to get to the train station by public transportation. The young man behind the desk wrote out the instructions for her so she wouldn't have any problems. When he handed her the piece of paper she said, "But I can't read. What am I supposed to do?" The young man looked frustrated.

"Miss, I'm going eastward on the train. If you wait till I pay my bill, I'll see to it that you get to the train station." Kenneth thought of the story his mother told him about the old woman on the train. *One good deed deserves another,* he thought.

When he left the hotel, the limousine was waiting for him. The little old woman was shocked when she found out what Kenneth was riding in. "You must be a millionaire. I have never ridden in one of these cars."

"No, I'm not rich," Kenneth said. "Didn't you stay at the hotel last night?"

"Oh, no, I would never pay those prices for a room when there are thousands of people starving just a stone's throw away, sir," she replied.

"Well, the ride is part of the hotel service. But you're right. There are thousands starving and the rich keeping getting richer." Looking at the woman for a minute he spoke quietly, "You aren't on a trip are you? You're here to ride with me."

"Is it that obvious? I was told not to let anyone know, especially you. Now I'm in trouble." She sighed. "Now I have to go through all that training again."

Kenneth chuckled. "No, I just have made it a private study. My mother had a visitor when she moved from a Midwestern town to the East Coast. You can tell a 'visitation' by the clear eyes, the shape of the mouth and the way they carry themselves. But let's keep quiet about it until we're alone,"

They rode quietly until they got to the station. Kenneth tipped the driver and called a redcap. The gentleman was a tall, clean-cut, Negro. Although he had broad shoulders, a reassuring smile and a straight back, Kenneth could see that he was in need. "How's your family Samuel?" Kenneth asked, looking at his name tag.

"Oh, sir, my baby is in need and my misses is worried sick. I just pray to the good Lord that a miracle happens. We waited twelve years for that baby. I just don't know what will happen to my Misses if the good Lord calls her home." Looking up to the sky he continued, "I'm not complaining Lord, you have doubled my tips, but I need a miracle."

"What miracle are you asking for?" asked Kenneth.

"Oh, I don't care sir. He can come and touch my baby and heal her or he can bring the money to pay the doctor's bills. You know He done 'own the cattle on a thousand hills and the wealth in every mine. A little problem like $1,750.00 is easy for him," Samuel replied with confidence but tears filling his eyes.

Is there a bank inside?" Kenneth asked.

"Yes, sir, two or three of them."

"Then let's stop by one of them before you take me to the ticket agent." Suddenly remembering the old woman, he turned and saw her standing at the door waiting. "Come on, my companion is waiting for me."

They stopped at a bank window, and Kenneth wrote a check and asked the cash be put into an envelope. Then Samuel, the old woman and Kenneth headed toward the ticket agent. Samuel asked if he was needed to take the luggage to the loading area, and the old woman said, "Thank you, it would make it a lot easier for us."

Kenneth told him the train and seat numbers, and then pressed the envelope into Samuel's hand. "Give your baby a kiss for me, Samuel, and when you can, help someone else."

"Why are you doing this?" asked Samuel.

"Because it's my ministry to this world, besides somewhere in the Good Book it says, 'Before I cried you heard me.' Obviously He heard you. Now go back to work, you have lost enough customers."

For about an hour the old woman and Kenneth talked about his life's service to humankind. The role his new friend Julie would have in his life. The effect he would have on the society of his hometown. It was clear that his sisters would do more than he would. When he brought up his life's end, the old woman would just smile and say, "Your life is in the Master's hands. I can only tell you that when your stronghold is called home you will soon follow."

He heard his train being announced and asked if he could

help her to the train, "I'm done here, Kenneth, but remember you are never alone, and you are loved by many." She reached up, pulled Kenneth's face to her level, kissed him on the cheek, turned and left. Kenneth just stood there with his hand on the spot that she had kissed him thinking, *I've been kissed by an angel.*

The trip to Chicago was relaxing for Kenneth. For the first time in many a year he could just sit and enjoy the scenery as it went by. He sat rubbing his thinking stone and studying the other passengers, their auras, and how they would change as the person spoke. He wondered if there was anyone studying him, or was he the only one with the gift?

As the train pulled into Chicago Union Station, his thoughts suddenly changed to Robin's Spices and the challenge of changing the power structure. What if Jacob wouldn't accept the role of President/CEO? Who would he hire to fill in the other vacancies that would exist when Kinston left the leadership? What was James doing? Would he be able to help out? And finally, Julie, should he see her again, or just deal with the problems?

As he stepped off the train the last problem was solved. Julie stood waiting for him. "I saw your name on the register. I hope you don't mind that I came down to welcome you back to the big city." Julie said.

"No, it's good to see you, but you know this isn't a social call to Chicago, don't you?" Kenneth replied as he kissed her.

"I assumed that when you sent the telegram to the hotel. It seemed hurried, cut and dry. Is everything okay?" She asked.

"Yes, yes it's just that I have a lot on my mind. I have to go to the university and then to the plant. I need to find an employment agency for executives. But my, you look good. Work has been good for you, I assume. How about dinner tonight and then dancing? God, I missed you Julie." Kenneth put his arm around her and squeezed her one more time.

"How about a nice quiet dinner in a small romantic restaurant on the west side of town, I don't feel like dancing tonight. Jim and Pete's in Forest Park would be so nice. You don't mind do you?" Asked Julie.

"The Westside, isn't that where the Family lives? I don't know...." Kenneth hesitated.

"Oh, come on. You've read too many gangster stories. It would be fun. I know the owners. The food is good and we can talk without anyone listening. Come on, be a good sport," Julie begged. "I'll have Jim make something special just for us."

Kenneth relented. "All right then, make it for 7:00 p.m.. What's the dress code?"

"Casual. People just walk in off the street. Is there anything you'd like to have? They make great pizza, or any Italian dish you can think of," Julie answered.

"Pizza, boy doesn't that sound good," Kenneth said more to himself than to Julie. "I haven't had pizza since I left Ohio State."

"Then Jim and Pete's it is. I'll be ready at 6:30, unless you want me earlier?" Julie got out of the limousine in front of the White Birch Inn, her skirt riding up a little too high as she moved across the leather seat.

"You're always welcome in my room, Julie. You know that don't you?" Kenneth took in her well-shaped legs and then, looking up, he noticed that she had unbuttoned her blouse enough that he knew he wouldn't say no.

"Then you check in and I'll freshen up. See you in thirty minutes." She kissed him once again and disappeared.

Looking at his watch, Kenneth realized that he needed to call Joe. Hurriedly he ordered a bottle of Dom Pe'rignon and got onto the elevator. What was he thinking of? He had so much to do and now Julie would be up in thirty minutes. Leaving the door open for the bellboy and Julie, he picked up the phone and called Joe. He was out but Molly said that Mr. Strowe had come home and was resting comfortably. The girls were staying at the main house to keep an eye on him and would like him to call them. Kenneth assured her that he would in the morning. He hung up the phone and then looked into the bedroom. There was Julie in all her beauty, barely hidden by the see-through teddy, lying on the bed.

"Come to me my love, my fair one, for I am sick for your love," she cooed.

Kenneth couldn't resist and quickly disrobed and joined her in bed. They made love passionately, and in the midst of it all Kenneth realized that Julie would be his downfall. She controlled him, physically, emotionally and psychologically. And there wasn't a damn thing he wanted to do about it; she was in complete control.

They showered together and got ready for dinner. Julie sensed that something was wrong. "What's wrong sweetheart did I say or do something that upset you?"

"Nothing that I can put my finger on, darling, but I think after tonight we better not see each other until I figure this out. Do you mind?" He asked hoping she would know that he wanted to be with her.

"Okay, if that will give you peace of mind," she answered as if he didn't mean anything to her.

They went down to the lobby and waited for the limousine. "You don't care do you, Julie?" asked Kenneth.

"Of course I care, darling," she smiled and squeezed his arm, "but it's business. If you need time, you need time. Now let's have a good time tonight."

They took the Kennedy west to Oak Park Avenue Exit and went north to Irving Park Avenue. Then driver pulled up in front of a small pizza parlor. "So this is River Forest?" Kenneth asked.

"Yes, did you know that Hugh Heffner and Kim Novak both grew up in this area?" Asked Julie. "And of course I grew up down the street about three blocks. My old home is just off the street about 300 feet."

They sat down and studied the menu. A heavyset Italian gentleman came up to speak with Julie. Julie introduced Kenneth as a friend from out of town. All Kenneth caught was Pete, one of the owners.

"Listen Julie, your uncle is coming over for dinner in about half an hour, are you sure that he should be here?" Pete nodded toward Kenneth.

"Oh, Uncle Sam will be delighted to meet Kenneth. If there's a problem I'll get up and leave immediately." She promised.

"Who's Sam?" Kenneth asked, feeling danger was all around him.

"Oh, Sam Lucaas, he's not only my uncle on my mother's side, but he also is my Godfather. You'll love him, sweetheart. Don't worry, he's gentle as a lamb," Julie said.

Kenneth placed his order, a stuffed Italian pizza with extra cheese. He wanted wine to go with it but was told that Forest Park was a dry community. "Uncle Sam wanted it that way because of the price the Family paid during Prohibition. Uncle Sam's father was killed by someone who either was into selling liquor or the Government thinking he was someone else. As Julie told her family's story, two large thugs walked in, looked at Kenneth, and then left.

"That's 'The Bull' and Kenny Vincent," said Julie. "Don't let them scare you. They're just looking out for Uncle Sam. They're his body guards. Exciting isn't it?"

"Not really. Matter of fact, maybe we should just leave so they can dine alone." Kenneth looked around and saw the place had been vacated.

"Oh, stop it. He'll be here in a moment and then we will dine," said Julie. "You know he's an important businessman here in Chicago. There are thousands who would be out in the cold if it wasn't for Uncle Sam, and having him as my Godfather has been such an asset in my life as well. Oh, here he is." Julie stood up. "Well, stand up stupid. He's my Godfather."

Kenneth stood up, but he didn't know why. He was just a

man with two thugs beside him. Mr. Lucaas stopped in front of Kenneth and looked him over. "Is this the man you've been looking for?" He asked, with a voice that was a hoarse whisper. Mr. Lucaas was shorter than Kenneth, about fifty-five or so, black hair with white temples, a mustache, and his suit was expensive and the diamond ring on his left pinky was almost like a signet ring. Kenneth suddenly started to smell death and felt anger attacking him.

"I'm Kenneth Edwards." He held out his hand, but the Bull brushed it aside. "I'm your Godchild's escort for the evening."

Mr. Lucaas turned to Julie, "I have some business to discuss here tonight do you mind eating outside? I hope this is the right man. I know you've been looking for a longtime, Julie."

"We'll be glad to, sir," Kenneth said, relieved of leaving the presence of this man.

"He wasn't talking to you. Don't speak to him unless he speaks to you first. Here?" Said Kenny Vincent, opening his coat enough for Kenneth to see his gun.

Julie kissed his ring and the two of them went outside to a table. "I wish you had kept quiet, Kenneth. No one speaks to Uncle Sam unless he talks to them first. Don't you have a Godfather? I thought you were Catholic?" Julie said.

"Yes on both accounts, but I can go in and speak to Mr. Strowe at any time. I don't have to stand in his presence or kiss his ring. And I don't have to live in fear of him," Kenneth replied with anger in his voice. Suddenly he realized that for the first time he mentioned Bill's name to an outsider. A cold chill went over him. "He's a businessman also, but you don't have to give up your life so that—"

"Oh, let's stop arguing sweetheart," cut in Julie, "this is a night for romance not fighting."

Jim brought out their pizza and introduced himself. They had some small talk and then he went inside. "I keep getting this feeling that I'm being examined for something. What did your

Godfather mean when he asked 'is this the man', Julie?" Kenneth asked.

"Oh, you know family. When you're my age and single they think something's wrong. Then they see you with a man and right away they hear wedding bells." Julie laughed nervously. The rest of the evening was just small talk of what happened since they last saw each other. Kenneth spoke of a young couple who were in need of help and said that he wished he could help. Julie surprised him with a cold remark about the underdog had to be kept in their place or you would have anarchy.

"So, what you're saying is that you aren't to help the poor or needy?" asked Kenneth.

"What I'm saying is that God put them there, so it is the upper class's responsibility to keep them in that condition. If it wasn't His plan, they would be like us." She replied.

Kenneth just shook his head. "There are thousands in this city that would only like a chance to eat three times a day, or have a roof over their head at night, and you blame the Almighty. What a difference between you and your family, me and my friends. I know of a man who left this city and is now spending his life helping others. And you would probably call him a fool. I would call him a saint."

Julie laughed. "Saint Strowe, I suppose. I don't remember hearing that name in church."

Damn she did catch the name. Now what do I do? Thought Kenneth. He decided to ignore the statement and change the subject. "I have to go to the university tomorrow and then to the plant. Hopefully I then can go home. Is there anything else you'd like to do tonight?" asked Kenneth.

"It's only 9:00. Are you sure you want to call it a night already?" asked Julie. "Oh that's right. You have concerns about us. I don't think tonight helped you any with your concerns, so maybe we should just go back."

"Thank you for understanding, Julie, but you're right, it didn't help. I'm cut from a different piece of cloth," said

Kenneth. Paying the bill and calling a cab he turned to see Julie once again talking to her Godfather. Once again she was kissing his ring. *What power does this man have over these people?* Kenneth wondered.

The cab ride back to the White Birch Inn was quiet, so quiet that Kenneth was about to start something just so he could hear Julie's voice. Finally they pulled up to the front of the hotel and got out. Kenneth paid the cab and kissed Julie's hand in a mocking gesture. "It's not funny, Kenneth. You don't understand and probably never will," Julie said with tears in her eyes.

"Then why are you crying?" asked Kenneth.

"Because of you, You, you stupid fool. Sometimes I just hate this job and what I have to do." She stormed past him and went into the hotel. Where she went Kenneth didn't know, but he did care and that bothered him.

In the morning Kenneth decided to go to the plant first, knowing that would be the biggest challenge for the day. He had to first speak to Jacob to see what his opinion was of the company and about him taking over the leadership role. Then getting Kinston out of the building with his colleagues would put a wrinkle in production immediately.

Arriving at the plant he found Jacob already at his desk. "Where is the rest of the office staff," Kenneth asked.

"Oh, the ladies will start getting here about nine and the others when they get here," answered Jacob.

"Okay, let's talk now before you get interrupted. Have you spoken to your sister?" Kenneth asked.

"Yes, she said that Poops is ill and he bought into her plant so she could survive another year. Is that why you're here?" Jacob asked.

"Yes and no. I plan on putting money into this plant, but we can't buy into something that we already own. What I'd like to do is put a million into the company and then sell it to you for a dollar. Now hear me out. For that to happen, we need to get rid of the leadership of the company. I understand that they weren't happy with the announcement of a freeze on executive pay. But we don't like them using women as their own pleasure commodity and then killing the babies. I don't know what you think of abortion but that is the Catholic Church's stand and we agree with it. What do you think?" Kenneth asked. "Can you run this company with a million in your account; turn it around so you and your ancestors will have a livable income?"

"Well yes. But why are you doing this? Mae said something about Dad, but I didn't understand," Jacob asked.

"Your father did something for, what did you called him, oh Poops, years ago. Now it's time for him to do something for you. Besides as he told Mae, he needs tax deductions," Kenneth said, "Now, should I go and get the papers written up for the sale? So I can have the joy of firing your old boss?"

"Yes, but I still don't understand," said Jacob as he handed Kenneth a dollar.

"See you in a couple of hours. It's been great doing business with you Jacob. Now pull down those barriers that remind you of Germany." Kenneth left.

He first went to the bank and transferred the funds to Robin's Spices and then went to the lawyers for the paperwork to be filed for change of ownership. There was a sense of peace and satisfaction to the transaction. While at both the bank and the lawyers he took care of a matter that was on his mind. At the bank he had an account opened for the education of James and his two sisters. At the lawyers he had a statement prepared for the State's Attorney's Office should something happen to him. He listed the things that happened to both him, and the things leading up to the sale of Robin's Spices.

Then going to the University of Chicago, Hyde Park Campus, he informed the business office of the account and gave them instructions on how they were to use it. If his sisters didn't come to U of C, then they could it use it as they wished. As he walked onto the campus, he felt as if he was in a different world. Surrounding the campus there was poverty and hopelessness, but the campus was a lush green with a sense of excitement and hope.

From there, he went back to the plant to exercise his final authority. He was looking forward to this since his last visit. To Kenneth, there was nothing as degrading as humans forcing other humans into deprivation of character. Here was a group of men using the women, not only as underpaid employees, but forcing themselves on them sexually.

As he entered the lobby, the receptionist quickly picked up the phone and announced that he was there, without even asking who he wanted to speak to. Mr. Kinston quickly came out of his office to greet him as a long lost friend. Kenneth just smiled and asked that all management personal be brought together, including those who worked in the plant. It took about ten minutes to get them together, then he asked the door be locked so that no one from the outside would interrupt the meeting.

Coming directly to the point, he announced the sale of the company effective at midnight that night. He announced that the new owner would prefer being anonymous for the time being. Then with a clear loud voice he said, "And as my last duty here at Robin's Spices, I have the privilege to announce that each and every one of you are fired. Your checks will be sent to you. Our attorneys have asked that we inform you that, if any woman would like to press criminal charges against you, the company will support them to their legal limit. Now go and get your possessions and be out in ten minutes or we will have the police remove you. That's all."

He then went out to the plant and announced that the plant would be closed for the rest of the day. All hourly employees would be paid for a full day's work. When he got back to the front office there was a hornets' nest waiting for him. Threats of law suits, his life wasn't worth a cent, etc. Picking up the phone he dialed the operator. "I need the police here at the corner of Western Avenue and 111th Street. There are fifteen angry men here threatening my life." Kenneth hung up the phone. "Gentlemen you have five minutes. The police are on their way. By the way don't try to open your filing cabinets I've already changed the locks. If you want what's in them, get a court order."

The police entered the lobby as some of the men picked up chairs to break up the office area. Seeing the police come in, it suddenly seemed as if the light went on: Kenneth wasn't kidding, they were fired. As they started to leave, Kenneth asked to look in their containers to be sure that no business information left the office.

As Jacob walked out he smiled and quietly said, "It's liberation day. See you in the morning."

Kenneth handed him a note to call him in the evening. He felt some things needed to be discussed before morning.

Back at the hotel Kenneth had a number of messages waiting for him, the first from James. He wanted to talk to Kenneth, so Kenneth invited him for breakfast. The others weren't as easy. Mae Parks had questions about Poops, and could she come and take care of him? Joe wanted to know if there were funds for improving the herd or should he just do it through careful breeding? Mercy's boyfriend was causing heartaches for her and Sarah said she should just drop him, no man is worth it. And then there was one from Julie asking to talk.

As he laid out the problems on the desk before him, the phone rang. It was Jacob, "I know you're probably either on the way out or swamped with decisions, but your note said to call." He said.

"Yes, Jacob, are you opening tomorrow? It might be good to stay closed for a day or two," said Kenneth. "Also, I'd like to suggest that you take a good look at my friend James, the man who came with me the first time. He is presently studying at the University of Chicago, School of Business. He worked at your plant years ago, as did his sisters, father and mother. So he does know a little of the business."

"I thought I'd go to the temp services in the area and get

people that are actively working in each field till I find permanent replacements. I'll certainly look at him though," answered Jacob. They then talked about Mae. Jacob got a call again wondering if he had heard anymore about Poops. "You know they were best of friends at one time Kenneth, if he doesn't have much time left maybe you could let her come down."

"I don't know what's going on with Bill. They were to call me if he got any worse. I had a call from one of the managers, and it sounds like more concern than need. But I'll check everything out I can from here and then call Mae. I don't mind if she comes, whether he's better or worse. The last time I saw those two together they were still dear friends." They hung up and Kenneth went for a glass of Port.

Julie knocked on the door and Kenneth opened it. "Listen Julie I have tons of work to do before morning—" Suddenly he realized she was crying. "Okay, come in. Let me get you something to drink. What's wrong? You aren't one to cry, so don't tell me 'nothing."

"It's you Kenneth, why do you treat me like trash?" Asked Julie.

"First of all it's you who constantly reminds me it's business. I understand that you're in the public relations business, but I just find it hard to connect emotionally with someone who reminds me 'it's' business. Secondly, after a wonderful time in bed, you take me where your Godfather will be to introduce me to him. Was that a trap for me? And lastly, this trip is not a social call. I have things happening that need my attention, so I can't be spending a lot of my time with you. However, I told you before and I'll tell you again, if you need me, call me and I will be there for you, Julie." Kenneth explained.

"But you don't say that to someone you only knew for a few days, Kenneth. At least we don't here in Chicago," said Julie.

"Then maybe you need to change either your location or your way of judging people. I look them in the eyes and within seconds can tell you if that person is honest and what their priorities are." Kenneth started toward the door. "Now as I said, I have a lot to do. If you'd like to continue this conversation, I'm dining alone at the Drake tomorrow night around seven. Should I change the reservation to two?"

"I'll be there, but you're wrong, Kenneth. There are people you can't trust, no matter what they look like." Julie brushed a kiss across his cheek.

"I know, and you're one of them," Kenneth said. "See you tomorrow night."

Chuckling at the fact that Julie didn't even flinch at the last statement, he picked up the phone to call Joe. "Joe, Kenneth here, what's going on in beautiful Ohio?"

Joe explained Mr. Strowe's condition and that he was always asking when Kenneth would be back. "He says he needs to talk to you about something important, laddie. So what do I tell him?"

"Tell him I'll be there in three days. Things here are a little more complicated than we had thought. Remember the conversation we had about you and Molly adopting my sisters? You need to call on Mr. Strowe's attorney and have have him start the procedure. Don't ask me why, I'll tell all of you when I get back. You are the man now Joe, so please follow my instructions. Tell the girls I love them. And when you're on the hill, say a wee one for me. Bye Joe, my love to Molly." Kenneth hung up the phone.

I guess I better call Mae, he thought, looking for the phone number that Jacob gave him. "Mae, or should I say Ma Parks, this is Kenneth. Jacob called and asked me to call you when I have some news about Poops. His condition hasn't gotten any better. Matter of fact, the doctors say he's holding on because he wants to tell someone something."

"Should I come and see him?" Mae asked.

"Mae, you are three times seven. You can do whatever you want. You gave me the impression the first time I was there that you just knew him on a business level. He talked of you as a good friend of the past, but when I saw you two together I knew it was far more than that in your eyes. So if your heart says go, then you're more than welcome at the Willow Creek Estate. I'll give the number to call before we hang up so Joe can pick you up at the station," Kenneth said. "I won't be back until the end of the week."

"We are more than just friends. That's probably what caused his heart attack," Mae said quietly.

"Nonsense, my friends that are heart doctors say the best thing for the heart is being around those we love, so stop judging yourself and get over there." He gave her the telephone number and hung up the phone.

After getting up at 5:30 a.m., Kenneth showered, shaved and headed downstairs for breakfast. As the elevator door opened, there stood James, smiling from ear to ear.

"Good morning, Kenneth, I beat you to the draw. Breakfast will be up in your room in about twenty minutes with a lot of coffee." James reached out to shake Kenneth's hand. "I ordered one order of hotcakes; one order of ham off the bone, browned; three eggs over-easy; and two slices of white toast, buttered with plenty of strawberry preserves, right?"

"What about you?" Asked Kenneth shocked that first James was there, and secondly he remembered his breakfast.

"That's for me, old man. You think I care about you or what you eat?" James laughed. "No, I ordered my favorite. You did want to talk in your room didn't you?"

"Your favorite, let me think, flapjacks; ham off the bone, warm but not browned; and four eggs over-easy on top of the ham. Oh, and plenty of coffee. It's good to see you again, James. Things have changed since I saw you last. Come on in and let me bring you up to date," said Kenneth. "How much time do you have to talk?"

"When Mr. Mertz called last night, I said to my Mrs. I'm taking tomorrow off to see my friend Kenneth. So you got me as long as you want me." Breakfast arrived and then James continued, "You know he said I should come over and talk to him about a job at Robin's Spices. I told him that I couldn't work for a company like that and he said I should talk to you before making up my mind. What's happened there?"

"Yesterday the company was sold out. All management was released immediately. Now they're looking for a whole new team. It would give you a chance to start on the ground floor, but I can't say if the new owner would hire you, after all you are in school. You still drive the cab don't you? Then the travel time to and from the plant would be a burden. Jacob would be more the one to speak to about a position there. I'm to be there in about an hour, want to come along?" Kenneth asked.

"Sure, let me finish this morsel and my coffee and I'll be ready to go," said James.

"Slow down I've had only two cups and I still haven't talked to you about your schooling. How is it going for you at University of Chicago?"

"Good, I'm holding a strong 'B'," James said, "and I applied for a scholarship next term. Whether I get it or not, I don't know. The company I'm working full time for has a program that will reimburse me for the courses I've finished. But it takes them up to four months to write the check. And now there are rumors that a layoff is coming. But school is coming along good. I love it, and I'm building relationships for the future."

"Good. Strong relationships are good, James. Stay in touch with those relationships. You'll never know when you might need them or they you. Now let's go down to Robin's Spices." Kenneth headed for the door. "We'll take a cab. I just don't feel right about the limo today. Do you mind?"

"No, but I would have brought mine if I had known. I like your tips." James laughed.

On the way to the plant Kenneth explained what had happened at Robin's Spices and that he had put money into a fund for James' education. He also encouraged James to pursue the job; he felt that Jacob needed someone he could count on.

"But why me, Kenneth. you got off a train, got into my cab and bang, my life is changed forever? No one had ever heard of you. You disappear without a trace. You're like an angel coming into people's lives and then you're gone. So why me?"

"I don't know," Kenneth began, "I walked out of Union Station needing a cab and there you stood. The cab had a few dents, but it was clean and polished, the inside was vacuumed and smelled cared for. I looked into your eyes and saw hope for a new life. Then when that doorman at the hotel called you common, I made up my mind to help you achieve that future dream that I saw in your eyes. My sisters say I have 'smuck' written across my heart, but I don't care. No one has the right to judge another by the job they do or where they live and work," Kenneth answered quietly. "Now my life is about over and loose ends need to be tied up."

"What do you mean your life is about over? You're young yet. You have a long life ahead of you," James said.

"No, I'm afraid not James. You see my parents had some enemies. I have this haunting feeling that they've found me and are following me." Kenneth sighed. "Here we are. Let's just drop the subject, okay?"

There were police cars in front of the plant; Jacob was talking with one of the officers. "Good morning Kenneth, we were broken into last night. There are officers in there right now with their dogs. So far all we know is that my office and the president's office has been ransacked," Jacob said. "Sergeant O'Grady, this is Kenneth Edwards. He's handling the sale of the company. He came yesterday and fired all the management personal."

"Isn't it a little strange to fire management just before you sell?" asked the sergeant.

"On the record or off the record, Sergeant?" asked Kenneth.

"On the record," replied Sergeant O'Grady.

"I was only following orders of my superior," Kenneth answered.

"Off the record?" asked the Sergeant.

"Management was using sex as a means of promotion and then having the pregnant women go through abortions, even though it was against their religious beliefs. The former owner didn't want that to be passed on to the new owner's headaches," Kenneth replied. "And if the offices of the president and Mr. Mertz have been ransacked, then I can tell you what they were looking for. They were looking for records of the abortions. They didn't find them because I have them in a vault at the bank."

"All clear, Sergeant," a young officer called out.

"Okay, take the dogs out of here and get the paperwork done. I'm going back to the station," said Sergeant O'Grady. "Using sex for promotion, were they Blacks?"

"No, Irish, it shouldn't make any difference," Jacob said. "Why do they always judge by race?" He asked.

"Because they're human, but believe me you won a friend when you told him it was his lassies that were being abused." Kenneth sighed. "You remember James?"

"Oh yes, we spoke last night on the phone. So Kenneth talked you into coming down?" asked Jacob.

"No, this is where my roots are planted. I'd like to see something good come out of this plant," answered James. "What do you have in mind for a job Mr. Mertz?"

"I need a plant foreman immediately," Jacob answered. "The ladies will be here tomorrow and I need someone to oversee the operation while I look into management. You know the word is already out about you firing everyone Kenneth?" Jacob said. "Oh, by the way Mae called. She's flying into Columbus this morning."

"But I hadn't been inside the plant until two months ago with Kenneth. I wouldn't know what to do," James replied.

"Oh, Martha, will be there to help. She'd be a good foreperson, but she doesn't want it. She said she'd teach you," Jacob said. "What about your schooling? Kenneth said you were at U of C. Can you handle both?"

"I handle a full-time job and a part-time job right now. My

courses are designed so I can go days or evenings, so I don't see any trouble," said James.

"Okay, see you in the morning, you too, Kenneth. I'd like to sign those papers as soon as possible," said Jacob.

"They'll be ready at 9 a.m. I'll take James to U of C for the changing of his schedule and then we'll come here with the papers," Kenneth said.

They called a cab and headed back to the hotel. James wanted to know more about Kenneth, but he wouldn't talk about it. "Just remember that if a Joe or Molly Murphy calls you, they will be telling you the truth," said Kenneth. "Anyone else, just let it slide."

Kenneth stopped at the front desk for messages; there was one from Mae and one from Julie. Julie's read, "I'll meet you in the lobby and ride over with you."

"Excuse me Miss, I need to get word to Julie. Tell her I'll meet her at the Drake at 7 p.m. She will not be riding with me," said Kenneth sternly.

"Sir, we have an excellent restaurant right here at the White Birch Inn, I am—" Kenneth cut the young lady off, "I've eaten in your restaurant. I'm dining at the Drake tonight." He headed toward the elevator.

He went up to his room to lie down for a while, thinking of what his parents had to go through dodging the Family. What about his sisters? Would they be safe with just an adoption or should he have to hide them out? There was a knock on the door, but he pretended not to hear it. It had to be Julie and that was the last person he wanted to see, but then the phone rang. The front desk was calling to inform him that a messenger service was on its way up for a signature. Kenneth got up and answered the door. It was the papers from the lawyer. Kenneth signed the register and took the papers. Looking at his watch, he saw that he had plenty of time to go back to the plant and make it to the Drake. Better yet, sign the papers and send them by messenger to Jacob. Or was he getting paranoid? Deciding that he was getting paranoid, he called Jacob and told him he was coming and went out and called a cab.

All the way to Robin's Spices he felt that someone was following him. Finally the cabdriver asked, "Sir is something wrong? You keep looking out the back window."

"No," said Kenneth feeling stupid, "I just thought someone was following the cab."

"There was until we got onto the Dan Ryan and then they passed us. You're not wanted for something are you?" The cabdriver asked, looking through his rearview mirror.

Kenneth just laughed and shook his head, but he thought, *If you only knew. Why am I so nervous?* He kept asking himself. Was it the fact there was still so much to do, or was he afraid of dying? The cab pulled up to the plant and Kenneth asked the cabdriver give him fifteen minutes and then take him back.

"As long as you know the meter will be running," he said with a smile.

Jacob had a notary present when Kenneth walked into the room. Kenneth took out the papers signed them in front of both men. Then Jacob signed them, and had the papers notarized.

"The company is now yours, Jacob. Good luck with it," said Kenneth, "and if there's anything you need in the future, we're there to help you. Now, I have a cab waiting for me outside. I'm leaving town, so I'll have James come by himself tomorrow." They shook hands and Kenneth left.

The ride back to the hotel was much more relaxing. *Maybe it was just the importance of the materials I was carrying,* thought Kenneth. *Or maybe it just doesn't matter anymore.*

Maybe the old woman in Cleveland was right. "We have a job to do and when it is done, all we can do is sit back and wait for the angel to come." *But that's crazy. I still have a lot to do,* Kenneth thought. The cabdriver pulled up to the front of the White Birch Inn; Kenneth paid him and went inside.

There were a number of messages, Julie confirming the meeting place, James saying he took care of school and would meet him at the plant in the morning and then one from Joe and one from Mae.

First he called Joe, and was told that Mr. Strowe's condition was weakening.

Then he called Mae. "Mae, Kenneth here, I hear Bill isn't doing too well. Do you need me to come home immediately?" He asked. "I can be on a plane in the morning."

"Please do Kenneth, he has been asking for you hourly. I don't think he'll last too much longer," Mae cried. They talked a little longer about what was going on at the

Estate and then said their good-byes. *Those two should have gotten together years ago,* Kenneth thought as he replaced the receiver.

He arrived at the Drake about five minutes early, but Julie was already there waiting. She looked stunning, hair pulled away from her face, diamond earrings hanging from her ear lobes, a low neckline lined with a string of pearls, a light blue dress not too short, and high heels. The perfume almost swept Kenneth into ecstasy as they came together and kissed.

"I wasn't sure if it was okay to kiss you," whispered Julie. "For some reason I feel you don't trust me."

"I don't, and I don't trust my heart either when you're around," Kenneth whispered back, as he gave her a gentle hug. "You look stunning tonight, my dear. Thanks for meeting me here."

As they were being seated Kenneth, noticed what appeared to be the honorable mayor dining with what looked like his wife. The maître d' was about to leave when Kenneth asked, "Can you ask the mayor if I may join him for a few minutes?"

"Sir, he doesn't like being disturbed when he's dining with his wife," he replied.

"Tell him it's a friend from Ohio," Kenneth said.

"May I come with you?" asked Julie.

"Sorry, business." Kenneth laughed; for once he was able to use that phrase on her.

The mayor nodded at Kenneth and Kenneth got up and walked over to his table. "Mayor Daley, I'm so glad you remembered me," said Kenneth as he laid an envelope on the table and covered it with a napkin. "I just wanted to say thank you for extending the bus line to Western and 111th. We do appreciate it." They spoke for another moment or two and shook hands. Kenneth left and went back to his table.

"Another job done?" asked Julie with a mischievous grin.

"I suppose you could say that. I just wanted to thank the mayor for helping me with the transit system," Kenneth replied.

"So how much more do you have to do here in Chicago?" Julie asked.

"You can tell your people I'll be done tomorrow night around 11:30 and plan on being on the 1:00 a.m. train back to Ohio." Kenneth looked into Julie's eyes. Her face didn't change, but fear flooded her eyes.

"You know! How did you figured it out?" She asked.

"The last time we made love," Kenneth said, "I suddenly just knew. And what scares me is that it doesn't matter. Although I don't think I will make love to you again. The physical desire is there, but something just doesn't feel right. Now let's have dinner and a quiet evening of friendship."

"I've never been out for just a quiet dinner and friendship," said Julie with tears in her voice.

"I have and it can be fun. Now just relax. There are rules. As friends we don't judge or try to hurt each other. Other than that, anything goes." Kenneth reached over and took her hand to reassure her.

"Are you crazy? You know who I am and you still sit there and pretend that you like me?" She got up to go.

"Sit down, Julie. I didn't say I liked you, but as you have often said, its business." Getting up he opened his coat. "See no guns. I'm not going to kill you or call the police. You asked for this evening and here I am. I just wanted you to know that I know."

Julie sat down. "I think I need a strong one. You're different, you're not scared?"

"I'm more scared of myself. You see, I think I am falling in love with you. But, how can a man love a woman he doesn't trust? I know what you're going to do has nothing to do with our relationship. I also know that no matter what I say, you'll do what you're told to do by your Uncle Sam. I can give in and say just kill me, but that isn't going to happen. I can also try to pick the place so my family can find me and I can have a decent funeral. And most of all, I can finish what I have to do so when I stand before my Creator I can say I did my best," Kenneth replied. "Am I scared to die? No. Am I scared of the dying process? Yes. But you see I know you well enough to know that you will have it done quickly with as little pain as possible. Will you do it? I don't think so. I feel you have the ability, but do you have the heart? Now that is the question. You will draw me into some area that is predetermined."

"Let's talk about something else," Julie sighed. "This is morbid."

So they spoke of little things, like growing up, school and dreams. As they talked Mayor Daley came up and said good-bye to Kenneth. Turning to Julie, he said, "Kenneth here is a good friend of mine. I'm sure nothing will happen to him while he's in my city."

Evidently Julie got the message because she excused herself to make a phone call. Coming back, she smiled and said, "We have the whole night if you want it."

"Have plans been changed?" Asked Kenneth.

"Let's say they've been delayed." Julie smiled back. "Can we go dancing? I love to dance and you are a good dancer."

"Sure, but remember I have a full schedule tomorrow. My train leaves at 1:00 a.m. and if I miss it, I'll be stuck here till noon," Kenneth said.

They went dancing, speaking little to each other. Kenneth enjoyed holding Julie in his arms. He felt that now that she knew that he knew, it didn't make any difference what would happen between them.

Finally at 11 p.m., he said, "I need to get some sleep. Can we call it a night?"

She didn't answer; she just walked off the dance floor with her head down.

Kenneth called her a cab. She protested, but he did it anyway. As they were parting, he reminded her that if she needed anything just call. With that she was gone and he knew he had to move fast or she would find out that he was leaving town.

15

The flight back to Columbus was uneventful, although Kenneth knew all he was doing was delaying the unavoidable. But he wanted to get back to the Estate and tell them it wasn't safe any longer. As he walked off the plane, a state trooper approached him.

"Kenneth Adams?" He was about two inches taller than Kenneth and, with his trooper hat, he looked like a giant. He had his hand on his weapon, and Kenneth wondered for a moment if that was to intimidate him or if he was going to draw it.

"There's been an emergency at your home and I was asked to get you there as quickly as possible. We'll have your luggage brought there later. Will you come with me, sir?" The trooper asked.

"Sure, but someone was to pick-me-up here. How am I to get word to him?" Kenneth asked.

"Joe Murphy, I believe, he is the one who contacted me. Now can we go?" He asked again.

Kenneth went with him, not knowing what to expect. With lights flashing and sirens blowing, they sped through the traffic and up Highway 30. As they came close to Crestline, Kenneth found the courage to ask, "Has Mr. Strowe died?"

"No, the Family found that you have skipped town and is out looking for you. Telling them you were taking the train but taking the plane instead only slowed their search. You may think you have your work done here, but you don't," replied the trooper. "You do know how to keep us jumping Kenneth. I'd think that with all the training you've gone through, you wouldn't be living on the edge all the time."

Kenneth took a sigh of relief and then started to think of what mess Julie might be in because he left town. Somehow he worried about her. Was she a part of the plan, and, if so, how could he save her from the mess she was in?

"Kenneth, you cannot save the world," said the trooper, "People have to make their own decisions and then live them out. This is true with your friend in Chicago. If she wants out, there are those who will help her. But for now you have to think of those who are depending on you." He pulled into the driveway of the Estate and turned off the lights and siren. "Now get a hold of yourself and do what you're told. Mr. Strowe has only two months to live."

"Officer, what is your name?" Kenneth asked, as he got out of the car. The man just grinned and said, "Gabriel." He turned the car around and drove off into the darkness.

Noticing the house's lights were out, he headed home, hoping he wouldn't wake the girls. The sun was about to come up and he knew where he would find his friend. He placed his briefcase on the doorstep and headed out to the hill. He had to pass Joe's house and as he did, Joe stepped out onto the porch and kissed his wife good-bye. Kenneth watched as Joe got into a car and started it up. He put it in gear and turned on the lights. When he saw Kenneth, he jumped out of the car without taking it out of gear. Before either Joe or Kenneth knew what was happening, the car was moving directly toward Kenneth with Joe in pursuit. Jumping into the car, he turned it off and it missed hitting

Kenneth by inches. "Well laddie, don't you know enough to get out of the way of a moving car?" asked Joe. They hugged each other and Joe invited him into the house. "The Mrs. will make breakfast."

"No, let's go up to the hill, she can make breakfast later." He didn't want Joe to know that he knew she was wearing her nightclothes and he didn't want to embarrass her.

"I'll go tell her, and then you have to tell me everything." Joe turned back to the house.

He opened the door and called out, "Molly my love, he is already here. Get breakfast on, and we'll be back in an hour."

Molly must have said something because Joe yelled, "Kill the fatted calf if you want, but you know what he eats in the morning. Four hotcakes, ham off the bone and three eggs over-easy."

"And coffee," called out Kenneth.

"Ah, that woman, I would trade her in, but it took too long for her to train me. I don't think I have that much time left. Now tell me about your trip and how did you get here so fast?" Joe asked.

Kenneth started telling him what had happened since they saw each other last, starting at the most recent, the ride. When he repeated the name, Gabriel, Joe's eyes got big. "The Archangel himself?"

"No, I think he was pulling my leg. I'm sure that when this gets told enough times, it will be the Archangel." Kenneth laughed.

When he got to the Family, Joe asked, "Do you think it's that bad, laddie?"

"Yes, and the sooner we get the paperwork done the better. So far no one but this community knows who they are. Maybe we can pull this off," Kenneth replied with much concern in his voice.

"I don't know, laddie, Mercy got into a fight over at the I'm Not Here Bar the other night. I'm sure there's a record of that.

The owner, she's a witch. She said she's going to press charges for the damage." Joe said.

"Joe, that 'witch' is Mercy's mother. She just doesn't know it. What was she doing there? She's a minor."

"Ah, she heard that her boyfriend was having an affair with one of the barmaids. She went there to see for herself, and when she saw it, she got mad." Joe explained.

"Poor girl," said Kenneth, thinking of his father and her mother.

"Poor girl nothing, she won the battle, laddie. You'd have been proud of her, but I'm not too sure of the war. That woman could cause her trouble."

"I'll take care of it. Now, what about the Estate? What's happened that I need to know about?" Kenneth asked. They talked for some time of the minor things that had happened while Kenneth was gone.

Suddenly Joe said, "Ah laddie, the hotcakes are on the griddle. Let's go home. The girls are there, you know. They'll be happy to see you."

They went back to Joe's house laughing and joking. *Ah it is good to be back home,* thought Kenneth. *There's something about the Ohio mornings that just can't be beat.*

As they ate breakfast, Kenneth explained what had happened in Mercy's and Sarah's parents' lives that was causing challenges now. Mercy was furious about Joe and Molly adopting them. Wasn't it enough that she didn't know who her real mother was? Now someone else was trying to take the place of the mother she knew from her. Turning to Kenneth she said, "You promised that I would meet my real mother. Where is she?"

"You have met her Mercy. The old woman at the I'm Not Here Bar is your real mother." Kenneth replied, expecting Mercy to explode in anger. "She didn't want you to see her at the bar. I couldn't set something up until I got back. Now that you have met her, do you still want to talk to her, sweetheart?"

"I, I, I don't know. I guess. Yes I do, I want to know why she wanted to get rid of me." Mercy started sobbing.

Molly went over to her and put her arm around her. "Now lassie, it wasn't that she wanted to get rid of you. You saw the building she lived in. She didn't have any privacy or money to take care of you and your father was the only safe person she could ask to do it. A mother thinks first of her child and then of her feelings or needs."

"How would you know? You never had any children," Mercy shouted and ran out of the house.

Everyone just sat there for a while, stunned at what Mercy had said. Finally Kenneth said, "I'm sorry Molly. I am so sorry. Let me talk to her."

"Ah, that child is cut to the quick, Kenneth. It will take a woman's touch to heal that heart." Molly's eyes were full of tears. "Why don't you talk to Mae? Maybe she can help. She is a wise woman."

Turning to Sarah, Kenneth asked, "What do you think of the adoption, Sarah?"

"I think it stinks. I'm an Adams and I always will be an Adams, but I don't have anything to say about it," Sarah replied.

"But you do, lassie. Molly and I won't adopt you unless you want to be. We can just become your legal guardians. Oh, those who hunt your brother will find you. But I feel they'll find you anyway. Yet there is no one Molly and I would rather have as children than you and Mercy. But at no time can we take your brother's place or your parents' either," Joe said.

Molly sat there nodding, tears flowing.

"Are you and Mercy going to sleep here tonight or at our house?" Kenneth asked.

"We were planning to sleep at home in our own beds," Sarah answered.

"We'll finish this conversation then. If either of you do not want to go through the adoption, you can keep the Adams name, I promise." Kenneth smiled. "Now go find your sister and calm her down, please. I need to go see Mr. Strowe. Oh, Sarah, don't tell Mercy about Molly's idea of Mae."

"I wasn't born yesterday, Kenneth." Sarah smiled. *If that isn't father's smile* Kenneth thought, *I don't what is. But Sarah has mother's ability to think through and then respond like her mother.*

Kenneth slowly went up to the house, not knowing what to expect. On one hand Molly said Bill was holding his own but on the other hand, she spoke as if he had one leg in the grave and the other on a banana peel. As he walked into the house, he smelled death. The rooms were all dark. Kenneth at first thought that maybe he was too late.

Just then he heard Mae's voice coming from the guest bedroom on the first floor. "Now Poops, as long as I'm here, you are going to obey me. Eat that breakfast or I will force it down you!"

"Things haven't changed have they? Give a woman an inch and she thinks she's a ruler." Kenneth said, laughing as he came into the room.

"Kenneth my son, you're back. Come over here and let me see you." Bill whispered.

"Not until you eat your breakfast." Kenneth winked at Mae.

"Mae, go get Kenneth a pot of coffee. And get that breakfast over here where I can reach it. What do you want to do, starve me?" Bill growled. "This food is terrible. The doctor said salt is bad for me, so now they won't let me have a single grain of salt."

"The doctor knows best, Bill. Now what's wrong with you? Everyone tells me a different story. To the best of my knowledge you and Mae were enjoying yourselves and then you had a massive heart attack. Now that I'm here, what are they telling you?" Kenneth asked.

"They keep saying any day now, he doesn't have much time left. But I'll tell you, Kenneth, I have at least two months left from today. I had a dream that you came back and I had two more months to enjoy the friendship of Mae." Bill shook his fork at Kenneth. "You know I loved that girl like a sister from the moment I saw her. She's the only woman I ever had as a friend."

Mae came in with a cup of coffee. "Poops, don't you go telling our personal business. What goes on between us is none of Kenneth's business." She handed Kenneth the cup of coffee. "They're making a new pot for you. When I told them it was for you, they sprang to life. They're also making you hotcakes, ham and eggs. Thanks for coming, Kenneth. I sure missed you and I know Poops has too." Mae smiled behind tear-filled eyes.

"It's good to be back." Kenneth gave her a kiss on the cheek. "Now can you tell me what's going on with Bill's health?"

"The doctor comes every day and takes his blood pressure, temperature and mumbles, 'Any day now.' He has put him on a bland diet and cut out his cigars and liquor. We try to keep him calm, but that Joe comes in and Poops gets all involved with whatever Joe has on his mind. So then we have to get him calmed down again, I think that Joe wants him to die," Mae answered.

"I'll deal with Joe. But what harm is there with a little salt in Bill's food if he's going to die any day anyway?" Kenneth asked. "When that doctor comes in I want to talk to him."

Suddenly there was a parade of staff bringing breakfast for Kenneth. He wanted to say, 'I'm not hungry. I had breakfast.' But looking into their eyes and hearing their welcome home, he didn't have the heart. Sitting down and eating, he discussed the trip with Bill, making sure he understood the part with Julie. Mae got upset and left the room.

"I'm glad she left," said Bill. "Women get to emotional. So you found someone you care about. That's good. She's a prostitute for the Family. That isn't good." Bill laughed, "Kenneth listen, when you lie here facing death, you do a lot of thinking. You got involved with the Family. We both knew they were looking for us. Now you know why I didn't want to go to Chicago. My work here is done. I can't answer for you, but let's just pretend from now on that 'they' don't exist. I need the lawyers to come down and dictate a new will. Also I need you to bring Bob and his wife, Alice, in to see me immediately followed by Joe and Molly. By the way, if it wasn't for Joe coming and talking to me, I would be dead by now. So don't you reprimand him. And another thing, do you have two one hundred dollar bills on you?"

"No, but I have them at the house," Kenneth said.

"Good, when the men come up, you shake their hands with a one-hundred dollar bill in yours. Don't let on that you know what it's for," he said with a mischievous grin. "Now go get the money and the men. I'm calling my lawyer before that infernal doctor gets here."

Kenneth went over to see Molly and asked her to find Joe. Both were to come to the house as soon as possible. Then he went home and got the money. Mercy was there by herself.

"Kenneth, I'm sorry for acting like I did at the Murphy's," she said, "but I don't want to be a Murphy. I'm an Adams. Is that so bad?"

"No, sweetheart," Kenneth hugged her. "I just wanted to protect you. If you don't want the adoption, then we won't have it. I love you, just remember that."

He went to the milk house and found Bob finishing. "Bob, have someone else finish your work. Mr. Strowe wants you and your wife at the main house immediately."

"He's going to let us go isn't he?" Bob sighed. "A baby finally on the way and I lose my job. Damn I hate my luck. How am I going to explain it to Alice?"

"I don't know what he wants, but Mr. Strowe has always been fair. You've turned his dairy around and he will show his appreciation somehow. Remember what you were told when we found those three cows sick? 'We have time to worry later. Let's handle the problem now.' So go get Alice and come up to the house."

"You know everything that man does. You just don't like me so you won't tell me." Bob grumbled.

"It's not that I don't like you Bob, I don't understand your's or Joe's business. That's why I stay away from you. I'm with Joe because we have other interests. We don't talk farming. And just for the record I hired you; I got you and Alice the better house and I got you the raise. So don't be so quick to judge me," Kenneth snapped.

He went back to the house with his brief case; he wanted to work on a number of things. One of them was the issue of his will. If the lawyers were coming up from Columbus, he might as well take care of that issue. Another thing was the issue of Mercy and her blood mother. How was he going to deal with that? Mercy was so angry about the subject and it was evident her mother wasn't much better. Then there was the police record of Mercy's fight at the bar; the court date was coming up and he wanted it settled out of court.

Deciding to deal with Mercy's fight first, he called the I'M Not Here Bar and asked for the owner.

"I'm the owner what do you want?" Said the voice at the other end.

"I understand that my sister and you had a disagreement the other day," Kenneth said, careful not to admit anything. "I'd like to know what the damages are so I can get them taken care of."

"There was at least five hundred in damages, and then of course there's the personal injury. My lawyer said that I should demand something for that," said Missy.

"If my sister is found guilty, then of course you should get personal damage," Kenneth responded. "In your eyes what personal damage did she do? She claimed the other party started the fight."

"Those spoiled kids all say that. I was there I saw what happened. She ordered a margarita, and that is what she got. She tasted it, said it wasn't what she ordered. That's what started the fight," said Missy.

"Okay, $500 for damages, how much for personal injury?" He asked.

"At least twenty-five hundred, I have a reputation to keep

here, you know," said Missy. "I can't let someone come and start a fight and not have to pay for it."

"So for three thousand you're willing to drop the charges?" Kenneth asked.

"Yes, well, plus lawyer fees, that will be another five or six hundred," Missy said.

"Listen, this what I see. You're asking $3,600 to have the case dropped. My sister is willing to stand before the judge and plead innocent and, if found guilty, have the record dropped in three months when she turns eighteen. That way you will have to explain to the judge why you served a minor a margarita, possibly lose your liquor license, or go to jail. I happen to know who the judge will be and he hates people who sell to minors. So, I'll see you in court, and don't forget to call that lawyer." Kenneth waited for the phone to click, thinking, *I should just go there and pay it.*

"Well, let's not jump to conclusions. Maybe it wasn't that bad." Said Missy. "What do you say to $500 for damages and a $1,000 for personal injury, no lawyer fees?"

"Would you like that in cash or check, large bills or small?" Asked Kenneth.

"Cash and small bills," said Missy, "and I want her to be there when I get it."

"Okay, I'll get back to you for the time and place. Have a good day, Missy."

As he hung up the phone, he heard Joe and Bob in the hallway talking, "So you're getting the sack too," said Bob.

"Ah, laddie, I don't count my chicks until I know they've hatched. I'm looking for good news." Joe laughed.

"Don't you go jinxing it, Joseph," *that's Molly*, Kenneth chuckled.

"I'm in the office folks," he called. He got up and reached into his pocket, taking the bills and folding them, he placed one in each hand.

"Bob, welcome to the house. You and your wife need to stop

by more often." Kenneth held out his hand to Bob. Bob took and shook it, grasping the bill from Kenneth's hand. Quickly he placed the other one in his right hand and shook Joe's hand. Both men looked confused.

"Now I honestly don't know what Mr. Strowe has in mind. What you have in your hand is there because he ordered me to place it there in the manner in which you received it. Joe, you and Molly are to stay here while I take Bob and Alice in to speak with Mr. Strowe. When he is done with you, please sit down and wait for him to speak with Joe and Molly. Those are the instructions I've been given, any questions?" Kenneth smiled at the stunned look on their faces. "Good, then let me see if he's ready, if so, it's the last door on the right." Kenneth opened the door and said, "Mr. Strowe, Bob and Joe are here with their spouses."

"Good, good. Mae you stay by the front door and hold off the doctor. This will only take a minute." Said Bill. "Okay, bring in Bob and Alice." He sat up in his bed.

"Bob and Alice, Mr. Strowe will see you now," Kenneth called from the bedroom door.

They came in hesitantly. "Good morning, sir," said Bob, fear on his face.

"Oh, Bob, stop that sir business. I don't eat people," said Mr. Strowe. "Alice, congratulations, I hear a little Robert or Alice is on the way, that's great. Now if I can get someone else married maybe we all can experience parenthood." He signaled Kenneth to sit down.

"I suppose you want to know what I wanted you here for. Well, it's not to fire you, so relax. What I want to do is offer you the dairy business. I can't give it to you because of tax laws. So if you want it, I will sell it to you for $100.00. But you have to decide right now," said Mr. Strowe, waiting for an answer.

"Sir, I mean, Mr. Strowe, that is a generous offer, but we don't have $50.00 let alone $100.00," said Alice, looking downcast.

"Kenneth," did you do what I told you to do?" aasked Bill.

"Yes sir," replied Kenneth. "Bob, if you would, look at that piece of paper I gave you when I shook your hand."

Bob reached into his pocket and, as he pulled his hand out, the $100.00 bill fell to the floor. Alice shrieked so loud that Mae came running thinking the worst.

"It's okay, Mae. The kids just got excited," laughed Bill. "So what's your answer?"

"Yes," shouted Alice. "Oh, Bob, I'm sorry it's your decision. What would you like to do?"

"I'm speechless," said Bob "Yes I would like to buy your dairy business, but what does the $100.00 include?"

"We'll discuss that in a minute. Okay, so you agreed on the price, $100.00 for the complete business. Kenneth you will be witness tomorrow when the lawyers come. Now let's get those Irishmen in here."

"Molly, Joe can you come in here?" Kenneth called. Bob and Alice sat down in the back of the bedroom.

"Ah, laddie, you're still alive?" asked Joe looking at Bob. "We thought they were trying to kill you." Joe stood next to Molly, playing with his pipe. "Now Mr. Strowe, how are you now the old man is back to cause you grief?" Joe chuckled, looking at Kenneth.

"Joseph, we are here not to laugh or play games," Bill said sternly. "As you know I'm going the way that all men go, good or bad. Most of my life, the wind has been at my back. But now I have to deal with an Irishman on my deathbed. What a curse."

"Ah, laddie, if you were lucky enough to be Irish you wouldn't say such a thing," said Joe.

"Quiet Joseph," Molly jabbed him in the ribs with her elbow. "The good man is dying and you want to make a joke of it. Mr. Strowe we will continue to pray for your soul."

"Molly, it isn't my soul that needs the good Lord's care, it's my money," Bill said. "You both know that I can't take it with me, so I would like to sell the beef business to you for $100.00. But you have to make up your mind right now."

"SOLD!" Joe reached into his pocket, only to find it empty.

"Ah, the black-hearted fool," laughed Molly. "Here is a $100.00, Mr. Strowe, and we will take your offer."

"Black-hearted fool am I, Missy? You're the one who took my money." Joe laughed.

"Okay, okay you two, these are the conditions: I have 800 acres here. This house sits in the middle. Now you two, Joe and Bob, will have to figure out how you're going to divide it. We have mostly two of each piece of farming equipment, so that won't be too hard to divide. But the house is going to a private organization to be used as a retreat center, which will include five acres. I don't care how you two divide it up, but it must be done by three tomorrow afternoon. Ladies I would appreciate it if you stay out of this part," said Bill. "When you come back tomorrow at 3:00 p.m., you can pay me the $100.00. Good negotiating. And by the way, if you can't get an agreeable settlement, then you lose the whole thing."

Mae came to the door of the bedroom. "The doctor is here to see you, Poops."

The doctor came into the room right behind her. "Why was I left out there waiting to see my patient?" He asked. "This man is dying and you are standing around as if he was going to outlive me, now out, all of you."

Kenneth stood firm.

"I said out! That means you, mister, whoever you are."

"I'm Kenneth, doctor, and I'm staying. Do you know why I'm staying? Because I'm the one who signs the check, and unless you can convince me otherwise, there will some changes here."

"Are you a doctor?" He asked.

"No, I said, I'm the one who signs the check, and that is all you need to know about me."

The doctor started to take Bill's vitals, blood pressure 140/90, temperature 98.9, and heart rate 78. "I don't know what's keeping you alive, William," he said. "You have a temperature, your heart is going a mile a minute, and your blood pressure is high. What you need is more rest."

"What he needs is a better diet, exercise and fresh air," said Kenneth.

"If he doesn't follow my instructions, I'm not responsible for his health," the doctor argued.

"You're not responsible anyway, doctor," said Kenneth as he ushered him out of the room. "Believe it or not God, and only God, has that responsibility. Now this is what we're going to do. As of today you will not be coming back unless we call you. Otherwise we will make appointments and bring him to your office. Now figure out what we owe you and be gone." Kenneth wrote the check and handed it to the doctor.

"I'm going to have to drop him as my patient. I can't keep him alive under these conditions," said the doctor.

"Good, I'll contact my friend Dr. Abram Schultz, at St. James in Columbus." Kenneth said. "Have a nice ride back."

When Kenneth arrived at home, Mercy and Sarah had dinner ready for him. "I take it you're getting me ready for the slaughter. All of my favorite dishes and you probably have strawberry shortcake for desert."

"No we couldn't find any fresh strawberries at the market, but we do have peach cobbler," said Mercy.

"Now, before the execution or the celebration dinner, let's settle this adoption issue. Do you girls want to be adopted by the Murphy's?" Kenneth asked.

"Well, if you think we should, I guess it's okay," said Mercy with her head so low that Kenneth couldn't see her eyes, but he knew they were filling with tears.

"Please answer the question, ladies, yes or no. Do you want to go through with the adoption?" Kenneth asked again.

"NO!" Said Sarah with such force that it even surprised her.

"Then it's settled. I'll tell Joe and Molly. Now, let's eat," said Kenneth.

"Oh, Kenneth, you're the most wonderful brother a girl could have." Mercy jumped out of her chair and gave him a big hug.

"And that goes double for me," said Sarah.

"Well, let's hope you're still saying that when they have you standing against the wall in front of the firing squad." Kenneth laughed.

"They don't do that anymore, do they?" asked Sarah.

"I don't know. I haven't been executed lately," Kenneth said.

The next morning Kenneth called his friend Abram and set up an appointment for Bill to see him. Then going over the paperwork that needed attention, he noticed a bill for $4,500 he didn't understand. He couldn't read the signature, so he had to call the business, the Sir James Detective Agency. The young lady put him on hold for a minute and then came back on the line. "We were commissioned to follow a Mr. Kenneth Adams to New York City, then Hoboken, New Jersey, then Cleveland, Ohio and Chicago, Illinois. Mr. James reported to the gentleman who hired us, a Mr. W. Strowe on November 3rd of this year. Is there anything wrong sir?" She asked.

Kenneth sighed. "No, I'll check with Mr. Strowe. If he confirms it, I'll have a check sent out today."

Walking into Bill's bedroom he found him getting out of bed and into a chair. "Look Kenneth my first time in a chair since my heart attack."

"And if you keep hiring detective services to spy on me, it will be your last." Kenneth growled.

"Oh, that. Well Mae thought it would be wise to have someone keeping an eye on you. If you knew how worried she was for your safety. . . Why she just couldn't sleep." Bill whined.

"IF you will excuse the French, Bill, *BULL SHIT*. They were following us from the time we left this house! Now what you do with your life is your business, but if I ever catch you spying on me again I, I, it will destroy everything that we ever had between us," Kenneth shouted. "I appreciate that you care, but I can take care of myself. And don't try to make me look like a fool. I can do that well enough on my own, blaming a woman. I'll go and pay the bill."

"They did do a good job, though," Bill said as Kenneth walked out of the room.

Mae was hurrying down the hall. "I heard the shouting, is there anything wrong?"

"Nothing that a brain transplant wouldn't cure, he's all yours," answered Kenneth.

Bob and Joe came into the back door of the house, Bob with his hat in his hands wringing it, Joe with his pipe. "I take it you have questions that you want answered before you talk to Mr. Strowe," Kenneth said. "You know he doesn't bite. Go ask him. He's in his room with Mae."

"We'd like to talk to you first, just to see what you think, laddie," said Joe. "We know how the man respects your opinion, and well, we aren't sure of what to say. Your tongue is much more eloquent. The Saints gave you a silver-lined tongue is what my Molly says." Joe tapped his pipe against his leg.

"Joseph, will you stop playing with that infernal pipe? Why don't you just smoke it? I know, when you become a man, and the Saints only know when that will be. What question do you two have? And Bob, put that blasted hat someplace. You are businessmen now, let's start acting like it," Kenneth snapped.

"Ah, laddie, if we came at a bad time—"

Kenneth cut Joe off."Damn it Joe, it's never time for indecisions. If you have something to say, then say it."

"Okay, we, Bob and I, want to set up a corporation, keep the 800 acres as one and we run both businesses on it, equal right down the middle," Joe said so quickly that Kenneth could hardly understand him.

"And the answer will be no," said Kenneth.

"Why?" asked Bob.

"Because 50/50 splits don't work in business, it has to be 49/51 percent to work. It's the nature of the beast, and Mr.

Strowe knows it. What I would do is take a coin and throw it into the air, heads one wins, and tails the other wins. That way, when you disagree on something the one with 51% has the last word. It will be difficult at times, but it does work. Here I have my lucky silver dollar that my father gave me. I'll throw it in the air. Who's going to be heads and who will be tails?" asked Kenneth.

"You call it, laddie," said Joe turning to Bob. "I'm always lucky in these so it won't make any difference."

"Tails," said Bob.

The coin went into the air and then fell to the floor, circling for a moment, and then stopping with the tail up. Joe laughed. "You're now the boss, laddie. That means you get to talk." Joe and Bob started toward the kitchen door.

"Just a minute, men," Kenneth walked up and took Joe's pipe and Bob's hat, "Now go with God's peace."

Mr. Strowe agreed to the plan of keeping the farm together, he was especially please with the name they wanted to give it, The Willow Creek Farm. "Where are your security blankets"? Mr. Strowe asked. "You two look naked without your pipe and hat."

"Ah, Kenneth, that black-hearted devil, took them from us. He said we needed to talk to you like businessmen," said Joe.

"He's right. The lawyers will be here at 3:00 and when you and your wives sign those papers, you will be landowners not hired hands. It will be whole new experience for both of you. By the way, from this moment on, you are to call me Bill, you understand?"

"Yes, sir," they responded.

"Now go and tell your wives of the final decision, and if you see Kenneth tell him I want to talk to the 'black-hearted devil'," Bill chuckled quietly to himself.

"No need to look for me, I'm right here. Men, here are your 'security blankets' I hope you don't need them anymore." He handed over the hat and pipe. "What can I do for you Bill?"

"Have you settled with the girls?" asked Bill.

"Yes, Joe you need to hear this. They don't mind being part of the Murphy household, but they want to keep the Adams name. I'm sorry Joe, but thanks for being willing," Kenneth said.

"We just want the lassies safe," said Joe. "However methinks Molly was hoping to have more women folks around."

"Okay, gentleman, 3:00 p.m. with your wives. Please don't be late, and Kenneth I need to talk to the girls now that they've made their decision," Bill said.

Kenneth called the house and told Mercy of Bill's request, suggesting that they eat lunch at the main house. That way it wouldn't draw attention to the other employees. Kenneth was surprised to see Bill coming down the hallway, leaning on Mae's shoulder.

"We're going to eat with the employees today, Kenneth," said Mae. "He misses them so much, and some of them just don't come in and say 'hi' anymore."

"He needs to get around. I spoke to Dr. Schultz this morning, and he is to be encouraged to live life normally. But he is to cut his cigars down to one a day and his drinking down to two a day." Said Kenneth.

Bill sat at the head of the table. Looking around, he asked, "Where is everyone? This table was always full of smiling faces."

"I'm sorry, Poops, but most of them left when you got sick," Mae answered.

"Well, okay, pass the salt please," Bill said.

"Hold it," said Kenneth. "You don't have any food in front of you and you're asking for the salt? The doctor said the salt issue will be resolved when he sees you, until then no salt."

The talk around the table was light and friendly. It was obvious that those loyal to the Estate had stayed. For this Kenneth was thankful. Mae announced that she had to go back home for a week or so after Thanksgiving. Sarah announced that she had been accepted at OSU for undergraduate work, starting in January. And Mercy said that she got a job at a women's clothing store in Mansfield.

"Congratulations girls," said Bill. "Oh, by the way, I need to talk to both of you for a minute after lunch."

They went into Bill's office, Kenneth following them. "As you know I'm about to leave this plane," said Bill, "so I'm trying to get as much done as I can before that happens. The day you were brought here, Mercy, and the day you were born, Sarah, I opened a trust for you two. A trust is a fancy name for a savings account that no one but the government can question. Your brother Kenneth is the executor. If he dies before you are twenty-eight, Joseph Murphy is the executor. The trust will provide you with enough money to live on for many a year, if you are wise. I have one piece of land left, and I want you two to buy it from me. It's the 125 acres of wooded land where your house is. It's time for the Adams to have a home. This afternoon my lawyers will tell me the best way of doing it. What I need from each of you is a twenty dollar bill. I suggest that you hit your brother for a gift, not a loan. Now Kenneth, help me back to my bedroom. I need to take a nap before the lawyers get here."

"Is there anything else I need to have cash for?" Kenneth asked.

"Yes, how many employees do we have now? The lunch table was bare, is it because of marriage or isn't anyone working here anymore? Also I need to know what our cash worth is right now. I mean before the lawyers get here," Bill said.

"What are you up to, Bill?" Asked Kenneth.

"You'll see," Bill said. "Now get me into this bed before Mae comes and starts scolding."

The lawyers of Gilken, Gilken, Hutch and Associates arrived at 3:00 sharp. So did Mae, Joe, Molly, Bob, Alice, Mercy and Sarah. The only one who was late was Kenneth; he had to go to the bank for some twenties. "The last few days have drained me financially." Kenneth winked at Bill.

Andrew Gilken, the spokesman of the group made a comment

that it looked more like a reading of a will than the writing of one. "That is one of the questions I have," said Bill. "What's the difference between an inheritance and a gift, tax wise?"

"That depends on the size of the gift, but probably three or four percent. The advantage in giving a gift is that it is immediate. The person or persons do not have to wait for one to die or the will to be read and then the bills paid to see if there is anything left."

"Kenneth, how many employees do we have now at the Estate and what is our cash worth at this point in time?" Bill asked.

"We have twenty-one employees, and our cash worth is a little over two hundred and seven million dollars," replied Kenneth.

"Okay, let me think while we settle the sale of real estate. Kenneth, get me a pad of paper and then sign the necessary documents to make everything legal. Oh, by the way Andrew, I have some land the two girls want to buy. We settled on the price, but they are under age what do we do?" Bill asked.

"No real problem, Kenneth is their legal guardian. He can sign in the Guardian area," replied Andrew.

All but Bill and Mae went into Bill's office. The farm was handled first, with Joe and Molly, then Bob and Alice. The land was labeled as the Willow Creek Farm. As Joe signed the paper, Kenneth handed him a small package. "Open it, Joe." Joe opened it and there was a pack of pipe tobacco.

"Now that you're a man, start smoking that thing or get rid of it." Kenneth smiled. "And Bob, I haven't forgotten you, this is an Australian hat. You can twist it and fold and it will always come back to the shape of your head."

The two girls came up without their twenty dollars. "Kenneth can you give me twenty dollars," said Sarah with her big brown eyelashes fluttering

"I need a twenty too," said Mercy, as she gave Kenneth a hug.

"I can't win," sighed Kenneth, "Okay I'll loan you each

twenty dollars. But I want it in writing that I get ten percent interest."

"No, no, no, that's not what you were told to do. It was to be a gift," said Sarah.

"Okay, here's your money, now where do we sign?" Kenneth asked. They signed the forms and the whole group walked out of the office talking excitedly, except for Kenneth and Andrew. "They sure seem happy don't they?" Said Kenneth.

"Why shouldn't they? They just bought prime land for pennies on the dollar." Said Andrew. "I just hope William lives long enough that these sales aren't protested." The two men walked back to Bill's bedroom, where Mae and Bill were arguing. It stopped as soon as they entered the room. Mae turned around and walked out her eyes were wet with tears.

"Can we start on the will?" asked Andrew.

"Yes, first I want fifteen percent to be divided between Ohio State University, University of Chicago, Michigan State University and St. James Hospital. Then I want twenty percent to be given to my beloved friend, Mae Mertz Parks, twenty percent to my dear friend, Jacob Mertz, and the remainder will go to my beloved friend who stood by me, Kenneth Edward Adams. Also I want this house and five acres for a retreat center, run by the Catholic Church. Now go write it up so I can sign it," said Bill. "Kenneth, can you get Mae in here for me, please?"

Kenneth walked the men to the front door. "Is this all legal?" He asked.

"Unless you can show cause to believe that he has lost his faculties, yes." Said Andrew. "We'll be back on the 27th of November for the signing of the will. If there's any need for our services before then, please call." Andrew shook Kenneth's hand.

"If you bring a statement, I'll cut you a check to cover your fees and expenses." Kenneth said.

With Thanksgiving in a week, Mercy bugging Kenneth about meeting her "blood" mother and Bill needing help with walking outside, Kenneth didn't get too much done. He closed

Mr. Strowe's account at the Board of Trade and the New York Stock Exchange. Went to the bank and ordered one thousand fifty, twenty dollar bills for Bill, and at the same time ordered for Christmas Eve pick up another two thousand one hundred twenty dollar bills. Then he took Mae to the Hallmark Card Shop in Mansfield to pick out appropriate cards for both post Thanksgiving and Christmas. Stopping at the I'm Not Here Bar, he asked Missy if he and his sister could have the honor of taking her out for dinner some evening.

"You know I work nights. Are trying to get out of me seeing her?" she snapped at him.

"No, if that doesn't work, how about an early lunch at the Brown Derby on Highway 30? We can pick you up and bring you back," said Kenneth. "Let's say Saturday, 11:30 a.m."

"No. I'll meet you there. I'm not riding with someone I don't know," Missy said. "And you're going to bring my little Sara Lynn, right?"

"Well she isn't little anymore, but I will bring her. You just be there and be ready for a surprise."

He then went to the police station. He wanted someone there in case something happened between the two women. The chief suggested an off-duty policeman in plain clothes. "Matter of fact, maybe a male and a female would be better. You know she can be a pain at times," said the officer. "By the way, Missy hasn't dropped the charges yet, do you know anything about that?"

"Yes, that will be settled before she meets Mercy." Kenneth shook his head. "You know, I just don't understand how people can get their lives so messed up."

"Isn't your sister under age?" asked the Chief. "We could take her license away from her for that."

"I know. That's how I got her from $4,500 down to $1,500. Personally, I would love to see that bar closed up, but I promised not to make an issue of serving minors if she dropped the charges. So wait till the charges are dropped if you don't mind, Chief," said Kenneth.

Kenneth went back to the Estate to find Mercy and talk to her alone. He found her with Molly, who was teaching her how to make Irish stew. Being noon, Kenneth had to stay and dine or be accused of having a "Black Heart". He didn't mind; Molly was a good cook. He just didn't want to hear the praise about the land and cattle. It was Bill's decision not his, and therefore they should be up at the house thanking him.

As they were about to sit down, a knock on the door sounded. "Get that, will you, Kenneth? It will be Mae and Mr. Strowe," said Molly.

"Poops said there was an excellent Irish stew being served here today," said Mae with a laugh. "We had to come and find out. I hope we're not intruding."

"This house will always be open to you and your loved ones," said Molly as she gave Mae a hug. "May the wind be always at your back."

They sat down at the table when Mae realized that Joe was missing. "Where's your husband, Molly?" She asked.

"Ah, that black-hearted lad, he decided to smoke that old pipe of his and now he's sick to his stomach." Molly laughed. "He'll be okay by evening."

They all laughed at Joe's expense. And then they spoke of the wonderful generosity of Mr. Strowe in selling the land and cattle to them. It was an enjoyable time together and Mercy's Irish stew turned out great. She beamed with pride as Mae and Molly complimented her and her cooking. Finally Kenneth excused himself and Mercy, stating that they had to go to New Washington to order the turkey, ham and the beef roast.

"Can't you just call the order in? That's what we always did," said Bill.

"No, I can't. I need to talk with Mercy about something that happened while I was gone, and I don't need someone interrupting or her running out on me," Kenneth said. "Plus, if she's going to cook like this, she needs to meet the butcher so he'll fill her orders right."

They rode silently for about ten minutes and then Mercy spoke, "You're mad at me for going to that bar aren't you?"

"No, I'm upset at you for allowing that woman to get you to start a fight. When will you learn that it takes two to fight? If you keep yourself under control, you won't get into trouble," Kenneth said.

"She called me a liar, said I ordered that drink," Mercy said. "I don't drink alcoholic drinks."

"Well, there's another reason I wanted to talk with you. I'll pay the $1,500 and the charges will be dropped. But you're going to meet your mother again on Saturday," Kenneth said.

"What do you mean again? I never met her, have I?" Mercy asked.

"Yes, you have met her and you had a fight with her," Kenneth said. "You see, Missy is your mother. I told you that, don't you remember? I wanted you to know before you see her Saturday."

"You mean that ugly old—"

Kenneth cut her off. "Stop it, Mercy. You can't pick your parents, and if you had to live the life that Missy has chosen, you'd look like that too. Now we're going to the Brown Derby. I'm going in and pay her off, and then you will come in. Don't start anything; be polite. I'll have two police officers there in case she starts something. But promise me you'll act in such a way that our mother would be proud of us."

"Yes, sir," Mercy said quietly.

They ordered the meat. Henry, the butcher, took time to explain how to pick out prime meat. He was about six inches taller than Mercy, had dark brown hair and broad shoulders. Kenneth noticed that Henry was always looking into Mercy's eyes when he spoke to her, as if she were the only one there.

On the way home Kenneth asked Mercy if she had any questions. Quietly she asked, "Do you think he's married?"

Saturday came. Kenneth and Mercy arrived at the Brown Derby at 11:20. When Missy came in, she looked like a painted hussy, but he was gracious. Seating her, he then handed her the envelope with the $1,500 in it. Missy was surprised. "You mean you have another sister, one that broke up my bar?" She asked.

"Yes, I have another sister, but she has never been in your bar. Mercy, your daughter, broke up your bar." Looking up he saw Mercy coming in looking like a princess. He smiled. "Here she comes now." Getting up he said, "Missy, I would like to introduce to you your daughter, Mercy Adams." Helping her with her chair he then went to the bar and sat down.

The two women sat for a few minutes. Suddenly Missy stood up and slapped Mercy across the face and headed for the door. Before she got there she was arrested for assault and taken away. Mercy just sat there crying quietly.

"Come on, sweetheart, let's go home," said Kenneth.

Nothing was said as they rode home. Finally, as Kenneth pulled up to their little house, she asked, "What did Daddy see in that woman?"

"I don't know, Mercy. All I know is that if it wasn't for her, you wouldn't be here, and for that I'm thankful," Kenneth answered.

From that day on Kenneth noticed there was a new Mercy. She walked and talked with a confidence that wasn't there before. Every move she made said, "I am here. I know who I am, and I care about you." The $1,500 and the meeting with Missy was worth it, even though Mercy wouldn't press charges.

The Thanksgiving dinner was a typical Strowe affair, too much food, a lot of laughter and surprises. One of the surprises was Bill calling all the people together and then handing out a Christmas bonus: 500 new $20.00 bills to each employee. Another surprise was the announcement that he and Mae were going to get married on Valentine's Day. Joe said it best when he said, "Molly, the wind is finally blowing on his back."

Kenneth was sitting in his father's chair at home that evening when the phone rang. Sarah answered it, thinking it was her boyfriend saying he arrived home. "Kenneth, it's for you long-distance, someone called Julie." A chill ran down Kenneth's spine as he got up to answer the phone. "Julie what a surprise, where are you?"

"I'm here in Chicago. I just wanted to call and wish you and your family a Happy Thanksgiving. Was that your wife who answered the phone?" She asked.

Kenneth laughed. "No, I don't have one of those, but I do have a friend. Her name is Julie. Happy Thanksgiving to you, too, how are things in Chicago?"

They spoke for awhile and then Julie said, "Kenneth, Uncle Sam had the contract removed from you and your family."

"What did you say? I think we have a bad connection. I thought you said the contract has been removed," Kenneth said hesitantly.

"I did, darling, I told him that you asked me to marry you. He had some trouble with Frankie out east, but everything is okay now. You can come and go without any fear for your life," Julie said.

"Does that go for my boss as well?" Kenneth asked.

"Yes, everyone," Julie said "I love you Kenneth, Happy Holidays." She hung up.

Kenneth just stood there for a while staring at the phone. Mercy and Sarah came into the room wondering if he was okay. "Yes, yes girls everything is fine. Remember the contract I told you about? It's been lifted. We're free at last. Oh, I wish mother was here to hear this."

"She is Kenneth, she is," Sarah whispered. The girls gave him a hug, crying for joy with him.

The next morning Kenneth got up and sat in the cold, rubbing his stone, waiting for his friend Joe. Looking over the landscape, he saw a grey cloud moving slowly toward the house. Joe showed up and, as he was about to sit down, he noticed it too. "Ah, laddie, a good deed never goes unpunished. We have sorrow coming."

"I saw it too. I just hope it doesn't arrive until after

Christmas," said Kenneth. "So what are you going to get Molly for Christmas?" Kenneth asked, hoping to change the subject.

"Ah, that black-hearted lassie, if I know her, she would want a younger man." Joe laughed. "But we were talking and we think maybe we should get her brother and his wife here from the Motherland. What do you think?" Joe asked. "He is a better farmer than me and he has two younguns just off his knee. They could be here for the spring planting."

"It's your decision, Joe," Kenneth said, "but you aren't the head of the farm anymore. How would your partner like it?"

"Ah, yes we worked some of that out, but he doesn't know about Molly's brother. We decided that we would put that 'Lucky Coin' of yours in a frame and each year move

it from one house to the other. The house that has the coin that year is the majority share holder. But what would he say about my brother-in-law?" Joe sighed and puffed on his pipe.

"Well, let's ask him. Isn't that Bob coming up the hill?" Kenneth asked.

"Bob, my boy, are you come to talk treason with us?" Joe called out.

"No, I need help. Alice is sickly this morning and I need someone to keep an eye on her while I finish the milking," Bob said.

"Kenneth, you go get Molly. Bob you get back to your wife before the devil gets there, I will finish the milking." Joe hurried toward the dairy barn.

"The devil gets there?" Bob asked.

"That's Irish for death. Now go, I'll get Molly. Has Alice seen the doctor lately?" Kenneth asked.

"No, not for a couple of months, why?" Bob asked, now looking worried.

"Okay, I'll call him. Now go, everything will be okay, Bob." Kenneth looked at the cloud once again. *"God, don't let it be the baby,"* he prayed.

It was a false alarm. The doctor ordered Alice to bed rest,

a regular schedule of appointments to see him and a blessing for a healthy child. Mae had gone back to Hoboken to take care of her employees and their holiday bonuses, but promised to come right back if needed. The lawyers came and the will was now official. Kenneth decided to take a few days off before Christmas.

"You're going to see Julie aren't you?" It was Mercy.

"Yes, why do you ask?" asked Kenneth being surprised by her tone of voice.

"I don't like her," Mercy said. "And what's more I think you could do a lot better than marry some prostitute."

"I'm not going to Chicago to get married, Mercy. I'm going to the opening night of the opera. One of the benefits of that is seeing the woman I love, who happens to be called Julie." Kenneth said sternly. "Now are you or Sarah driving me to the airport?"

"It's my turn," Mercy sighed. "Anytime you're ready, I am too."

"I'm sorry for talking about Julie like that," said Mercy after about fifteen minutes on the road. "I just don't want to lose you."

"Don't worry you'll always be my baby sister." Kenneth chuckled. *It sure is nice to be needed,* he thought.

The trip to Chicago was far too short. He stopped to pick up the tickets for the opera and found that they were sold out. Calling Julie, they decided to just be together rather than him going to a scalper for tickets. As they walked the streets of Chicago, they spoke of life together. Beside the huge Christmas tree in Daley Plaza, Kenneth slipped to his one knee and asked if Julie would marry him.

"Have you asked Uncle Sam for my hand?" asked Julie. "I can't say yes until you do."

"I don't want to marry your Uncle Sam. I want to marry you." Kenneth said.

"Yes, but in the Family, you must first ask the father," Julie said. "Mine is dead, so you have to ask my Godfather. Don't worry, he'll say yes."

The next day Kenneth found himself at Jim and Pete's having pizza for lunch. Julie had instructed him how to approach and speak to her Godfather. And as they left, he was the happiest he had been in years. The answer was yes from both Uncle Sam and Julie.

"You know, I have to go to Tiffany's to buy a diamond for Bill and Mae. Want to come along and find one for the future Mrs. Kenneth Adams?" asked Kenneth.

"After New Years, can I come down and meet this Bill?" asked Julie.

"It would be a honor," Kenneth replied.

They picked out the rings and then went back to the hotel for dinner. As they discussed their future together, Kenneth suddenly felt that something wasn't right. He mentioned it to Julie and they decided to finish dinner and then he would call home.

It was Mercy. She had an accident. While she was driving, an extreme pain appeared on her right side and she lost control of the car. No one was hurt, but she was in surgery for an appendectomy. Kenneth promised to come right home in the morning. He would call Joe for a pick up at the airport.

The next morning he picked up Bill's ring and gave the address for Julie's to be sent to him when it was complete. After paying the bill, he hurried out to the limousine and went to O'Hare Airport.

Joe was waiting for him when he got off the plane. "The operation has gone well. She'll be released tomorrow," Joe told him. "But we have other problems. Bill has been doing things that don't seem natural. Saying they killed his son and he was going to kill them."

"His son, died, thirty, forty years ago," said Kenneth.

"Ah, laddie, I don't like it. He seems like a crazy man, and

Mae's coming tomorrow. I don't think she should see him like this," Joe said.

"Okay, let's go see Mercy, then I'll deal with Bill," Kenneth picked up his luggage at the baggage claim area.

They stopped at Mansfield General Hospital, where Mercy was doing fine. She was glad to see him; Sarah was sitting beside the bed sleeping. They spoke for a few minutes and then Kenneth went home to deal with the other problem.

Bill was sitting in his office, hair all messed up, spills on his shirt, mumbling about his son. Kenneth slowly walked up to him, wondering what was going on in that mind of his. "Kenneth, they didn't kill you. You got away. I told you Joe that they couldn't kill my boy," Bill shouted.

"Joe, why don't you go and help your wife, tell her I'll be down to dine in thirty minutes," Kenneth said.

"Bill, why did you scare the daylights out of everyone?" asked Kenneth.

"I called Mae, she didn't come. I called you, and you didn't come. Where is Mae?" asked Bill.

"She had to go home for a few days. She'll be back tomorrow, but do I have to tell her how you behaved?" asked Kenneth.

"No, she'll think I care and then there won't be any peace in this house," Bill growled. "I'm okay now. Go to the Murphy's for your 'meal' I'll get by, by myself."

"Okay. Oh, I have Mae's ring. It's in the suitcase in the car. I'll bring it up after dinner." Said Kenneth.

"Good, have fun without me," Bill called as he walked away.

As usual, dinner was delicious. One thing about Molly, she could cook. They laughed and when Kenneth told them of Julie, Molly got excited and started to talk in Gallic. Joe brought out a letter from his brother-in-law, saying that they would be happy to come to America, and asked that he be told what to do to speed the arrival. Kenneth said he had a friend who could help. And as far as the money was concerned, they would work things out later. Suddenly, there was a knock on the door. Bill had walked from the main house and obviously had fallen a number of times.

"I know I wasn't invited, but Molly, the poison they wanted me to eat would kill a rat," said Bill.

As if out of nowhere Molly had a plate in front of Bill loaded with food, "Now, laddie, who said you weren't wanted at *MY* table? This may be Joseph's house, but this is *MY* table. And you are always welcome to put your feet under it." Molly kissed the old man's forehead. "Joe, in the back of the cabinet is a wee bottle of spirits. Get it. Mr. Strowe is coming down with a chill."

"A wee bottle," said Joe as he came out with a half gallon of Brandy. "Woman, what is a bottle if this is a wee one?"

"Never you mind, you black-hearted drunk." Molly poured out hefty drinks for all.

"To our families," said Joe as he held up his glass, "may the wind be at their backs so they come back to us quickly."

"Here, here," said Molly and Kenneth. Bill just looked at his glass and whispered, "To Mae, the woman, the best friend I ever had?

Kenneth and Bill went and picked Mae up at the airport the next day. Bill was a different man; he once again had a slight spring to his step. He leaned on Kenneth every time Mae wasn't watching, and it seemed that she purposely looked the other way a lot. *Bless her, Lord,* thought Kenneth, *for being so sensitive.*

The days before Christmas were busy for Kenneth. He went to Chicago to do his Christmas shopping, taking the girls with him. They got to meet Julie; Mercy still had trouble accepting her. Then back to the estate for decorating and gift wrapping. Kenneth went to the bank and asked for the twenty dollar bills. He was told that they couldn't get them without Mr. Strowe's signature. He went back, got Mr. Strowe, got the money, and then removed all his money from the bank. The president was frantic, on Christmas Eve losing his biggest depositor, but Bill wouldn't be reasoned with and Kenneth couldn't blame him.

Calling the girls up to the house for help, he, Mae and the girls wrapped $20,000 in twenty dollar bills in bundles. It was getting dark when they were almost done. There was a knock at the door, and Mae answered the door. It was the local auto dealer. "Is there a Mercy and Sarah Adams here?" asked the gentleman. Mae called them to the door and then motioned Bill and Kenneth to come.

As the girls got to the door, the man said, "Merry Christmas," and handed them each a set of keys. "These keys go to those two Corvettes," he said with a smile.

"Oh, my God, who, why, they're gorgeous," said Sarah. Mercy just stood there in tears.

"Bill and I talked about it and decided it was time for you to have your own cars," said Kenneth. "Thank you Fred. Do you need a ride home?"

"No, I have a ride down the driveway. If you have any problems, just call." Fred waved as he went to his ride.

"How can anything get better than this?" asked Mercy.

"Oh, I have a feeling that things will improve." Kenneth had a twinkle in his eye. "Are you going to church tonight?"

"Oh, Henry asked me to go with his family to St. Bartholomew's in New Washington."

"Are you still seeing that meat cutter?" Kenneth asked, as if he didn't know.

Sarah laughed. "Only every other day, but he doesn't mean a thing to her."

"Oh, be quiet Sarah, or I'll tell about James," said Mercy as she hurried out of the room to get ready for church.

Kenneth looked at his sister; she just shrugged as if she didn't know what Mercy was talking about.

Back at home, Kenneth finished his wrapping and then called Julie. Sarah made some excuse about having to go to the barn. Things were quiet in the house at last. He just sat there, thinking of Christmases that had gone before, especially his sister's first one. It was the first time he could remember peace within the Adams household. He must have dozed off because suddenly he was being shaken by Mercy.

"You knew, didn't you? You knew and you wouldn't even give me a hint of what was going to happen. I should hate you for allowing me to go into a situation like that," she said as she landed on his lap. "Oh, I love you so much. What I did do to deserve a brother like you? I thought you'd say no, after all he isn't rich and probably never will be. But I do love him, Kenneth, thank you."

"Just for the record young lady, he is rich. When a man finds a woman who loves him, he's the richest man in the world," said Kenneth. "Does your sister know?"

"She does now," came a sleepy voice from Sarah's bedroom.

Mercy ran into Sarah's bedroom and closed the door. Kenneth got up and went to bed. "One down, one to go, Mother." He said as he looked up to heaven.

The next morning, being Christmas, Bill and Mae held the traditional Christmas breakfast. After breakfast and the presents for the children were opened, Bill called everyone together. "This will be my last Christmas here at the Estate, so I would like to give my bride-to-be a gift." He handed her a small box, holding their engagement ring. As she opened it, she let out a gasp and threw her arms around Bill's neck. After Bill caught his breath, he went on. "And for each of my faithful employees I have a small token of my appreciation. I was going to put each of you in my will, but I was told how slowly an executer can move. So without any further ado, pass out the rest of the gifts." The room became silent as they opened their gifts. "Well, isn't someone going to say something? Like Merry Christmas!" Bill laughed.

"Merry Christmas," everyone shouted at one time. Then each and everyone came up and thanked him personally. Finally Kenneth came up and kneeling down so he could look Bill in the eye he whispered, "Merry Christmas, Dad," and hugged him, "I love you."

Slowly the room emptied. Mae and Bill sat in the quietness, enjoying the beauty of the moment. "You know Poops, you are one special man. Did I tell you that I love you today?" Mae asked.

"No, and if you keep looking so beautiful I will take you up to my room and have another heart attack." Bill laughed.

The phone rang at 3:30 the next morning. It was Mae, "Poops died about five minutes ago, can you come up, Kenneth?"

Kenneth stood there for a moment frozen, "Yes, sure. Let me get dressed. Are you sure?"

"Yes, the doctor just left and I don't want to be alone. Can you come up and maybe Molly?" She asked.

"Yes, I'll call her right away," said Kenneth, still in shock.

He woke up Sarah and told her where he was going to be, and then called Joe, explaining Mae's request. He hung up the phone and started to get dressed. There was so much that had to be done, and the holiday season being in full swing, it would be a challenge. Turning around, he thought he saw his mother standing in the hallway.

It was Mercy. "Kenneth you will do fine. Mom is with you, you know that don't you?"

"Yes sweetheart, but suddenly I feel so alone. He was my pillar, my stronghold in the face of all odds. He was always there for me." Kenneth wept unashamed before his sisters.

"We'll go with you," said Mercy.

"No, I'll go now. You two can come up when you get dressed. Remember if this ever happens to me, I love you two." Kenneth smiled beneath his tears.

"Hello, Mae. I'm here now. Don't worry we'll get through this," Kenneth called as he walked into the house, trying to reassure her.

"I just don't know what he wants. When I would bring up the subject, he would get mad and say his funeral was all planned. I was supposed to be his bride in two months and he wouldn't even tell me what he wanted for his funeral," Mae sobbed.

"I know. He wouldn't discuss it with me either. He said it was in the safe." Kenneth got up to go to the office. "He made me promise not to look at it until now. You know he knew that he was going to die tonight didn't you?" asked Kenneth.

"What? How did he know that?" asked Mae.

"I don't know how, but he did. Here let me read this to you," said Kenneth as he opened the sealed envelope.

> Dear Kenneth,
>   You are at OSU now, but there will be a day that you will be reading this, for it will mean that I died. The date will be December 26th, the year I don't know yet. But I'm asking you to do me a favor. There is someone who is dear to my heart, her name is Mae Parks. Call her and tell her of my passing. She will be hurt, so be gentle as you only you can. Tell her I love her and wished things could have worked out for us.
>   The funeral arrangements are on the paper enclosed, but I want to tell you how proud I am of you and although you aren't my son, I still love you, son.
>   Love,
>
>   Eugene Golbal
>   aka William Strowe

The funeral was all planned out and paid for. Only the family and workers were allowed to attend. He was praised by the priest as a man of God. But Kenneth knew the priest was only trying to comfort the grieving. Bill never was that holy.

The day after the funeral Kenneth and Joe went to the lawyer's office. Kenneth wanted Joe to know everything for he knew Joe would be taking over the job of executing the will. It was simple. The four institutions were to divide fifteen percent, Mae and

Jacob were to get twenty percent each and finally the remainder went into the trust for Mercy and Sarah. Five acres and the house would be set up for retreats one year after his death. The executor of the estate would get five percent for services rendered before anything went out.

As they rode back to the Estate, Joe was quiet for some time. "Laddie, do you know what we're talking about, moneywise? Are we talking thousands or ten thousands? What are we talking about here, Kenneth?"

"As of this morning the estate of the late William Strowe is worth $212,000,000 and some odd cents. So each person or organization in that will is going to receive millions. Millions with an M, and every person in that will would give up their millions to have him back this moment," Kenneth said with a sniffle.

When Kenneth walked into the house, Mercy handed him a note from Julie, explaining her feelings of his loss and that she understood why he couldn't come for New Years. She ended the message with something that he knew but didn't understand how Julie knew: "When we see each other again there will be no parting."

The three families had New Years together at Bob and Alice's house. After all, she wasn't to go out and she wasn't to work. So all she could do was open her door. It was a quiet evening. The girls had their dates and the adults had their memories. Joe and Molly were excited about her brother coming under a job visa. Bob and Alice about the baby, Kenneth, just sat there and thinking, wondering how did Julie know? Mae had gone home, the house was shut up, his work was done.

Everything seemed so empty to Kenneth. "Joe, did you see the cloud this morning?" Asked Kenneth.

"Now, laddie, don't start talking about death on the day of celebration," said Molly with a worried look in her eyes. "There has been enough death to last us a lifetime. Now just hush!" She gave Joe a look that said, *I will kill you if you say something.* So Joe just sat there as if he didn't hear.

Alice was about to say something when Bob gave her a look, also. No one wanted to speak of the subject. "Well it was over my house," said Kenneth, "so I guess I can talk about it. You two men need to think about the future. Get wills written so no one can take what you earned from your family. You two have over $500,000 in land and livestock, and equipment. What would happen if something happen to you, Joe?"

"I would shoot him, the black-hearted fool. Now you stop talking about death Kenneth. We know you're grieving. So are we, but it is New Years Eve," Molly ordered.

Two days later Kenneth had just finished writing his will and paying for his funeral. Coming back home, he hit some black ice at the same time a semi did. There was nothing he could do. He grabbed his crucifix and said, "Forgive me, Father, for I have sinned." He died on impact. Almost immediately he felt his spirit being lifted out of his crushed body. Looking around he saw the light that was there when he was in his mother's womb. Slowly he followed it, up, up, until he saw the Gates and heard the trumpets. Then he remembered—his work was finally done.

As he entered the Gates he looked and saw Gabriel standing with his head bowed. Looking farther down the street paved with gold, there was a procession headed his way. Led by the Son of the Master, in his hands were beautiful white wings. Placing them on Ken's back he said, "Well done, my good and faithful servant, welcome into your rest."